THE MAN NEXT DOOR

Maida Lovell is a loyal secretary in love with her boss Steve Blake; one of the strongest passions in his life is patriotism and it looks like he is a killer. Walsh Rantoul and Maida had spoken with mutual animosity and shortly he is dead. Then his bruised and bloodied body disappears.

Wartime Washington DC is full of spies and saboteurs which threaten military and civilian life. Someone is after secrets, and Maida has no shortage of information the enemy would like to get their hands on . . .

THE MAN NEXT DOOR

Mignon G. Eberhart

M

First published 1944
by
William Collins, Sons & Co. Ltd.

This edition 2004 by BBC Audiobooks Ltd
published by arrangement with
the author's estate

ISBN 0 7540 8654 2

British Library Cataloguing in Publication Data available

Printed and bound in Great Britain by
Antony Rowe Ltd., Chippenham, Wiltshire

CHAPTER ONE

SHE RANG and waited. The house seemed very still in the shadows of the spring twilight and, somehow, empty. Steve had said the servants might be out.

Standing on the doorstep with its white pillars, Maida remembered that, and it struck her as rather unusual. Christine Blake—Steve Blake's lovely, widowed sister-in-law, in whose house he lived—was one of those housekeepers to whom no detail is too small for perfect arrangement. Why, then, was it ever possible to come to her house and find no one to answer the bell?

Washington in wartime was different; there were many instances of adjustment to the pressure and pace of the times; possibly there was some compromise Christine had had to make in her household routine, owing to the employment situation. Maida dismissed the thought, put her small gloved thumb on the bell again, and again waited.

Through the soft twilight there was a murmur of traffic from across the park, the shrill little whistle of a frog somewhere, the indescribable, moist and tender fragrances of a warm spring evening. It wasn't quite dark, already, though, a faint mist, rising perhaps from the broad Potomac, seemed to veil in soft blue the yet bare, brown shrubs pressing around the house. A few tulips were up, shooting slender green stalks from the winter's leaf mould along the iron fence and around the doorstep. It was rather an imposing doorstep, but then, it was Christine's home; then Christine Favor, she was born in that house, and after her marriage to Harcourt Blake, Steve Blake's older brother, she had continued to live there as Christine Blake. Whenever she could, for Harcourt had been in the navy, she joined him for a week or a month, always returning to her house in Washington while Harcourt was at sea.

She was there when he died—in action—only a few days after Pearl Harbour.

It was that that really persuaded Steve Blake to accept the arduous, exacting and important job the government had required of him. Harcourt's death, and Steve's patriotism. For Steve too had wanted to get in the navy; he had wanted to see active service ; he had already made his plans, taken his physical examination, applied for a commission—any commission—that would take him into the war.

Then a new government post had been created, had arisen from the need for it, and Steve Blake had been the obvious man, the first choice. He was well known ; he had been a brilliant lawyer before he became interested in aeronautics and swerved from politics and his law practice to, first, counsel for an airline, then director in an aircraft manufacturing company—and then its executive president. He was young, only in his early thirties ; but his brilliance of mind and integrity of character were unquestionable.

In the end he had been, actually, drafted. The telephone call from Washington had come on the heels of the news of Harcourt's death in that far-off Pacific. One of the strongest passions of Steve's life was his patriotism ; he had been brought up on the stirring oratory of the great American leaders and lawmakers. The death in battle of Harcourt, his only close relative, moved him deeply. He dictated sheaves of notes to Maida, in order to leave full and complete office memoranda for his successor, made plans for the securing of that successor, gave up his cherished hope for active service and went to Washington.

It was all swift and hurried ; he had a whole department to organise, a new department with its work cut out for it but without standards or precedents to guide it. He plunged instantly into the mass of work ahead of him.

Washington had changed, owing to the war, from a gracious, quiet, dignified and beautifully ceremonious Southern town to a seething, crowded, vibrant city, the most important city in the world where decisions were being made which would affect human life for generations in the future. " Come to my house," Christine had said to her brother-in-law. " I'm so lonely."

Maida had heard her say it, for Steve brought Maida to Washington with him. She had been his secretary for three years ; he had known her and her people since she was a child of ten and he, twenty or so, was in law school. He had gone to the debut party rich Aunt Jason had given her ; had employed her when, because she had to earn money, she had completed a secretarial course. Aunt Jason had staked her to it—albeit complainingly. (" A girl with a face like yours ought to concentrate on getting a rich husband," Aunt Jason had said frankly and disapprovingly, tapping her cane smartly on the arm of her chair. " However, if you must be independent, I'll give you your tuition—but not a cent more, mind you.")

Maida liked working for Steve Blake. She had come immediately to Washington when he asked her, to act as his confidential secretary. She found herself a small apartment on Connecticut Avenue not far from Taft Bridge. But Steve, because there was no time to find an apartment for himself or perhaps mainly because Christine insisted and he felt sorry for her, had stayed at Christine's. When, thought Maida suddenly, he was not at the Chichester where Angela Favor, Christine's beautiful younger sister, lived in a small and luxurious pent-house, and mainly occupied herself with being a beautiful ornament of society. Maida had sent orchids to Angela only that morning, and had told the florist to enclose Steve's card. She had to resist an impulse to tell the florist to put in also a nice large and vigorous branch of poison ivy.

Orchids to Angela ! She thought with a flash of rather rueful amusement that if anybody got the poison ivy it would be herself, Maida Lovell, secretary to Steve Blake.

She shrugged, moving her shoulders impatiently in her neatly tailored grey tweed ; there was no excuse to feel sorry for herself, and she didn't. She rang the bell again and reached in her big alligator bag (a present from Aunt Jason) for the house key. She had taken it and the small key that opened the desk in his study, from the desk in Steve's big, pleasant office.

As she did, she glanced upward along the windows of the Georgian house with its mellow brick and narrow high windows, facing Rock Creek Park, and something moved behind one of those windows.

She stopped. It had been the barest flicker of a motion. In the waning light it seemed to her now that the curtain hung perfectly straight and unmoved. Certainly now, and so far as she could see, no one was there. Yet she had a swift and rather unpleasant impression that someone had been looking down at her. Failing to answer the bell, vanishing swiftly and with a certain surreptitiousness when, drawn perhaps by that stealthy regard, she had looked up in time to see the barest motion of that withdrawal.

She waited a moment, perplexed and rather disturbed. But she must have been mistaken. If anyone were in the house, he'd have come to the door.

No ; it was some glancing reflection of light from—she glanced around, and saw no light except those in the windows of the Lister house—well, from somewhere, she decided. put the key into the door quickly, unlocked and opened it.

The hall was shadowy ; the pleasant fragrance of a well-kept house floated to her nostrils—the blended, clean fragrances of wax and potpourri and fresh air with a trace of woodsmoke. She groped around for a light, found some crystal-hung, electrically-wired candelabra on a table near the door and turned them on. Instantly the long, wide hall leaped into soft light, with the stairway stretching upward in a graceful curve of white and mahogany, and the prisms of the candelabra striking small gay lights from the long, gilt-framed mirror behind it. Her own reflection moved too in the mirror : a slender, trim figure in her grey suit and small blue hat ; the furs over her arm swung gently ; her light, pompadoured hair caught gleams from the lights, too.

She closed the door. The deep jar of it seemed to emphasise the emptiness of the house. No, she had been mistaken about the motion she had glimpsed in the upstairs window ; it was only imagination, she told herself again, or a reflection from somewhere.

But when she turned again from the door and looked down the hall past the stairway, she saw that a room at the end of the hall was lighted.

Well, then, she hadn't been mistaken ; but whoever was here was certainly stone deaf. In any case, she'd better announce her presence and her errand.

She walked down the hall, past the stairway and came to the door of a small library. It was at the back of the house—a small, informal room, opening upon the garden and the brick terrace with french doors. One of the french doors stood open now, letting in a soft current of moist spring air. A man was standing at a table where there was a tray with glasses and a siphon. It was a man she recognised instantly, a young, slender man, small, really, with blond hair and impeccable tailoring. It was Walsh Rantoul. The man next door.

She stiffened with dislike and the wish she hadn't come.

Or at least that she had gone straight upstairs and so avoided him.

He lived in the cottage next to Christine's ; their gardens adjoined and, in fact, at one time the cottage had been part of the old Favor place, and it was only recently, in the face of the housing situation that the war had created in Washington, that Christine had had the cottage renovated, rebuilt, decorated, and then had let it to the man standing there. He was a man Maida strongly disliked, and a man who was not only Steve's rival in Angela's affections, but whose rivalry had been widely and distastefully publicised.

Obviously he was waiting for someone. Before she could move and escape, he turned, saw her and smiled.

His face had small, almost doll-like features—startlingly regular, with round, shallow eyes, and a trace of something fragile and effeminate around his small mouth and chin. He came forward at once.

" Why, Miss Lovell, I thought you were Angela. I'm waiting for her here." He smiled and indicated the tray beside him. " I've just poured myself a drink ; will you have it ? "

" No, thank you. I only came on an errand for Steve."

" Oh, really. The perfect secretary. Isn't it after office hours ? I think Steve works you too hard." He came nearer—so near she could see the rosy highlights on his small, pink mouth and the tiny, unexpectedly numerous lines around his eyes. " Come on, Miss Lovell, take pity on me while I wait for—for Angela. She's always late, you know. She said to be here at a quarter to six. Talk to me until she comes. Steve can wait. . . . "

" No, he's—in a hurry." He wasn't, really ; he'd only told her to get the notes for a radio speech he had to make and bring them to him at the Chichester, where he was to have dinner with Angela. (" Try to get them to me before nine," he had said. " I'm to be at the broadcasting studio at a quarter after.")

She had entered the room and now, as she spoke, turned back toward the door. And Walsh Rantoul said suddenly, in a voice that was thin and soft and, again, feminine : " You don't like me, do you, Miss Lovell ? "

" Why, I . . . " She turned toward him, taken aback a little. " What an odd thing to say ! " She laughed a little,

not very successfully, and told herself she wasn't going to be
trapped in any sort of conversation with this little, blond
man with the pretty, doll-like face and shallow, suddenly
calculating eyes. Calculating? It was an extraordinary
adjective to use for Walsh Rantoul, who was supposed to be
anything but calculating. He went to parties; he was seen
everywhere; he was liked by ladies; he gave small, intimate
dinners—otherwise, Maida thought suddenly, she knew
nothing of him. Except, of course, that he was an admirer
of Angela's and thus Steve's rival. He had managed to get
in the gossip columns once or twice in that capacity, and
lately (the week before, in fact), very prominently. She bit
her lip, thinking of that; the trouble was that Steve was
important and his job was important. Too important to be
linked in such a way with a man like Walsh Rantoul.

He was watching her, his eyes sharp and cool. Then he
said, smiling, but still watching: " You're trying to evade.
You know you don't like me. I've known it from the beginning. Since the first time I saw you, in fact. It was at a
cocktail party that Christine gave. Remember? Right in
this room. You came with Steve, and several people, I
remember, congratulated Steve on the good looks of his
secretary." He kept on smiling; his voice was soft and
thin. " Good looks in a secretary are a great asset, you
know, Miss Lovell. Or may I say Maida? Everybody else
calls you Maida—Christine and Steve and . . ." He glanced
at his watch. " Dear me. Angela *is* late. She's always
late. I suppose Steve has found that out."

Maida could feel herself flushing with anger. But he wasn't
really worth anger. She said, deliberately cool, deliberately
impersonal, ignoring his insistently provocative words : " I'll
go on and get the notes Steve sent me for. Apparently the
servants are out."

" What . . ." He blinked, then turned the glass in his
fingers and watched the amber liquid swirl. " Yes, I believe
they are. It's Monday, you know. And servants are independent just now. Everybody's out. I came in the garden
way from my own house. You must come to dinner sometime, Maida." He put down the glass suddenly and came
toward her. " Will you come to dinner sometime? Just the
two of us. Alone." He caught at her hand and leaned
toward her, smiling.

He was barely her own height; he was very self-satisfied, very sure of his charm, a little condescending to the secretary. Her fingers itched to come into sharp contact with the rather girlish cheek leaning now so near her own as he put his arm rather closely around her. Probably that was the way Steve had felt the week before—only Steve actually had slapped him, knocked him down at the entrance to one of the best of Washington hotels.

She drew back so quickly and definitely that his arm dropped away at once. After all, it wasn't her place to get herself in a row with a friend of Christine's and Angela's. She said: "Thank you, I don't go out to dinner," and turned away but he followed her. His face flushed, but the rebuff did not appear to anger him; instead, his eyes still looked merely calculating—a look that puzzled her even through her distaste for the little scene and the position it thrust her into, and her exasperation. Why should Walsh Rantoul look like that?

"Oh," he said softly, still smiling, smoothing one ringed, manicured hand over his yellow hair. "So you don't go out to dinner? Except with Steve, I suppose. Is that why you don't like me? On account of Steve?"

"Really, there's no point in this . . ."

"You do hate me, don't you? Most women like me. Why don't you? Is it because of that row with Steve last week?"

"That exceedingly well-publicised row?" she said sharply.

"I didn't publicise it, if that's what you mean."

"It was all in the columns. I'm sure Steve would try to keep it out."

"My dear girl, when a man deliberately assaults another man, and knocks him senseless in as public a place as that, there's no way to keep it a secret. Especially when the object of their quarrel is as lovely and well known as Angela." He smiled again. "Angela didn't mind."

"And neither did you," said Maida. "It's only Steve whom such publicity hurts."

"What a lovely little face you have, my child," he said slowly. "When you're angry, at any rate. Your eyes are really like stars. I always thought you were a funny, cold little thing. Now I see I was wrong. Of course, your mouth ought to have given you away." Again he put his arm toward her. "Such a beautiful mouth," he said. "Warm and . . ."

She really would have liked to slap him ; it was a childish, swift, petty and utterly futile impulse—and one which would have given her much satisfaction. She said swiftly : "My mouth is my own, thank you," and felt as childish as she would have felt had she followed the other absurd impulse. The only thing to do was to get away ; stop talking to him ; end this preposterous conversation. She moved quickly away from him.

He didn't follow her. But he said, just as she reached the doorway, in a voice so soft that it was curious how penetrating it was in that dark and empty house : "You're in love with Steve yourself."

CHAPTER TWO

A CLOCK struck in the hall. The slow deep notes were measured and deliberate, giving time its due of respect and dignity. There was a solemnity about those slow and measured notes that was almost a warning of the implacable swiftness of time, of the incredible shortness of man's allotment.

The french door moved a little and the black glass winked and caught a moving light behind Walsh Rantoul's slight, dapper figure. The air seemed suddenly less warm and balmy—became charged as the clock marked that irrevocable hour with something chill and ominous.

No one was there, of course. No one was in the house except herself and the man opposite her.

The clock stopped striking. The last note died away slowly and lingeringly ; it was exactly six o'clock ; that hour would never come again.

Maida said slowly : "I'm going upstairs now. Steve will be waiting."

Walsh Rantoul said : "Steve's not the only man in the world, you know. I guessed you were in love with him the first time I saw you together. There's something in the air, in the way you look at him. I can always feel it between two people." He smiled, but this time uneasily. It seemed to Maida that he was listening ; not to the clock, for that had

stopped striking, but for something else, something perhaps
as intangible as the passage of time.   He said in a preoccupied
way : " It must be rather unpleasant for you, seeing Steve
go off the deep end over Angela. 'But, my dear, as I say,
he's not the only man in the world."

She moved into the hall, and he followed her and said :
" Stay with me. I'm lonely. Have a drink with me—until
Angela comes." But he was thinking of something else,
something urgent, something, she thought, of which the
striking of the clock had reminded him.

He lounged in the doorway, holding his glass in one small
hand, smiling at her. Listening. Behind him the room was
lighted and gay with flowers and cushions and books strewn
about—perfectly commonplace, perfectly everyday. She
reached the stairway and turned upward. It was dark above,
and she saw no electric switch for lights at the lower part of
the stairs. As she went up, sliding her gloved hand along the
polished bannister, she was conscious of that slight figure in
the doorway, the light distinct on his blond hair, his grey suit,
his cornflower-blue tie and the neat corner of cornflower-blue
handkerchief in his pocket, watching her, until she reached
the landing and turned again.

Up there it was silent and perfectly dark. Even the
windows at the front of the hall showed merely pale rectangles
of twilight—the window, she thought suddenly, where, as
she stood at the door and rang, she had thought someone
moved, quickly, out of sight.

She had been at Christine's many times and knew the
general plan of the house. The room—or rooms rather, for
it was a small suite of bedroom, bathroom and tiny study—
that Christine had allotted to Steve was on her left. She felt
her way into the open doorway, groped for and found a light
which showed her a large room, with an old-fashioned mantel
and lovely mahogany ; she crossed it and entered Steve's
study.

But first she closed the bedroom door. She didn't know
exactly why she did that, but she made very sure it was
closed. She closed the study door too. As she lighted the
desk lamp there, the small room, with its bookshelves and
Steve's broad desk, came out of what had been a well of
darkness. She went to the comfortable red-leather desk
chair and sat down.

After a moment of staring at the millefiori glass paper-weight before her, she leaned over and put her face in her hands.

So it was that clear. So clear that even Walsh Rantoul, not very brainy, certainly not very sensitive, could see it.

Did Steve know, then? Did Christine?

Did Angela?

Steve could have no idea that she had anything but the frankest, friendliest affection for him. Thinking back, she felt sure that Christine was too preoccupied with herself, her quite real grief—and her somewhat moderated but still rather plentiful social activity, to pay much attention to anyone else's emotional state. " I mustn't let myself give in," she had heard Christine say, touching her eyes with a wisp of handkerchief. " I must make myself go on living. Besides," she would add, " I can't refuse the Smiths . . ." or the Charmlays or the Harrises. " And they do have rather nice dinners." Upon which she would put away the handkerchief, have her beautiful golden hair done and get into a dinner dress—black, since she was so recent a widow, and black was very becoming to Christine's blonde beauty.

In a very real sense Christine was right ; she was innately sensible and kind. Certainly she had gone out of her way to help Maida get settled in an apartment, to make her feel welcome at all times in her own house, to show every gracious and generous courtesy to a girl who had no claims upon her whatever. Perhaps Steve had asked her to do so, but Maida was inclined to think not. Maida liked Christine, in spite of Christine's facile manner, for the good-natured kindness that lay below it.

No, she was quite safe with Christine.

Angela, like Christine in many ways except she had more strength of character and charm, shared a kind of frank self-absorption and self-assuredness that, although less strongly, was one of Christine's characteristics. Angela, of course, had more excuse for it. She was ten years younger than Christine ; she had an independence Christine had never had—as witness her refusal to live with her ier sister. In her small pent-house, a little too full of exactly the right things, she lived her own life. She had an inheritance, as Christine had, from their father. She had from that a competent income, more than competent, indeed, for it permitted her furs and gowns

and jewels such as her famous star sapphires—famous because
everyone said, instantly, that they matched her eyes. As
a matter of fact, thought Maida, overcome by a feminine
twinge of satisfaction, Angela's eyes were her only bad
feature ; they weren't at all like star sapphires. They were,
instead, a bright, turquoise blue, a little hard and small,
even when carefully shadowed and made up. But she was
tall and slender ; her features were flawless, her yellow hair
like a cap of gold, her smile and expression full of warmth
and a frank, candid kind of charm which was very attractive.
Maida was too honest to pretend to herself that she liked
Angela, but she had to admit her beauty and her charm and
her generosity. She gave money and she gave time and effort
wherever it was asked and wherever her name would help a
charitable cause.

Angela had a wide range of acquaintances, but if she had
few intimate and close women friends, then it was perhaps
owing to her universal popularity, or that she had a kind of
vanity which does not make for loyal, intimate friendships ;
she might praise a woman friend lavishly—and somehow leave
her deflated, less attractive, a mere satellite to herself. Once,
when a young navy lieutenant had taken a fancy to Maida
at a cocktail party and insisted upon taking her home, Maida
had heard Angela. " Maida's such a nice little thing," she
had said warmly to the young lieutenant. " She's Steve's
secretary, you know. A dear girl, really ; so conscientious.
I'm afraid she's having rather a dull time in Washington,
poor child. Do be nice to her."

Needless to say, having been transformed from an attractive
and desirable young woman to an object of charity, something of the first fine careless rapture on the young lieutenant's
part had diminished. Not that Angela cared for the young
lieutenant, either.

But then, neither did Maida. That was because Steve
dwarfed and dimmed every other man in the world in her
eyes and always had. And Angela took Steve, too—or
almost took him.

Maida wasn't quite sure that Steve had actually, as the
unpleasant little man downstairs had said, gone off the deep
end over Angela. Steve had a brilliant mind and so little
vanity that flattery warned him rather than deceived him.
You could never be sure, with Steve, what he was thinking or

how much he saw and understood. He was certainly attentive to Angela ; he dined with her, he sent her flowers, he let her take him to cocktail parties or went to her penthouse to see her, lounging, resting, smoking, while Angela talked. And Angela was useful to him ; there was no getting around that. Useful in a way in which Maida herself could not be, for Angela knew Washington ; she knew the ropes ; she knew the people who knew the people. No one knew better than Angela Favor the winding paths, the feuds and the factions, the hidden significances, the silken fabric of compliment and of ceremony ; and in the end the most direct way to a goal. Steve was not personally ambitious ; but he was intent upon doing the thing he had been brought to Washington to do, and in the accomplishment of almost any public office and duty, there is a background of political knowledge it is well to know.

Angela knew that ever-changing, ever-shifting background. Angela had influence, of a certain kind ; possibly not as much as she claimed, but the mere claiming goes far in an easily convinced world. And she made the most of the knowledge that a life in Washington, the moving, changing, glamorous, sometimes cruel, always exciting city, had given her.

Maida was not sure how much of himself Steve really gave Angela, or how much he liked her. The quarrel (that oddly public quarrel, so unlike Steve) had supposedly been about Angela. Steve himself of course hadn't even mentioned it ; he wouldn't.

Well, she wasn't the first girl to fall in love with her boss ; and really the only thing she could do about it was to go along, doing her job as best she could—not only for Steve but because it was, too, her only way to serve her country at war. Eventually she'd either get over it or not. The day was long past when maidens languished and died of unrequited love. " Nuts," muttered Maida explosively to herself. " That's enough of that." She sat up and got out the mirror from her handbag and touched her nose with powder and looked at herself for a long moment. She wasn't really bad-looking. In fact, she decided, she was prettier than Angela ; but then, unfortunately, that depended upon one's taste. She put a little more lipstick on her mouth, looked at it critically, removed it ; lighted a cigarette, took three or four steadying breaths before she put it out in the bronze ash tray beside her hand and addressed herself briskly to the business at hand. The notes for the speech—where had Steve said they would be ? Oh, yes, in the upper right-hand drawer. She took the smaller key she had brought with her at Steve's telephoned directions and started to unlock the flat-topped desk, but, to her surprise, it was already unlocked.

It opened readily. She frowned a little, remembering Steve's words. Yes, he'd said definitely the desk was locked. It was his habit to lock things, for much confidential and highly important information passed through his hands. It was one of the reasons why he had brought Maida to Washington with him ; he knew her and knew he could trust her. She decided at last that he had been, that time, mistaken.

The notes were not there. She had clipped them together herself and corrected them. As she ruffled again through the sheaves of papers, the front door, below, opened and closed with a loud jar. She stopped and listened. Obviously some-one had come into the house ; Christine, perhaps, or Angela arriving to keep her appointment with Walsh Rantoul. It occurred to Maida that Angela was running her dates rather close together ; meeting Walsh Rantoul at six at Chrinstine's house, and dining with Steve at eight.

But it was not Angela. Almost at once she heard quick footsteps on the stairs, heavier than a woman's. Someone came along the hall and into Steve's bedroom and, as Maida half rose from her chair, Steve himself opened the door of the study and stopped, looking at her.

He'd been hurrying, for he was breathing quickly. His hair was untidy ; he'd apparently been to a formal reception, for he was in striped trousers and cutaway coat with his overcoat slung across his shoulders. A dark-red carnation was in his lapel ; Maida had ordered it that morning at the same time she had ordered the orchids for Angela. ("Those small white ones," Steve had said, and added, with what was for him a lyrical outburst, "like white butterflies.")

Steve, tall, thin, brown-faced, caught his breath and said quickly : " Oh, hello, Maida. Where's Christine ? What's wrong ? "

" Why, nothing. Christine's not here. I—don't under-stand. . . ."

" Not here ? " he cried. " But she telephoned. She said

for me to meet her. Right away. I got the impression that it was rather urgent."

"But she—Steve, I don't think she's here at all. I rang and rang and nobody answered. I'm sure she isn't here."

"Not here, huh?" He frowned, thought for an instant, and sat down opposite her, stretching out long legs. "It's funny." He thought for another moment and then grinned: "Oh—I remember now. She was going to a cocktail party somewhere and it's the servants' day out. She must have sent word for me to pick her up in the car. Yes, that's it. No chauffeur. Message was garbled by the time I got it. Well . . ." He yawned vigorously and shook himself a little. "I'll go around and get her."

"Taxis are still running," said Maida, thinking how tired he looked and how in moments of relaxation the look of youth left his face and he became grave and preoccupied.

"Oh, well, you know Christine."

"Steve—it's none of my business, but you do drive yourself too hard."

He looked at her rather sharply and then unexpectedly yawned again. "I'm all right. Everything's working. I'm not the only one."

"I know. But it's—things like that that tire you. Christine and . . ." She almost said Angela; she practically bit off the end of her tongue.

He laughed shortly. "Bless you, Maida. But Christine—well, it's so short a time, you know. She misses him so much. Anything I can do is very little." She knew he was thinking of Harcourt. There was a moment of silence. Then he sat up abruptly. "Well, I'll be off. I think she was going to the Slaters'. I'll take the notes now, Maida."

"Didn't you say they were in the top drawer?"

"Yes. Why? Haven't you found them?"

"No." She glanced through the papers again.

"That's funny," said Steve. He watched her a moment frowning again, his brown face instantly taking on the look of keenness and concentration she knew so well. "I was sure I put them there," he said, and got up and came around beside her. His hands were long and brown and firm. She always liked Steve's hands; she wanted to touch them—so near her own. The light shone on his black, ruffled hair;

with something like horror at her own impulse, she wanted to touch his hair too.

She said rather stiffly : " I've looked, Steve. They aren't there."

" Oh. Well . . . " He paused, then glanced at his watch. " Hell—if I'm going to pick up Christine and then go on to . . . The notes must be somewhere in the desk, Maida. Look them up, will you ? And bring them to me as I told you to—at Angela's, before nine. I've got to run along."

" All right, Steve. If I can't find them, I'll get the carbons from the office."

" Thanks." He glanced at his watch again, and then looked directly down into her eyes. For a second or two he said nothing.

The house was very quiet ; Washington and the whirling life of the city seemed miles away, in some distant, remote world. Steve's eyes were all at once very dark and very searching. Then he leaned forward and put the back of his hand against her cheek.

It was the briefest touch—light, warm, gentle. He said, still looking into her eyes : " I do thank you, Maida. For much . . . "

It was queer how shy she could turn with Steve She said, almost coolly, for fear perhaps her voice would tremble— for fear she would put up her own hand to hold his against her, for fear she would turn her head and nestle it against his arm : " It's nothing, Steve. Good-night. I'll leave the notes at the desk and they'll send them right up to you."

His hand lingered another fractional second. Then he said : " All right. Good-night, then," and all at once he was gone.

The little room was just a room. No longer a small, enchanted island. She could hear his footsteps crossing the bedroom and then the door closed again.

After a moment she remembered Walsh Rantoul, waiting for Angela below ; she hadn't thought to mention it to Steve. She hadn't, as a matter of fact, really thought of anything, since his hand had touched her face.

And that was a fine thing. A fine how-do-you-do. A fine kettle of fish. To let the merest, most casual touch of a man's hand affect you like that. Now then—where were the notes ?

Perhaps because she was telling herself, self-derisively, such things as that, she was never sure later whether or not she heard Steve leave. She didn't consciously hear the front door close ; she didn't consciously hear his car, which must have been parked on the street outside, start away. She did, sometime later while searching through the desk, hear a car backfire. Quite loudly and sharply, somewhere near.

In the end she found the notes, shoved beneath the blotter and not in a drawer at all. It took time, for she had looked rather thoroughly through the desk drawers first.

She identified them at once—her own typing, with Steve's written additions in the margin. She put them in her handbag, stood up, locked the desk, and turned out the light.

It wasn't till she reached the top of the stairs that she became aware of two things. One was that there was now no light at all downstairs. The other was that she didn't want to descend into the silent black pit below. It was as if the steps had been taken away and a bottomless, horrible black gulf stretched below and some deep atavistic instinct warned her of it. Warned her so poignantly, so urgently that she stopped still, there at the very top of the steps, afraid to go down.

In the silence, she heard something whimper, like a dog in pain. The sound came from below.

CHAPTER THREE

CHRISTINE had a dog, a cocker spaniel named Rosy. Maida thought that out quite clearly. Then she realised that she was groping along the wall at the head of the stairway, still standing poised above that somehow dangerous and threatening black brink, trying to find a light. Turn on the light— there must be a switch somewhere here—turn on the light. Her fingers encountered the small button and pressed it.

At once the black and threatening chasm was gone ; there was just a hall below, exactly as it had been when she entered ; the stairway was just a stairway.

And again someone—something—below gave a strange, half-strangled sound, a whimper that brought her heart pounding in her throat, that stirred the nerves along the back of her neck, that made her want to run—out of the house and away.

But that was fantastic. She must take a hold on herself. She must go down there and find out what it was that whimpered like that. . . . And why.

The dog, of course. It had been out in the street (for it hadn't barked or come near her when she entered the house) ; it had been out in the street and there'd been an accident and the beast had crept around through the garden and into the library at the back of the house through the open french window. Yes, that was it. Obviously no one but herself was there. If Angela had come to meet Walsh Rantoul she had gone again ; both of them had gone and Steve had gone and Maida herself, busy and preoccupied, hadn't heard them leave.

As she was thinking, she was going downstairs, one step after another, making herself go. Her hand gripping the banister all the way down. The sound didn't come again.

She didn't pause when she reached the tall newel post, for by that time she had nerved herself to go to the library and find the dog. Something would have to be done for it at once ; she began to think of a veterinarian. Was there one fairly near ? She'd find the dog and then telephone there in the library. After that she would telephone for a taxi and if necessary take the dog there.

Unless it was too late . . . She reached the doorway to the library, and it was dark. Walsh Rantoul and Angela had gone then. And the dog made no further sound— perhaps it was too late to do anything for the little dog. Only an anguish of pain, a mortal wound, could drag from any throat a sound like that.

She found the electric light button by the door and turned it on. The table lamp made a downward pool of light. The bright cushions, the books, the flowers, the glitter of glass on the table were still there.

Walsh Rantoul lay on the floor, sprawled like a sack, his tie oddly spotted, his head turned at an impossible angle. He lay just behind a flowered sofa that stood at right angles to the door.

Nobody moved in the house. Nothing happened. The clock in the hall ticked huskily—still measuring time. The clock that had measured Walsh Rantoul's last hour. For she knew that he was dead. She wasn't conscious of any reasoning process. She wasn't conscious of anything, really ; except that slight, awry, grey figure sprawled there with the blotches on the blue tie, and the light spring breeze coming in the french window.

Nobody who wasn't dead could lie like that—so supine, so broken, so *dead*. All life was gone ; not a spark of that mystery of all mysteries remained. He looked shrunken. There was no question but that the last little tremble of life had gone—just gone—but gone completely.

Then it wasn't the dog that had moaned like that, high-pitched, half-strangled. It had been Walsh Rantoul, dying.

Then she was moving. Quite steadily, really. Probably she could only move because she'd been thinking of the dog and what she must do for it. She must do something—it was a kind of inner compulsion. She went to his side and bent down, behind the sofa. She must touch him and make sure he was dead. Then she saw that his doll-like face had been bruised horribly ; that his eyes had no life, but were merely blank, bright reflections of the light above.

The bruise was a queer blotch. That couldn't have killed him. A bruise like that couldn't have killed him, yet he was dead. The blotches, the red smudges on the cornflower-blue tie caught her eye, and she followed them and saw the slowly spreading blotch of dark, viscous red on his white shirt, under the loose hanging grey coat.

So that was it. She knelt there, frozen again, but thinking. A knife wound—or a revolver shot could have made that. She hadn't heard a revolver shot. Still she'd heard something—something loud and sharp. A motor, she had thought, had back-fired. But really—she was looking away from that slight, sprawled figure, looking around the room, searching. She saw the smashed glass, the glass probably he had had in his hand when he'd watched her out of sight—only twenty or thirty minutes ago. It had smashed and lay on the edge of the rug, and there was a dark patch of liquid on the rug. There'd been no struggle in the room—or had there ? There was that bruise on his face, and it didn't look sharp, as it would have looked if he'd fallen against the sharp edge of a table. Besides, the only thing near him was the padded and cushioned sofa. But the room looked orderly, except for the dreadful disorder of violent death that lay within it.

There was only that smashed glass that was different. The french door was still a little open. The flowers, the magazines, the books, the thin old rugs—nothing was different except the thing beside her.

Then she saw the revolver.

The glitter of it caught her eye. It lay a little under the sofa. She put out her hand toward it and then realised she mustn't touch it and lifted the pleated flounce of the gay slip-cover and looked at it. It was a revolver ; it looked like one that Steve had. She looked closer and discovered that it was Steve's revolver.

She knew that because she had seen it many times ; usually it was in his office and he had joked about it. Someone, sometime, had given it to him, and it was what Steve had called too fancy. This, because it wasn't just a plain, businesslike revolver ; it was done up with a silvered handle and Steve's initials engraved upon it. S. B. She could see them now, in the shadow under the slip-cover.

Steve's revolver.

But Steve hadn't shot Walsh Rantoul. Somebody had taken Steve's revolver and shot him. Somebody . . .

Again two things happened.

She saw Steve's red carnation. Broken and lying on the rug, its dark red so near the colour of the design in the rug that she hadn't seen it until then.

There was a step on the terrace outside the open french window.

There was another step on the terrace ; someone was coming, lightly and rather slowly.

She reached first for the carnation. It was quite near ; she had only to put out her hand, take it quickly and hold it, crumpled in her hand behind her as she rose. The revolver too—that was Steve's, but there wasn't time to do anything about that. She had to stand—quickly—before whoever was approaching could reach the doorway, see her rise, wonder why she had been kneeling like that, out of sight, behind the sofa.

Again she wasn't reasoning. She had to act, follow conclusions—without travelling consciously, step by step, the path that had led her to that conclusion.

She got up quickly, swaying a little, clutching the cold, crumpled petals of the broken red carnation in her bare hand

and holding it behind her. What had she done with her
alligator handbag ? Oh, there it was, by the door, on a
chair, with her short brown gloves and her furs. She hadn't
known where she put them down. The steps came nearer,
scuffled, and a voice said : " You little devil, you hold
still . . . "

It was Nollie Lister. He stopped in the doorway in full
view against the spring twilight. He was wearing wrinkled
grey slacks and a sweater and smoking a pipe, and carrying
Rosy, who was wriggling furiously in his arms. " Mrs.
Blake," he began, blinking nearsightedly through his spectacles in the sudden light. His voice was angry and high-
pitched. His thinning brown hair showed a gleaming round
bald spot. " Really, Mrs. Blake," he said, " I must ask you
to keep your dog at home. It's the third time. The third
time. And you know how difficult it is now to get really
good tulips. Mine were sent from Holland before the war
and are prize bulbs. There's no excuse . . . " Full-tilt, he
stopped, blinked again and said flatly : " Oh."

Rosy wriggled and gave a shrill yap. She was fat, overfed,
and somewhat spoiled. Her paws were muddy and she had
an air of complacency. Maida was swaying a little—as if the
floor vibrated. She put out her hand, and steadied herself
by holding to the back of the sofa. Nollie Lister said in a
disgruntled way : " I thought you were Mrs. Blake."

" No . . . " said Maida. At least she thought she said it ;
and then realised that only her lips had moved and her throat
and that no sound had come from them. She tried again
and said, " No. Mrs. Blake is—is not here." Her voice
sounded very strange in her own ears, tight, strained. Nollie
Lister didn't seem to notice anything out of the way—either
about her voice or the room. Of course he couldn't see what
lay there behind the sofa, at her feet. But surely he—surely
anyone could sense the horror. The presence of death. It
was almost tangible, almost it had a voice, almost—she caught
herself quickly. She had to steady herself. She had to
protect Steve until—well, until she knew what else to do.
She couldn't let anyone see that revolver, that red carnation.

Steve had been in the house. Steve had quarrelled, publicly,
violently, only the week before, with Walsh Rantoul. Steve's
red carnation—Steve's revolver . . .

Her mind was whirling now, not very sensibly, altogether

like a dream. She must get rid of Nollie Lister with his peering, nearsighted gaze roaming the room. She must give herself—*and Steve*—time. That was it, time. She'd acted instinctively when she heard the footsteps on the terrace. Now she knew exactly why she'd acted as she had. Get rid of Nollie Lister ; don't let him see or know.

"Well," he said slowly, eyeing her strangely. (Did he notice anything wrong about her ? Her eyes ? Her colour ? Her voice ?) "Well, I wish you'd tell Mrs. Blake that I simply won't have it. She's either got to tie up her dog or make good the bulbs, and she can't really replace the bulbs. I hate to complain to the police but, really, I shall have to if this keeps up. You're Mr. Blake's secretary, aren't you ? "

She didn't trust herself to speak this time. She only nodded. Why didn't he go ?

"I thought so. I remember you at one of their cocktail parties. Living here, are you ? "

Oh, good Heavens, she thought. He's going to turn conversational. He's going to come into the room, stay, wait for Christine, perhaps, chat. Why doesn't he put down the dog and leave ?

Well, she must get rid of him. She said : "No. I only came on an errand for Mr. Blake. I'm leaving now."

"Oh," he said, but didn't move or turn away. Something puzzled him—without perhaps his knowing he was puzzled. He was exploring, searching, sending out little tentacles of curiosity. He lingered, hesitantly, there on the threshold, still holding the dog.

Rosy too had stopped wriggling and looking self-satisfied. Instead she was alert, all at once, sniffing the air, turning her head this way and that.

Then Rosy growled—softly, puzzled, inquiringly.

Nollie Lister looked down at the dog. "What's the matter ? Doesn't she know you ? " he asked. " I shouldn't think she'd growl at you. What's the matter, Rosy ? "

"Nothing's wrong," said Maida in desperation. " She's all right. She always growls like that. I'll . . ." Her throat was so tight with anxiety she could hardly speak. The effort to do so made her voice come out hard and harsh. " I'll tell Mrs. Blake about the tulips. I'm sure she'll see that it doesn't happen again. I must go now. If you'll give me the dog, I'll just lock the french door; she—Mrs. Blake asked me to do so."

" Oh. Then she's not been gone long. I was going to wait for her. It's much better, you know, for me to talk to her about it while I'm really upset. If I wait a day or two I'm not so likely to make her understand that it simply must not happen again. Mrs. Blake is a very positive woman as perhaps you know . . ." He stopped as Rosy growled again.

This time it was a real growl; the hair on the back of her neck had risen and she was staring at the sofa.

" Good gracious," said Nollie Lister. " She sounds quite savage. She . . ."

Rosy was struggling, trying to get down, growling and staring at the sofa.

The room rocked again. I'm going to faint, thought Maida. I've got to get that dog away from him. I've got to . . .

Somehow she left the sofa and moved, still holding one hand crunching the red carnation behind her back. She went around the end of the sofa as Nollie Lister stooped down with the dog. She reached him just as Rosy's feet touched the rug and scooped up the wriggling, snuffling dog in one arm. " Thank you," she said. " Thank you, Mr. Lister. I'll tell Mrs. Blake. Now, if you don't mind, I'm in a hurry . . . I was to lock this door. . . ."

He backed away, looking really perplexed now. " Why, of course . . . Why, naturally . . ." He said, stammering, watching her. Later he'd remember how she looked, what she's said, how she'd made him leave. He'd remember the way the dog had growled and the way her hair had risen along her neck. He'd remember . . .

" Good-night," she said, and almost forced him away from the doorway. He was on the terrace, his face white against the soft spring night, his eyes wide and questioning. She closed the french door. He was still out there, probably, standing on the terrace, revolving in his mind the oddness of the little scene between them—her look, her voice, her anxious determination to get rid of him quickly.

She hadn't been very adroit. But she had got rid of him. Rosy was struggling in her arms, watching the sofa, growling softly in her throat. She must get rid of her, too. Lock her up safely somewhere. Suddenly she had a horror of the soft, fat, spoiled little dog, which had reverted to its native instinct, its wild knowledge of the presence of death in that room—lying hidden behind a flowered sofa with blood upon it.

She was steady now that Nollie Lister had gone. If he was still out there, peering through the black window-pane, she must wait till he'd gone before she did whatever it was she was so sure she had to do. And she must act as if she were leaving, as she had told him she was doing. She reached to lock the french door, and the key wasn't there and there was no bolt. And there were things she had to do. Quickly. At once. Before anyone else came.

She could have reasoned about Steve. She could have thought deliberately and honestly that his life was worth ten of Walsh Rantoul's. She could have decided that if Steve had killed him then there must be a reason for it. She could have merely said to herself, I love Steve. Whatever he's done, I love him.

She thought none of those things actually. She was thinking only of how to get the revolver and the carnation away from the house so no one could find them. And that she must look—quickly, so carefully—for anything else that Steve had left behind.

Nollie Lister was probably expecting the light to be turned off. Besides, that would indicate to him, if he were still watching, that she had gone. Surely blackness in the room would convince him that whatever puzzled him was nothing.

Holding Rosy tightly, she crossed to the electric light switch again and turned it off. The bright, commonplace room (commonplace, except for that one way in which it was so horribly not commonplace) faded into dusk. It was not quite dark, for the light from the hall streamed into the room. This path of light, however, fell between the french doors and the sofa. So, if she approached the sofa on the distant side of the light, she couldn't be seen from the terrace and, at least, she could get hold of that terribly condemning evidence, Steve's revolver.

Rosy surged out of her arms and down upon the floor, bumping and thrown a little off her balance by her plunging descent. Maida bent quickly and seized the little dog again. She'd better put Rosy somewhere, shut her in a room. She scooped her up and went swiftly into the hall and toward the dining-room.

She didn't turn on lights as she went ; the light from the hall also fell through the broad, arched doorway into the dining-room.   It was no good leaving Rosy there ;   she'd only follow her back into the library.   Where was a room with a door ?

She went on to the butler's pantry, turning on that light. But only a swinging door intervened there between the pantry and the dining-room.

Eventually she put Rosy in a broom closet in the kitchen ; a closet that had a door that latched securely.

She turned out the light again in the butler's pantry, thinking, as she did so, how steady her hands were, and feeling as if she had done nothing but turn lights on and off again for hours.   She went quickly back to the library—and stopped in the doorway.

The light was on again.   A man stood with his back to her, his hat pulled rather low over his head.   He was standing behind the sofa, looking at Walsh Rantoul's body.   He heard her and turned around.   Then she saw that he had Steve's revolver in his hand.

It was a man she had never seen before

CHAPTER FOUR

As IT HAD done once before while she stood in that doorway, the clock in the hall struck slowly, emphasizing the silence. This time, however, it struck only three times.   That meant that it marked the third quarter hour ;   it was a quarter to seven.   She'd been in that house forty-five minutes.   It seemed an incredibly long time ;   it wasn't possible it could be only forty-five minutes.

Her hand was on the door casing, clutching it.   Her other hand still held the crumpled red carnation.   She moved slowly, under the steady gaze of the man before her, and put that hand in the pocket of her jacket, carefully, so he wouldn't see the flower, slowly, so he wouldn't guess that she was hiding something.

He didn't move for a long moment.   He was a bulky man, rather short.   He wore a light overcoat and his hat shaded heavy features.   His hand, holding the revolver, was thick and stubby—a forceful hand, brutal somehow and ruthless. The light fell strongly upon it and upon the revolver where it left his face in the shadow.

She said at last : " Who are you ? "

He moved then. He came a step nearer her, turned to glance down at Walsh Rantoul, and said quickly and almost conversationally : " How do you come into this ? "

She saw then that he was holding the revolver in a peculiar way, that he had a handkerchief around it in such a way that it was interposed between the grip of his fingers and the steel.

That was for fingerprints. And that and his question made her think suddenly that he was a policeman, a plain-clothes man.

There was no way for him to have known what happened, or to have arrived so soon, unless Steve had gone straight from that room and that house to the police.

Up to then she had been almost hypnotically composed ; she had moved, talked, got rid of Nollie Lister without letting him see Walsh Rantoul's body ; she had thought to hide the red carnation ; she had even in a way planned. She hadn't questioned her own acts and hadn't actually thought of the fact that everything she did made her, literally and legally, an accessory after the fact—and even if she had she would probably still have gone along the path that every instinct laid out for her. But Steve himself must have gone to the police and certainly he had confessed.

Steve, and all that was Steve ruined, destroyed, his name made a catchword, emblazoned in the headlines. Did they give the death penalty in the District of Columbia if you confessed ? It was queer how little one knew of the laws of the District ; it was like being in a foreign city.

Steve—all she could think of was Steve—all that bright future of Steve's was gone. *And his job*—that was important too ; terribly important in wartime ; where would they find another man so patriotic, so selfless in his interests, and who knew that job with its peculiar and difficult requirements ?

The police wouldn't think of that, of how much more value he was to them free and alive than in prison, tried, convicted. They'd have to obey the law. They'd have to carry out that horrible, inexorable process that ended with such ignominy. Steve—with his tall, easily moving body, his black head, his grave, kind eyes, his fine mind—put in prison—for murder.

And for the murder of a man like Walsh Rantoul. It wasn't fair; oh, it wasn't fair.

The man opposite her was watching her; gradually his features were becoming more distinct; they were strong, with heavy lines, intelligent but cold and, just then, vulpine. There was no mercy in that face.

The false strength that had buoyed her up until then suddenly deserted her; she had needed to act—now the need was past. Steve himself had confessed. Her knees felt like jelly, and she sat down slowly, not knowing that she did it, in a chair near the door.

" I said," said the man, eyeing her from the shadow of the hat brim, " who are you ?   How do you come into this ? "

He could easily find out; anyway, there was no point in trying to evade.   " I'm Maida Lovell," she said, her lips numb and stiff.

" Maida Lovell.   How did you happen to be here, in this house ? "

She moistened her lips.   " I came to get some papers Steve—Mr. Blake wanted."

" How long have you been here ? "

" Since—about six, I think."

He waited a moment in silence.   She noticed suddenly that the corner of the sofa shielded the grey, horrible heap that lay behind it, and she was thankful, with a kind of wave of nausea, for that.   " Did you get the papers ? " he asked suddenly.

" What ?   Oh, yes," she nodded toward her alligator handbag.   His eyes seemed to follow her own and linger there for a second before they returned to her.

" Did you see the murder ? " he said suddenly and bluntly.

" No," she said.

" Where were you at the time ? "

" Oh—I don't know."

" You must know.   You knew Rantoul was in the house; you knew Blake was in the house.   Where were you when it happened ? "

In another moment he'd try to make a witness of her; make her testify against Steve.   She clutched at her chair with both hands.   " I came into the house," she said slowly, thinking that she must tell a story which, later, would hold up but betray nothing.   " I came into the house.   I went upstairs to Steve's study. It took me some time to find the papers he sent me for. Then I came down . . . " Her voice independently and of its own volition just stopped, completely, there.

He waited a second or two and said : " You knew Blake was in the house. You knew he "—he jerked his head over his massive shoulder—" was in the house. What did you hear and see ? "

" Nothing. I was upstairs . . . "

" Yes, you said that. I happen to know that you knew Blake was in the house ; that he talked to you. I happen to know that you came down here and either witnessed the murder, or found Rantoul immediately afterward. That's true, isn't it ? "

She couldn't answer. Searching for an answer, where no answer existed that might not, later, be incriminating to Steve, she met his eyes helplessly but without speaking. He said : " Don't be so afraid of what you say. I know Blake killed him. I know that you know it. I even know . . . " the shadow of a smile touched his hard mouth, " I even know what you put in your pocket just now, as you came in the door."

With an effort of will she kept her hand from going to that pocket in her jacket. " It was a dark-red carnation," he said. " It was broken when the two men struggled, and it fell on the rug. Then Steve Blake got out his revolver—it was in the drawer of that table over there—as you see the drawer is open a little . . . " She followed his gesture toward a table across the room, a large book table with another lamp on it and a substantial drawer below. It was, as he had said, open a little as if it had been jerked out. It conjured up the whole picture. A struggle between two men, Steve beside himself with anger, walking over to that table where his own revolver was kept, jerking open the drawer and levelling it at Walsh Rantoul.

But there was a falseness in the picture ; it simply wasn't like Steve to shoot a man down like that, in cold blood, a man who couldn't likewise defend himself. Yet he and Walsh Rantoul had fought once before, she remembered ; quite publicly and violently, and Steve had never offered any explanation for it. So it wasn't in cold blood at all, but in fury and blind rage.

Steve, ordinarily self-controlled, cool, observant, was on occasion overtaken with gusty, quick-acting anger. The man, watching her, said quietly : " I don't know what their quarrel was about. Do you ? "

She shook her head.

He said : " Well, I see you don't want to talk. And I know why ; you're afraid of being made to turn witness against Blake. Will you give me that carnation or must I take it away from you ? "

Still she sat in stony, motionless silence. He waited a moment and then said, shaking his big head a little : " Look here, Miss Lovell, there's no point in your acting like this. You see, I saw the whole thing."

" You . . . ! " she whispered. " But I thought . . . ? "

She'd thought he was a plain-clothes man ; he *was* a plain-clothes man ; he must be. But then how had he seen what had happened in that room·?

He went on : " Did you notice that bruise on Rantoul's face ? I see by your eyes that you did. Well, Blake did that. And Blake himself has a bruise where Rantoul got home to his jaw. Rantoul was little but "—he shrugged—" wiry. Listen, Miss Lovell, I don't believe you are really paying attention to me. And it is essential," he said, spacing his words with a peculiar intentness that, in itself, compelled her attention. " It is essential," he said, " that you listen to me. Will you ? That's better. Now then, Miss Lovell, do you want Blake to go to prison for this ? I see you don't. I watched you, you know. I saw you get rid of that nosey little fellow who came in with the dog. I saw you take the dog away. First I saw you take the flower, to hide that. My guess is that you were coming back to hide this revolver— Blake's revolver with his fingerprints on it. The revolver that was used to kill Rantoul.

" Who are you ? " she said. " Are you a policeman ? "

He shook his head. " No. I'm a friend of Walsh Rantoul's."

So Steve hadn't confessed. From that blinding thought it was scarcely a leap to the next one : there still may be a way to save him.

The man opposite her went on so slowly and directly that she knew he had determined his course. " I'm a friend of Walsh's   I was staying at his house for the night. He came over here and I—followed him after awhile. I could see easily through the french window, over there. I stood in the shrubs that edge the terrace ; if you want to prove my state-ment all you have to do is take a flashlight and go and look ; the soil is soft there and I'm a heavy man ; you can easily find my footprints, if you're of a mind to do so, and if you're a smart girl "—suddenly he spaced his words again so they were freighted with significance—" as—I—think—you—are—you'll note that I stood there for some time. In short," he said, " I saw the whole thing. I saw Blake enter this room. I saw him exchange a few words with Walsh. I saw them fight, briefly. I saw Blake get this revolver and kill him."

" Steve "—she overcame a strange lethargy of speech—" Steve wouldn't have done that."

He lifted his eyebrows and smiled a little. " Oh, yes, he would. He nearly killed him last week. Don't forget that. If he'd hit Walsh just a little closer to the temple there'd have been a homicide charge then and there."

" But he . . . " she fumbled through horror, through fear for Steve, through a sudden, dreadful weariness, as if all her nerves had been put to sleep and all her blood had been drained away. " Steve wouldn't have left clues to himself, like this. If he killed a man he'd have the—the intelligence to see to it that no clues were left. He wouldn't leave his own revolver here for someone to find. He wouldn't lose the—the carnation he'd just worn. He wouldn't kill a man right here, in the house where he lived and where the murder would be certain to be traced to him. You aren't giving him credit for intelligence."

He was shaking his head, smiling again. " You forget, Miss Lovell, that the murder was done in the heat of anger. It was not premeditated. In fact, I doubt if Blake could have done a premeditated murder. If he gave himself time to think about doing a murder, he wouldn't do it. No—he didn't intend to do this. Therefore, all your arguments are false. He didn't intend to do it, therefore he didn't choose his place and time and weapon. . . . . "

" He would have gone to the police at once. He. . . . "

Again he was shaking his head. " How little you under-stand the most natural impulses in the world. No, Miss Lovell. He's gone now. He rushed out of the house—horrified, probably—when he realised what he'd done. That's natural; that's the way men really behave. He's rushed away to cool off, to get himself together, to realise what he did. No, he didn't intend to shoot Walsh. But he did shoot him. He'll be back presently, to clean up the place. He'll remember the revolver; he'll remember the flower; he'll remember that the body will be found here, in the house where he lives, and there'll be questions. Inquiry. Police. He'll remember that he's left a blazoned trail straight to himself, and he'll come back to efface that trail. But," said the big man softly, " he'll come back too late. Because, as you see, I was watching. And I got here first."

" Steve will confess to the police. You don't know Steve."

" I know men, Miss Lovell. And, in this case, I think I know Blake. You see there's something you've overlooked. He's a lawyer; he knows what happens when the law takes its due course. He's a man, and won't look forward to being the self-confessed prisoner at the bar, to be convicted as he certainly would be. And furthermore—Steven Blake is a patriot."

There was something unsaid, something new in the atmosphere, something significant and intent and purposeful in his eyes and in the thing he said. Something that stirred and moved and was about to come into being, so she could see it. She was sitting forward in her chair now, tense, listening. He said slowly again, as if to be sure that she would hear and understand every word: " Steven Blake is a patriot. Even if he had the weak—and I consider not at all human motive to confess—his patriotism would confound him, would keep him silent, in other words. You see—but you know this, Miss Lovell; I don't need to tell you this: right now his country needs him. Alive."

After a long silence she whispered: " Yes."

" His country needs *him*—not a man who's imprisoned for life for murder. Not, to all intents and purposes, a dead man. He—Steve Blake—is needed. He knows that. And he's deeply and sincerely patriotic." He waited a moment to let the force of the argument sink into her, while he wrapped the revolver. very deliberately, very slowly, so the action fascinated her and she could not look away from his great brutal hands and the gentle way he was wrapping the white handkerchief around the revolver. and slipping it carefully into the pocket of his coat, inside his overcoat. Then he

looked fully at her. " You realise that I'm right. Even if
he's different than any other man in the world and willing to
confess to murder before he needs to confess and take what's
coming to him, he'll think twice before he does it because of
his job. His very important job, Miss Lovell."

Steve *was* patriotic ; it was his breath of life ; it was bred
in his blood ; there was perhaps no other love that ran so
deep in his heart ; it outweighed self and personal ambition ;
it outweighed everything with Steve. She knew that.

And the big man moved a little closer to her and said
quietly : " The trouble is, of course, that *I* know the facts.
I can go to the police. *I* have incontrovertible proof. I
don't even need to go to the police myself. All I need to
do is write a letter—an anonymous letter, telling them that
Walsh has been murdered ; telling them the fingerprints of
the murderer are on the revolver which I can also mail to
them ; telling them what happened. I won't even need to
appear in the case. Blake was here in the house ; he can't
build himself up an alibi that wouldn't break down. The
police would get in the F.B.I. men ; the combination would
pin down Blake as the murderer within twenty-four hours.
He wouldn't have a chance. . . . "

Again something new moved and stirred in the room,
lay half-hidden behind his words. She whispered :
" *Wouldn't . . . ?* "

" Wouldn't, if I did that. I've got something to offer
you, Miss Lovell. I'm an opportunist, you see. I take
advantage of the things that fall my way. I can't say that
I expected a plum like this to drop into my lap. But it has
dropped, and I'm not a man to hesitate or "—there was something cold now back of those easy tones, something cold and
implacable as steel—" or to attempt to deceive."

" What are you getting at ? What do you mean ? "

" That's good. I like your question. You're an intelligent
girl, Miss Lovell. I can see that you'll grasp the situation
intelligently. No hysterics. No silly—and utterly futile, I
may warn you—attempts to evade. I'll put it simply, so
you'll see the force of it. The fact is, I'll keep silent about
this murder. If I'm paid . . . "

" Paid ! " Dazedly she thought of money, and he followed
her thought swiftly and exactly.

" I don't mean money," he said. " I mean—information."

Information! She knew instantly, exactly, like a flash of lightning out of the night lighting up a murky scene, what he meant. Heaven knows they'd been warned of it often enough! "Be careful—be discreet—never talk. Enemy ears may hear you." Horrible pictures flashed through her mind; planes laden with army and navy officers, all of them important; planes laden with replacements bent for some beleaguered, desperately fighting spot; planes for the faraway sight of which soldiers, hard-pressed, would be scanning the blue skies, hopefully and prayerfully, begging their God for the sight of that distant speck of silver which meant their lives, their fight, their victory, perhaps. Passenger lists—so when somebody important was on a plane, something would happen; something mysterious, something that couldn't be traced because the plane was burned. Burned with everybody on it; gone, souls going up in clouds of instantaneous black smoke. Sabotage—information—killing. This was war.

She felt sick; for the first time in her life she knew that the word heartsick is real and literal, and has a meaning.

The man before her was in the pay of an enemy government—German, Japanese, Italian, what did it matter? She didn't even accuse him; it was obvious; there was no need to talk of that. Steve—or those crashed and smoking planes—crashed and smoking whenever there was something important to go on them, important material, important plans of campaign, worst of all, important men, men who meant something to America, men who could not be replaced. The time of their departure secret, but Steve always knew; the air routes, their landing and refuelling stations—secret again, except to Steve and a few others. In his newly created job he had such information; it was part of his job which was, in effect, nothing more or less than that of a kind of liaison officer between the military and civilian air force, co-ordinating the two to best serve a nation at war, with its great demands and great need of every airplane that was capable of flying—not only to fight but to keep factories making war materials going at full tilt, turning out more planes and more guns until we could catch up with an enemy who had for so long subordinated everything else in order to stack up reserves of fighting equipment, before their treacherous attack upon a peace-loving country.

The big man, watching her, his face like a horrible bird

of prey, said suddenly : " Blake's life—or information. It's an easy trade."

She got up. She was perfectly steady and had no hesitation at all about her reply. It would be Steve's reply, too. She said, rather quietly : " No."

It didn't shake her to see the casual, unsurprised way in which he accepted her reply. But it did frighten her a little ; as if even below the monstrous suggestion he had already made there were other, more monstrous threats. He was altogether unperturbed ; he even smiled a little. He said : " I thought you'd say that."

She gathered herself together for attack. " Besides," she said, " you've admitted that you are an enemy agent. Can you possibly fail to see that I shall immediately report you to the F.B.I. ? And that they will not believe your accusation of Steve ? They can't believe it. The word of a spy . . ."

Again he took the wind out of her sails by smiling in a perfectly unperturbed way, and replying as casually and as matter-of-fact as before. " No. You won't report me. Although, if you want to, I've no objections. But I've said you were intelligent ; please do me the compliment of respecting my own intelligence. You have no evidence against me but your own word ; and you'll have to believe me when I say that none exists. Telephone to the F.B.I. now if you choose. They'll only investigate me—perhaps— and certainly release me. I'm telling you the truth when I say I am perfectly in the clear. But your Steve Blake— will be convicted upon incontrovertible evidence. I'll even explain to the F.B.I. exactly why you told them I was an enemy agent—because you were determined to cast doubt upon my word. My word," he said, and looked at the sofa. " Yes," he said softly, " I knew you'd refuse my demands— at first."

" At first ? There can't be any other answer. Ever. Steve himself . . . "

He wagged his head, as if some ugly amusement touched him. " Oh, yes, Steve. Steve Blake might be a fool ; he might admit what he's done and take his punishment. But you see *you* love him. Are you really going to sacrifice the man you love for "—he spread his hands and lifted his shoulders—" for a little harmless information ? " And again he watched her.

After a moment, because with diabolic shrewdness he'd
made her see again, in spite of herself, the man she loved—
Steve, with his gravely smiling eyes and long brown hands,
condemned to a dreadful living death (if it wasn't death
itself)—she said, in a queer, half-whisper : " Harmless ? "

He nodded. " Quite harmless. Only a few small things.
You aren't likely, you know, to know anything that's very
important. You're only his secretary."

In the very act of rising to the bait, she caught the look
in his face and realised he was trying to trap her into admitting
just how much of the information that passed through Steve's
hands was available—if she tried to secure it—to her. Play
dumb, she thought swiftly.

" Well, of course," she began, fumbling for the words of
her role, " I take his letters. And I can get into one of the
filing cabinets."

" *One* of the filing cabinets ? "

" It's—got important things in it," she said. Could she
play up to the sudden, half-visioned idea that had come to
her ? Could she deceive this man before her ? From that
she went swiftly to another question. Could she evade,
could she put him off until—well, until what ? Until, at
least, she had gained time.

He said : " *Very* important ? "

" Well-l-l," she said, trying to give the impression both
that what information she had access to was not important,
and that she was trying to convince him that it was, " yes.
Yes, I . . ."

He cut swiftly through that. " I said you were an intelligent young woman, Miss Lovell. Don't try to deceive me.
You really have access to almost every bit of information
which Blake has. Well, now—do you trade ? Or shall I
telephone to the police ? And disappear, after mailing them
the gun ? Don't think you can have me traced. I've
covered myself too well ; there is no danger for me. But,
meantime, Blake will be taken by the police. And Blake,
I don't need to say, is *not* in the clear." He went to the
telephone and put his hand out toward it.

And Maida's heart quite literally stopped. Steve.

There was no question in her mind of loyalty. She couldn't
give him the information he asked—not for Steve, not for
herself, not for anyone. She couldn't even consider it ; it

was simply a mental hazard she could not leap ; it came within the realm of so deep and instinctive a taboo that the mind failed even to take the breaking of it into account. Even if she had wished to do it, some physical wall would have arisen to stop her.

And it was that way with Steve, too. He'd give his own life, yes, readily. But dicker in that shameful way with the enemy, even for an instant, even in his thoughts—never.

And he would despise her for it, even if she could bring herself to consider such a course.

But it meant Steve's life, too. The evidence was conclusive against him ; there was no question of that. Men have been hanged on far less direct evidence. There was no way out.

Or was there ?

It was there again, like a blinding flash of light in her heart—running along her veins. She lowered her eyes quickly, for fear the man watching her would see the flash of change and hope in her eyes. And she saw that, since she had moved from the chair, she could now see that grey, terrible heap behind the sofa.

Whether Steve had killed him or not, there was that evidence, horribly conclusive against him. Time—she might fight for time. She must find Steve, tell him, together they could work something out. Some escape. Some plan. They must do it.

She said, eyes still lowered : " How will you hide—that ? "

His hand was still at the telephone, but he sensed a change in her voice. He said, very quietly, very watchfully : " There are ways. I'll see to that. Unless . . . " He took the telephone, but carefully. She saw that he interposed a fold of his coat between the grasp of his hand and the instrument. He was taking no chances. " You haven't long to decide," he said, and started to dial. She said stiffly : " Don't call the police."

He put down the receiver slowly, watching her, accepting her decision but watching her. He said finally : " I knew you were an intelligent young woman."

As he spoke the heavy front door opened and someone entered, closed it with a bang, paused for a moment and then started down the hall toward the library. Toward them. Whoever it was was walking quickly and purposefully.

CHAPTER FIVE

IT WAS NOT STEVE. She knew his walk. And it had to be someone familiar with the house—someone with a key, either Steve or Christine or Angela. All at once Rosy, in the broom closet, burst into a series of shrill, demanding yelps, clawing and yapping, giving tongue to the world that somebody had entered the house, somebody she knew, and that she was shut up and wanted out.

In the sudden clamour Maida looked at the man. He had frozen into immobility ; only his eyes showed that his mind was grappling with the unexpected turn, exploring it, deciding a course.

She held her breath, and the man across the room held his breath too, she thought, to listen. And, as Rosy's clamour to get out waxed higher and louder, the quick, light footsteps stopped. There was an instant's pause, and Maida thought the pounding of her heart would choke her. Then the person approaching evidently turned, walked back a few steps and into the dining-room. There was the light click of a high heel as whoever it was stepped momentarily off the rug in the hall and on to some bare, polished space of floor before the footsteps grew light upon the thick rugs in the dining-room and then suddenly, as if the swinging door had been opened, Rosy's barks grew briefly louder and then softer.

Maida took a quick breath. Christine—if it was she—was momentarily out of the way. If she had come in, everything would have been lost. There would have been no way to warn her of the desperate, small hope that Maida had clutched at, no way to quiet her, no way to cope with her. With that clarity that comes in moments of great need, Maida saw that if the thing that she had grasped at, the faint small hope, the dangerous—perhaps mad—project she was going to undertake had any chance for success no one else must know of it.

No one but Steve. She'd go straight to Steve—tell him— make him consider ways and means of saving himself and the trust committed to him ; keep him from going to the police, if she could. And the man across the room moved with lightning agility, and so quickly, he was like an enormous shadow moving toward her.

He too had caught the significance of the light click of a high French heel upon the strip of bare floor. " Who is she ? " he said, in a whisper that barely reached her ears.

" I don't know. Christine, I imagine. Christine Blake."

" The sister-in-law. All right. Get rid of her. Telephone to me to-night. At Monrose 2—0901. Remember that. Monrose 2—0901. Telephone to me. Get out of here now. I'll see to everything." His great hand went past her and quickly snapped off the light. Only the faint path of light from the hall now touched his face. He whispered as lightly as a zephyr again, yet with horrible clearness : " Don't try to cheat. Get rid of her, whoever she is. Keep her out of this room for ten minutes—five. Remember, though—I've got all the evidence. I've got it and I can use it. Don't try to double-cross me."

He put a hand like steel on her shoulder, as if to emphasize the implacability and strength of the force against her. He pushed her into the hall as easily as he would have moved away a leaf. She could hear Christine now, talking to the dog in a low, distant murmur. Rosy had stopped barking. Christine would be coming back into the hall. Numbly she started in that direction when the man in the library caught at her and thrust her alligator handbag into her hands, and her brown gloves and her furs. " It was careless of you to forget these. Don't be careless again," he said. " You must learn."

His voice was perfectly easy and matter-of-fact.

She thought suddenly and horribly : So that's how they make enemy agents ! As easily as that. Using love as a threat and a lever. Using life . . . Christine swung open the door into the dining-room and came across it and Maida walked quickly away from the library door. It happened that she reached the newel post just as a woman appeared in the wide, arched doorway into the dining-room—at the side of the house opposite to the drawing-room and the library. It looked as if she herself had just come downstairs, Maida thought swiftly ; she would make Christine think that. And then she saw that, although the golden aureole of carefully coiffed hair was the same colour, it was not Christine who stood there. It was Angela.

She was dressed for the evening ; glittering sequins dotting the delicate blue marquisette gleamed beneath her long, white

ermine coat. Her face was freshly powdered and beautiful,
and her lips and eyes were carefully made up ; a blue sequin
flower perched on top of her golden curls. She held Rosy in
her arms and Rosy was quiet. All at once Maida saw again
that Rosy was ominously quiet—not wriggling, not struggling
as she usually did to get down, but instead watchful and
uneasy, staring past Maida down the hall toward the now
dark library doorway, her ears alert.

With utter horror, remembered too well, she saw the little
dog's brown hair begin to rise along the back of her neck.
She had to get hold of Rosy If Angela put her down and
she ran to the library . . .

Angela said coolly : " Oh, it's you. I didn't know you
were here. Where's Christine ? "

Where was Christine, thought Maida ; she'd forgotten
Christine ; she'd forgotten the absent servants who ought,
soon, to be returning. But Christine had telephoned for
Steve to pick her up at the—where had he said ? Oh, yes,
the Slaters'. She said, quickly : " Christine is still at the
Slaters' ; I believe they're having a cocktail party. . . . "

" Oh, yes," said Angela. " I looked in. But I left ages
ago and went home to change. It's seven o'clock. Christine
ought to be at home by now—unless, of course, she's gone
on somewhere." Her thin, arched eyebrows were frowning
a little. " That's what she's done, I suppose. But where is
Steve ? Is he here ? "

" No. Steve—I thought—went to pick up Christine.
Then he was to go to your place for dinner."

" Well, really, Maida, dear, don't you suppose I know that !
But he . . . " She looked at Maida, and her eyes became a
little brighter and harder so the pupils were agate-sharp black
points. " You didn't say how you happen to be here."

Rosy gave a struggle and Maida held her breath, literally.
But Angela was of a nature to subdue anything that struggled
—even a little cocker spaniel. She held the dog firmly in
her ermine-clad arms. Maida said : " Steve sent me to get
some papers from his desk. I'm just leaving."

" Hasn't Steve been here ? "

Better not admit his presence ; better not admit anything
in case, later, there was a question of it. She listened behind
her ; the library was perfectly still ; there was no sound of
motion whatever. Yet it seemed to her that a slight, small

current of air touched her, as it would do if the french doors had been opened wider softly. Wide enough to permit—she caught back that thought as if it might communicate itself to Angela. She said quickly, seeing the impatience in Angela's lovely regular face and bright blue eyes: " Steve ? Why I thought he was with you. At the Chichester, I mean. He said he was going there, and I was to bring the notes to him there. I—as I say I was just leaving."

Rosy gave another determined wriggle. Maida had a swift and frightening mental picture of the dog leaping to the floor, making a brown streak to the library, stopping to bark and bark. She started toward the door, hoping Angela would follow and, to her great relief, Angela did so, still holding the little dog. Maida said : " I was just going to walk across the park and get a taxi."

She put her hand on the door. If only Christine didn't choose that moment to appear.

Angela said, frowning : " I came in my car. I'll take the notes to Steve. I expected him before now, but I expect he was held up somewhere. I thought he might possibly be here with . . ." she paused, almost imperceptibly, and said, " with Christine." Her lovely, full-throated voice hardened a little on the name.

Was she, then, a little on guard about Christine, a little jealous, a little afraid that Christine so newly widowed, so definitely an object of affection and sympathy from Steve, would tighten her claim upon him ? Christine was Angela's sister ; but sisters had been rivals before now. It was the smallest, briefest thought that went through Maida's mind and disappeared. Christine really grieved for Harcourt, as much as she could grieve for anything, and Steve was not at all likely to make love to his brother's widow. And, in any case, it didn't matter to Maida ; nothing mattered except that she must see Angela out of the house—and find Steve.

Hurry. Hurry. It was like a voice admonishing her. She opened the door and the soft night air, laden with a thousand, gentle spring fragrances struck her face. How much had happened since she had stood on that doorstep, ringing !

Angela's long car, with a uniformed chauffeur, was drawn up at the kerb, its engine running. As the door opened and the two women were outlined against the light from the hall, the chauffeur sprang out, tossed away a surreptitious cigarette, and opened the door of the tonneau and stood there, at attention, waiting. Angela said rather reluctantly : " Well, I suppose if he isn't here he must have gone to the Chichester. I expect I just missed him. I only thought that Christine might be keeping him here. That is "—she caught herself quickly with a side glance from beautiful—and hard—blue eyes at Maida—" that is, Christine is so determined to make Steve feel welcome in her house and home. And, poor darling, she was accustomed to so much attention from Harcourt. But she mustn't demand attention from Steve ; he hasn't the time for it, really. And she, poor dear, doesn't realise that Steve's an important man. That he's frightfully busy and frightfully . . . "

She was going to go, thought Maida, scarcely daring to believe it.

Angela paused, thought for an instant, and frowned absently into the mirror, turning her head to one side to observe her hair and the set of the diamond ear-rings she wore. Then, as Maida watched, she decided. Perhaps the waiting car, the open tonneau door, showing its lighted and luxurious interior, as much as she thought that, somehow, she had barely missed Steve and that he was waiting for her at the Chichester, decided her. She bent, put down the little spaniel, and, as Maida stepped aside to hold the door open for her, swept past her. And failed thereby to see that cocker go down the hall, rather slowly, her head low and cautious.

Maida's heart seemed to clutch itself together as she saw the dog's queerly savage advance—almost as if a hand had tightened upon it. But Angela must not see. She stepped outside quickly. The man in the library could deal with the dog. She closed the big front door heavily and finally. Now, surely, Angela wouldn't draw back. If she could get her away before Christine arrived !

She did. Angela, holding her skirts high, went down the sidewalk to the car.

At the door, with the chauffeur giving her his arm, Angela turned to speak to Maida who had followed.

" I'll take the notes to Steve," she said. " Give them to me."

Maida hadn't thought of that ; she must see Steve herself

Yet she mustn't let Angela know that it was urgent—so terribly urgent. She said: "Steve asked me to bring them."

"But, really, my dear!" A quick shadow of annoyance and impatience came over Angela's face, lighted from the light in the tonneau. "Can't you trust me with them? Don't be a silly girl!" She laughed a little lightly, but she was annoyed just the same. Maida said quickly: "Oh, of course. I think he wanted to dictate a letter or two that I was to get out on the night post. That's all."

"Oh," said Angela, tapping her slippered foot on the step. Then she got quickly into the car. "All right," she said. "Come along. Get in. I'll take you there. Steve will be waiting. That will be quicker than getting a taxi."

Maida hesitated. Somehow, going alone, walking across the park, getting herself a taxi eventually, would have given her time to think. But it was better to get to Steve at once. "Thank you," she said, and got into the car. The chauffeur closed the door; instantly the little lights at either side of the deeply cushioned seat went out. There was only a gentle gloom, lighted faintly by the dashlight before the driver's seat ahead. The chauffeur got in and the long car pulled easily away from the kerb, leaving Christine's house. Leaving the thing that lay there—huddled, with blood upon it and sightless blank eyes. Although by this time, it might no longer be there. "I'll see to it," said the man with the hat pulled low over his lined and heavy face. "I'll see to that," he'd said, with a finality that argued complete adequacy.

The darkness became darker as they passed into shadow, grew lighter as they turned and went under a dimmed street lamp, dimmed because Washington was a city at war, the centre of a great government at war. Angela's perfume wafted across the little space between them as Angela moved impatiently.

Well, she'd got to think. Plan. Think. As never in her life before she had thought.

Suppose Steve was not at Angela's, waiting. Suppose he'd gone straight to the police and told them that he'd murdered a man. Suppose—her heart turned over—*but suppose Steve hadn't murdered him!*

No matter about the evidence. Suppose that had been arranged—deliberately to trap Steve. And she'd swallowed it—hook, line and sinker. Suppose the whole incredible and horrible thing had been intentionally arranged to force her to give the enemy that valuable information that lay in her power and Steve's to give.

She'd been frightened—horrified—taken by surprise. She'd been an easy victim. Her shock—and her love for Steve—had been played upon accurately and surely as a man plays upon a well-known instrument. Knowledge of human nature—that was the stock-in-trade of a successful enemy agent, of a man like that one who had stepped in from the terrace, out of the night, and had taken command of the situation.

He had said he was a friend of Walsh Rantoul's. He had said he'd been watching and had seen Steve murder Walsh. He had picked up the revolver, and it was undoubtedly Steve's revolver ; she had seen that herself. But it might have been planted.

There was the carnation. But she still had that. She put her hand in her pocket to make sure.

It was not there. She searched, so anxiously that she could feel Angela, through the dusk in the tonneau, turn to eye her.

" Lost something ? " said Angela suddenly.

" No," said Maida. " No."

But she had ; the dark-red carnation was gone. Somehow, probably when the big man had pushed her toward the hall, he had slipped his other hand in her pocket and taken that carnation. He'd had her bag, too, for an instant or two ; the bag she'd put down without knowing she had done so when first she saw Walsh Rantoul's huddled body, and then forgotten along with her gloves and furs. The big man had remembered, had thrust them at her, had warned her that she must learn to be careful. She opened her bag and felt for the notes of the radio speech, and they were gone, too.

Steadily, now, she closed the bag and surveyed the situation. The notes themselves were not important ; nothing that Steve or anyone would say over the radio could be of a nature to give the enemy any information it didn't already have. That was clear.

It was the ease, the stealth, with which he had taken not only the betraying red carnation but the notes, too, from her bag, that emphasized the kind of organisation that the man in the library represented. It gave her for the first time, really, a glimpse of the net that had fallen around her and of the smallness of its meshes. There was not only one man against her (and against Steve) ; there would be very soon any number of men. An organisation, working secretly, working swiftly, working ruthlessly, working for the most part from venal motives.

They were running swiftly and silently through the park now, and time was passing. Steve's radio address was scheduled for nine-thirty ; he was supposed to be at the studio at a quarter after nine, and the notes were gone. You can't make a radio address by *ad lib*bing, especially if you are a public official whose every word must be weighed, in times of war. She'd have to go back down-town to the office, let herself in, get the carbon of the speech. Steve's notes along the margin, of course, were lost. But the speech had been, naturally, composed of generalities. He'd have to do with a copy of it on which he'd made no notes ; in any case, Steve's memory was sharp and clear—almost photographic ; in all probability he would remember the notes he'd made.

It was comforting to reflect that the notes that had been taken from her handbag were just what they were : notes of a radio speech, scheduled to be delivered publicly to whoever cared to listen. It was of no value whatever to the organisation the man in Christine's house represented.

At the same time she'd better hurry. Get the carbon of the notes ; find Steve ; tell him everything. Steve would know what to do. Steve was a fighter. Steve could be as resourceful, as wily, as hard-hitting as anyone working openly or secretly against him.

She turned to Angela. " Can you let me out here, Angela ? "

" Let you out ? Why ? " said Angela after a rather long stare through the dusk.

" I've made an idiotic mistake," said Maida. " I got the wrong notes."

" Oh. Well, that was stupid of you. But, really—Steve's depending upon the notes ; radio speeches are important. How did you ever happen to . . .? Well," she was biting her crimson lips which were artfully made up to look fuller.

' Yes, it really was very stupid of you.   I don't know why
Steve puts up with things like that."   Her tone had a distinct
flavour of proprietorship ; it implied she would speak to
Steve about the inefficient secretary he had employed.
" Well, the best thing to do is to go back to Christine's house
and get the right notes.   It's much quicker than to go to the
office.   I'll tell the chauffeur to turn around."   She was
actually leaning forward.

" No," said Maida sharply.   Too sharply.   Angela's golden
head jerked a little toward her again ; she could see her eyes
narrow so that they looked calculating.   Calculating—Walsh
Rantoul had looked like that.   Maida's heart gave a kind of
lurch as she remembered.   She said firmly : " No, there's a
better copy at the office, and I'll get it.   If you'll stop the
car I'll pick up a taxi."   She hesitated.   Then added : " I
expect Steve will be waiting for you at your hotel.   I don't
want to hold you up.   Will you tell him I'll be along with
the notes ? "

Angela thought that over for a moment.   Then she said,
on a tangent : " Do you always call him Steve ?   Even in
the office ?   I shouldn't think . . . "

" That," said Maida, " is Steve's business, don't you
think ? "   She said it very gently, but she wouldn't have
said it at all if she hadn't been so frantically anxious to get
out of the car before Angela could tell the driver to return
to Christine's house.   That fated, death-haunted house—
where Heaven only knew what was going on just then.
Again she shuddered away from that thought.   And then
she was aware that Angela was eyeing her thoughtfully, her
mouth tight but perfectly self-possessed.   " I've always said,"
said Angela calmly, " that it was a mistake to employ anybody with whom one feels bound to maintain a certain
friendly relationship.   I shall tell Steve what you've just
said.   Certainly you can take a taxi, if you want to.   There'll
be one presently on the street we are just coming to."   The
glass was up between the tonneau and the driver's seat.
She leaned forward and picked up the little speaking tube
and gave the chauffeur concise, swift directions.

They stopped in another moment.   It was the corner of
a traffic-laden street.   Lights from cars were going swiftly
in both directions.

" It won't be long before you find a taxi, I'm sure," said

Angela, conspicuously not offering to wait. " I'll tell Steve
that you'll bring the notes ; be sure you're not late."

Maida got thankfully out of the long car, and as thankfully
watched it roll away.

And, as a matter of fact, although owing to the congestion
of population in Washington then and the demand for taxis
it could have been a long time before she managed to find
one, it was really only a few moments.

She gave the driver the number of Steve's office building
on H Street, leased by the government when the war expansion
overwhelmed the city, and sank back against the cushions.
The taxi driver took it without comment ; he probably knew
it was an office building. The Washington taxi drivers know
everything—or almost everything. But he was accustomed
to people working at all hours, at night, all night. Picking
them up in the cold grey dawn, taking them to some all-night
lunchroom where they could get coffee, returning them to
the office for more work. He whistled cheerfully and wasted
no time at the traffic lights.

She had keys both to the outer offices and to Steve's
office. The carbon, however, would be in her own desk,
not yet filed. There would be a watchman in the building,
at the door probably, and several other offices lighted. It
was always that way. She would get the notes and go
straight back by taxi to Angela's hotel. She'd simply tell
Steve she had to talk to him alone, let Angela think what
she chose.

The familiar, blue-uniformed building guard, with
registration book, had not yet become a fixture of this newly
established government agency, born of the sudden war
emergency. However, a watchman was on duty, as she had
expected him to be—but in a little cubbyhole at the back of
the wide entrance, having himself some coffee and a doughnut.
He looked around the door as she entered, her heels tapping
along the bare floor, nodded and told her which elevator was
running. The boy running the elevator said, rather glumly,
something about her working late.

She saw no one in the wide corridors. She opened the
outer offce door and all was in order with little black covers
over the typewriters. She went on into her own office and
sat down quickly at the desk. Before she even put down
her bag or took off her gloves she saw it. The cover had

been removed from her own typewriter; that drew her attention to the paper that was slipped into the roller. A paper upon which someone had typed—with her own type-writer: " Find out what ocean-flying planes the government is to take over from the Interstate ; their size and description ; and the date of transfer.

CHAPTER SIX

SHE didn't believe it. She saw it ; she reached out in-credulously and touched it. She noted the devilish clever-ness with which traces of the writer had been evaded by the use of her own machine, her own yellow copy paper. But she still simply didn't believe it.

Yet it was there—unsigned. It hadn't been there when she left the office, and anyway, no one in the office would have typed such a demand. There was no question as to its origin.

It had been at the most—even allowing for more time between the moment when Angela let her out of the car and she managed to pick up a taxi than, at the time, it had seemed—twenty minutes since she'd left Christine's house. Well, make it twenty-five ; she'd been engrossed in thought, terribly engrossed. Perhaps she'd really walked further than she'd thought before the empty taxi came along and she hailed it and got in. But even twenty-five minutes wouldn't suffice for the big man at Christine's to do what it was neces-sary to his own scheme to do—cover his own and Steve's tracks, get downtown, and into her office.

But then it was simple for someone to get master keys, duplicate keys, skeleton keys. The locks of office doors were meant to keep people out, yes ; but they were not absolutely burglar proof. It was the steel filing cabinets ; the great steel safes with secret combinations that did that. Or were intended to ; at least they made it harder.

But she was thinking in circles—and thinking idly ; thinking things that didn't matter. The point was that, somehow, he had got there ; somehow, he'd left that message where she would see it. Somehow, he'd given her her first assignment.

Her first assignment ! The phrase struck her with utter horror. It was such a poignant thrust that she rebelled completely against it. Nothing was worth that. She read it again and again : " Find out what ocean-flying planes the government is to take over from the Interstate ; their size and description ; and the date of transfer."

The Interstate was one of the biggest of the commercial airlines ; it was known far and wide simply by that name. The Interstate. As a matter of fact, however, it was not merely interstate, it was international ; it flew wherever planes could fly, binding countries together, soaring above the highest mountain chains, cruising trackless oceans, travelling everywhere. It was a source of great pride to every American ; it had a record for safety that was unsurpassed.

Naturally, when the war began so suddenly, with such ugly treachery and dishonour when those Japanese planes streaked out of the sky on a golden, sunny Sunday morning over Pearl Harbour—naturally at that time the Interstate had been one of the airlines that was remarkably well equipped. They had planes, land planes of the latest type. But what was at first of chief importance was that they had planes which would fly over oceans, mammoth flying boats of long-range cruising speed and power, capable of carrying large cargoes of men and material.

They—the organisation the man at Christine's must be a part of—knew then that the government was about to take over some of those planes. She knew that, too. And Steve knew the details ; he knew what planes ; their capacity ; their ceiling, range, power, speed ; he knew when ; he would know the routes ; the destination ; the men they were to carry.

She was cold. It was queer how cold anybody could be on a warm spring night. She was so cold that she couldn't move ; even her heart, somehow, seemed to stop. So that was the kind of thing that was now lined up against her. Against Steve.

Walsh Rantoul wasn't worth it. Nothing was worth it.

Somebody—not Maida but somebody in her body— moved. Turned about in her desk chair. Reached for the telephone.

She knew the number of the F.B.I. She had memorised

it weeks before. She was in possession constantly, through Steve, of various items of information the enemy would like to know. If anything happened ; if she suspected anyone ; if there was the faintest reason to suspect anyone, she had already determined her obvious course. She had memorised the number. Call it any time, she'd been told ; night or day ; any time. There'll always be a man there, ready— waiting—for just such calls. Don't hesitate. Call it.

She took the telephone off the cradle and began to dial. Steve would do that. Steve would have done it at once.

As she dialled the third number, however, she thought : then let Steve do it. That will be better.

And remembered with a stab that it was Steve's life.

She put down the telephone slowly. If Steve had killed Walsh Rantoul, the man back there at Christine's would not hesitate. His plan, seized as a true opportunist does seize upon a plan, might fall through completely, fail utterly ; but he was without mercy,. he was implacable ; he would betray Steve. He meant that. And he had the evidence. No ; she'd see Steve first. He would call the F.B.I. There was no doubt of that ; he'd do it at once.

She tore the paper from the typewriter and folded it up carefully and, after a moment's hesitation, slipped it into the soft, fragrant hollow under her brassiere ; it would be safer there than in her handbag. With a kind of wry smile she remembered the old-fashioned novels ; ladies always put their love letters in their bosoms, under the lace and (as a rule) violets that nestled there.

Well, that day was past and the horrible thing that she mustn't lose was not a love letter. She glanced at her watch. She was vaguely surprised to find that it was only a little after eight. She was still cold and very conscious of being alone in the offices, with Steve's darkened office opening from her own and the outer office, through which she had passed, bare and strange without its usual clatter of typewriters, and chat and visitors coming, waiting to see Steve, and going again. Someone—not long ago—had entered that outer office, had entered her office, had sat right there at her desk where she was sitting.

She pushed back the chair with an abrupt motion and got up.

Oh, yes—the notes for the radio speech. She unlocked

the desk and took out the clipped sheets. Scrutinising each page, she decided that the carbon was clear enough for Steve to read. That was that then ; she wouldn't have to stay in that suddenly haunted office and make a new, fresh copy. With a grasp at the sensible, everyday, commonplace kind of life which had been so fantastically and madly destroyed during the past two hours, she told herself she was hungry. She was cold, and she was hungry.

She'd feel better, she'd find her own wits again, she'd be able to think clearly if she had some food. And there was time. Instead of going to the hotel she'd go direct to the broadcasting station. But first she'd telephone to Steve.

Suddenly it seemed queer to her that Steve hadn't either brought Christine home, or arrived at Angela's apartment. On second thought, though, that could be easily explained. He must have been on his way to one place or the other at the time when Angela came.

But she put the notes in her handbag ; they'd be safe this time, she decided. She took up the telephone and dialled Christine's house.

She could hear the repeated buzz several times. What was going on there ? What had happened ? Where was Steve ?

Christine answered. Her voice was as always, when she was thinking of it, very soft and melodious. She said : " Mrs. Harcourt Blake's residence."

" This is Maida. Is Steve there ? "

" Oh, Maida." Christine's voice altered slightly ; it wasn't quite so musical. " No, he isn't. I think he's at Angela's. He was going to have dinner with her to-night. Why ? "

" I—I had a message for him," said Maida. " Has Steve been there ? "

" Why, no," said Christine. " I just got here a few minutes ago, but I'm sure he hasn't been here. That is—well, on second thought, I suppose he could have come in and gone out again ; the servants were out to-day—such a nuisance. Rilly Delbert had to bring me home from the Slaters' party."

" Slaters'," said Maida. " Oh, yes, I thought Steve was to pick you up there."

There was a kind of silence at the other end of the telephone. Then Christine said ; " No. He didn't pick me up.

He had to go to a reception this afternoon. Poor Steve, you know how he hates being made to leave the office when he's so busy. No, I didn't see him at the Slaters' at all. Try Angela's, Maida, if you want him. I'm sure you'll find him there."

Her voice was untroubled. But perhaps she'd just got in ; perhaps she was talking from the telephone in her own room, upstairs. Perhaps she hadn't gone into the library at all. Perhaps—Maida's heart gave that sickening kind of lurch again—perhaps the huddled grey heap was still there, still staring with blank bright eyes that merely reflected the light from above and didn't see anything. She had to know. She thought quickly, and said rather desperately : " Christine, I stopped in to get something for Steve . . . " An admission that ; she realised it too late. She had to go on : ". . . and I—I lost my gloves. Brown gloves. I wonder if . . . "

" Well," Christine sounded annoyed. Probably she'd just got into one of her clinging, chiffon tea gowns and settled down on the chaise longue for a rest.

" I thought," said Maida, " that I might have left them in the—in the library. Downstairs."

That was an admission too. But she had to know.

" Oh." There was a pause. Then Christine said rather crossly : " I suppose you want me to look for them. Well, hold on a moment. I'm using the extension in my room. Really, Maida, it seems to me an efficient secretary wouldn't —oh, well, never mind. Hold on and I'll look myself. . . . "

Angela would have told her coolly that the maid would look for them the next day and hung up. Christine demurred, but went to look herself. It was the difference between the two women. Yet both of them were incredibly lovely to look at—Christine only a little older, a little more matured in her figure, a little lazier and less likely to exert her will. She was going downstairs now. Maida could see her, chiffons trailing around her, little satin mules stepping carefully down the steps. Christine was proud of her small, high-arched feet, and white, dimpled hands. What would she find in the library ?

What would Christine's lazy, lovely voice sound like when it spoke again into the telephone ? Or would she take down the telephone in the library at all ? Wouldn't she scream, stare, run for help. . .?

Maida's throat was so tight it hurt as if she were choking back tears. Her hand clung so tightly to the telephone that it was numb and—again—cold. Then all at once there was a click and Christine said : " They aren't here, Maida. You must have dropped them somewhere else."

And her voice was unchanged. Possibly a little irritated, a little put-upon, but otherwise unchanged.

Maida made herself make doubly sure, and said in a voice that sounded amazingly natural, she thought, and casual : " I thought I put them down on the arm of the sofa. Perhaps they dropped behind it."

" Wait . . . " said Christine.

Again it seemed to Maida that the throb in her throat would choke her before Christine came back. Her voice tinkled irritably into Maida's ear. " No. They aren't there. They're nowhere in the room."

Her voice was irritable, but that was all. So that thing that had been Walsh Rantoul was gone—taken away. The big man in the library had fulfilled his part of the bargain, and expected her to fulfil hers.

She must have thanked Christine and hung up, for she was standing there staring at the telephone.

She wondered rather vaguely how he could have done what he must have done and still have come all that distance to the office, found his way in and left the message on her typewriter. But that was simple, she saw at once. It was the telephone ; he was not working alone. He had merely telephoned to someone—someone equipped for just such a chore. Someone to whom, again, opening an office lock was more routine. All in a day's work.

She took up the telephone again and dialled the number of the hotel on the top of which nestled Angela's lovely little penthouse.

" Miss Favor's apartment, please," she said, when a voice said, " The Chichester " in a bored way. Angela's maid answered. She was a coloured woman of about fifty—discreet, well paid and self-effacing. But Steve wasn't there.

The maid left the telephone to speak to Angela and came back. Miss Favor had said to tell Miss Lovell that Mr. Blake wouldn't be there for dinner, after all. He had just telephoned and said he was detained and would Miss Favor meet him at the broadcasting studio at a quarter after nine.

"Detained," said Maida. "But didn't he say where? I —it's a business matter. I've got to see him."

The maid's voice was smooth as jelly and respectful and uncommunicative.

"That's all Miss Favor know, Miss Lovell. He jus' say he detained."

Again Maida put down the telephone.

The one thing to do then was to go to the broadcasting studio and wait for him.

Perhaps it was then, really, that the first premonition of utter disaster, utter catastrophe, entered Maida's heart. If so, she dismissed it—quickly, almost desperately. She pulled her furs around her throat to warm her and left the office.

Going down in the elevator the boy said something about working at night; he didn't like it, he said. The hours got long, after midnight. He stood in the doorway of the elevator and watched her start down the wide corridor to the entrance. On an impulse she swung back to question him. Had anyone else gone up to that floor since he'd been on duty?"

"Nope," he said. "Do you mean Mr. Blake?"

"Anybody," said Maida. And he said again, losing interest: "Nope. Place is dead as a doornail to-night."

But there were ways, of course; the fire stairs; even the fire escape and a corridor window. She went out on to the street and, again, eventually found a taxi and went to a little restaurant where she made herself eat.

As she had suspected, the food was heartening; she was less chilled, less completely surrendered to the nightmare that had engulfed her by the time she'd swallowed some hot soup and steak and coffee.

But her face, in the little mirror behind the cashier's desk when she left the small, warm restaurant, looked white and tired and she saw herself glance quickly and with a horrible scrutiny at a man who walked up behind her to pay his bill as she paid hers. He didn't look at her. Outside the little restaurant he walked briskly away, intent on his own business. It was the message on the typewriter that had done that to her; that had made her feel that the net had already enwrapped her. She took another taxi and reached the brightly lighted broadcasting studio a few moments before Steve.

To give herself something to do, something to employ her thoughts while she waited, she read through the speech he was to give, watching for mistakes. It was all clear. She was sure Steve could read it with ease before the microphone, and at a quarter after nine he arrived.

Angela was with him.

He smiled when he saw Maida.

" I knew you'd be waiting," he said, coming toward her.

" Have you got my notes there ? " He was still wearing the cut-away of the afternoon and the striped trousers, and his overcoat again was slung across his shoulders.

But the thing that, mainly, she saw was the patch on his chin. A little white square of medical gauze held in place by adhesive.

" Steve—*what* . . . ? "

He looked straight at her, his grey eyes bright and dark and inscrutable. " I ran into something," he said, and smiled briefly again. " Give me the notes, Maida. I've got to run through them with the announcer for time."

She gave him the notes.

Without knowing it, really, she followed him—and Angela, still dressed and glittering in blue sequins and white ermine, so the elevator boy and the men in the control room and the young announcer himself all looked at her with interest and admiration.

Somebody gave Maida a chair, just behind Angela. Somebody told her to be quiet when the red light came on, because that meant that Mr. Blake was on the air.

And then all at once the red light did come on. There was a complete, deadly hush. Someone in the control room waved through the glass in a signal that the young announcer seemed to understand, for he stood in front of the microphone and began to talk in easy, nicely moderated syllables.

Maida didn't hear them. She didn't even hear Steve when he took the announcer's place, his notes in one long brown hand.

For he'd slipped back his overcoat and put it on a chair. And from where she sat she saw that there was no dark-red carnation in his buttonhole.

That—and the gauze and adhesive on his chin. I ran into something, he'd said.

She got up. Ignoring the gesture of caution from the

announcer, the lifted eyebrows which Angela turned toward her, she slipped very quietly to the door and (taking care to make no rustle, no sound at all to be magnified a thousand times by the all-hearing microphone) out of the room.

Afterward she didn't remember walking through those wide, echoing corridors or going down the elevator.

She didn't remember the street, the people, the lights, the little crowded drug store that eventually she must have reached.

She did remember fishing in her bag for a nickel and the knell-like sound it made as she dropped it into the box of the pay telephone. She remembered making certain the little folding door was closed, too.

Then she began to dial. She couldn't have forgotten the number, Monrose 2—0901.

CHAPTER SEVEN

AGAIN she had reached a conclusion, swiftly, because she had to, and only then began to go back over the steps that had led her to that conclusion. They were, however, there, hard, solid, incontrovertible and completely convincing. She had known that Steve would go straight to the F.B.I. as soon as he heard her story.

If he heard the rest of the story, nothing else would matter. He would stop the scheme that the man at Christine's, the enemy agent, had instantly set in motion by seizing upon the circumstances of Walsh Rantoul's death so quickly and so daringly. Yes, Steve would go straight to the F.B.I. She had known that; she had counted on it. And there she had made her mistake, for that meant that he would tell exactly what had happened. And he would tell *all* that had happened. It meant that the unknown, the enemy agent, would instantly send in the revolver, which almost certainly had Steve's fingerprints on it; it meant that the weight of circumstantial evidence would instantly be brought to bear against Steve.

The telephone buzzed, a regular, short ring.

She'd been mad to think of telling Steve. He would instantly, without pause, walk straight into the trap. They would arrest him at once. How could they fail to arrest him?

They would. . . . Suddenly she realised that she'd been waiting too long for a reply. She hung up and quickly dialled again.

She must have made a mistake in dialling the first time ; perhaps her fingers slipped, for this time almost at once there was a click at the other end, and a voice she remembered too well said easily, rather pleasantly, indeed : " Miss Lovell . . ."

Maida caught her breath. It was not easy, now she had to launch it. It was a tricky, dangerous thing she planned to do ; one which might well turn into a boomerang and ruin herself and Steve. She said in a whisper : " Yes . . ."

" I was expecting you. Would it interest you to know that everything is done ? "

" Everything ? " She whispered it again and looked through the little glass in the door. But there were only two or three people in the drug store—a clerk selling some throat gargle, somebody sitting at the lunch counter over a cup of chocolate. Every day, normal people, living in a quiet, beautiful, normal world, such as she had been living in only a few hours ago.

" Everything, Miss Lovell. You need have no worries on that score. Mrs. Blake will not dream of the scene that took place in her library." There was actually a kind of throaty chuckle in the bland tones. Maida said :

" Why did you tell me to call you ? "

" Only to establish contact, my dear. By the way, you've been to your office ? "

" Yes."

" I thought you would go there when you found the notes gone from your pocketbook. Not very interesting notes, I'm afraid ; nothing that all the world couldn't know."

" Naturally," said Maida. " It was only a radio speech. I could have told you that."

" Ah, but you didn't. You must learn to repose more confidence in me. You got my order ? "

" Your . . ."

" Yes, yes—my order. I'm sure you got it. I telephoned immediately. See that you have that information for me. To-morrow at the latest."

To-morrow. And time was the weapon she was playing for. " But I . . . It may not be possible. You don't understand . . ."

" Nothing is impossible," he said softly. " I'm sure you
can get that if you try. And if you don't try—Miss Lovell,
I trust you have no doubts of my intention. I'm not a man
to be trifled with and the people I represent do not propose
to be trifled with. This very fortunate little incident has
come very luckily into my hands. Don't think for an instant,
my dear, that I don't intend to utilise it to the very fullest
degree. You do understand me, don't you ? "

She made some sort of sound. It didn't satisfy the man
at the other end of the wire, for he said sharply, with something that was suddenly vicious and cruel in his voice so the
words were like a whiplash, designed to bring her to her
senses : " *Don't you understand ? Everything . . .* "

" Yes," said Maida.

The voice purred again. " I thought you would. I hold
all the cards, my dear. Don't forget. Even the thing you
in America insist upon using a Latin phrase to designate.
In other words the . . . "

" Yes. Yes, I . . . "

" The *corpus delicti*," he continued, and chuckled again
softly.

" Where did you—what have you done ? "

" Ah," he said. " That's my part of the bargain. Suffice
it to tell you that I can always prove what I've said I'd prove.
If it becomes necessary."

" But that wouldn't help your cause," she began. " That
would be only revenge, totally without value to yourself or
to the—the people who pay you."

Again there was a note of something vicious and savage in
his voice. " Don't deceive yourself, my dear. Now then,
to business. You found my order. Very well. Someone
will telephone to you some time to-morrow. Be ready to tell
them the answers."

" But—how shall I . . . ? "

" You'll know," he said. " Don't worry about that."

" Who are you ? How shall I get in touch with you if I
want to—if I—if I have something important . . . "

He saw through that at once and chuckled softly again.
" Oh, come, my dear. Don't pretend you're so eager to fall
in with my plans that you would even try to contact me in
order to tell me of some bit of news that comes your way.
No, no. I'm too old a bird to be caught by that. However,

if you must have a name for me you can call me "—he
hesitated and then said almost laughingly—" Smith. How's
that ? A good American name. Smith. That's all now."

" But—but wait. Won't there be inquiries about—about
him ? Won't there be . . . ? "

There was no chuckle in his voice now. Obviously he
wanted to end the conversation, thinking perhaps she had
had the telephone tapped or that someone else was listening.

He said : " There'll be no inquiries about him ; that is all
settled," and hung up.

Maida waited and then hung up too, and left the drug
store. She walked home. It wasn't far and she had a vague,
unrealised hope that the fresh, balmy air of the spring night,
the ordinary, everyday act of walking briskly along ordinary,
everyday streets would brush away the webs of the extraordinary, of the fantastic and the incredible, from her mind.

It didn't. She was only desperately tired and dreadfully
certain that there wasn't any way out of the ugly tangle.
The big man's voice was so horribly wise, so cognisant somehow, in itself, of pitfalls, of traps, of plots against it. Any
slight attempt he had recognised and stopped. Instantly.

Smith. She wondered what his name really was and where
he lived. Well, that should be easy ; she had the telephone
number and that could be traced. But what evidence was
there against him ? He had assured her with an unruffled,
unshaken certainty that was convincing that there was no
evidence against him ; that he was in the clear, as Steve, he
had added, was not.

She reached her apartment house off Dupont Circle.

It was actually not an apartment house but an old residence with the high ceilings and narrow halls and stairways
and multitudinous fireplaces of its period, which had been
done over into small apartments. Maida had taken one of
them mainly because the whole atmosphere reminded her of
the houses of her childhood. Aunt Jason had still, although
she never lived in it now, such a house. Maida had gone to
dancing parties and New Year parties and for week-ends to
such houses.

Her rooms were on the third floor at the back where the
sun poured in ; it was why she had chosen them and, like
hundreds—no, thousands—of other Washington girls, she
had let her instinct for domesticity make a home of it. It

was a little home to be sure ; not very elaborate but it was quiet, it was peaceful and it was her own. It was also rather charming, but that was mainly, Maida felt, because Aunt Jason again had gruffly but thoroughly relented and sent her one or two lovely pieces of furniture, telling her at the same time that they would eventually have been Maida's in any case so they might as well be sent to her now. So the big, lovely secretaire against the wall was an old Chippendale, gracious, enduring, dignified. The table in the old-fashioned embrasure of the window had the lines and elegance of the same period. There were two or three small but good rugs, a handful of elegant old china and some silver with the Lovell initials on it—or at least almost on it—for in most cases it was very worn. There was a little good linen, too, in the chest of drawers beside the mantel. The fireplace didn't work very well ; something was wrong with the draughts ; still, on occasions, Maida lighted the everlaid fire of birch logs and pine cones and felt as if it were her own hearth fire, warming her, and enclosing her little home in peace and loveliness. Only it was rather a lonely little home.

She had been extravagant to the extent of taking an apartment which had a tiny bedroom. It was so small that when the flat wide bed was open (for she'd followed the advice of another girl in the house, Hortense Wigglesworth, and got herself a double studio couch for a bed) she had barely room between it and the dressing table to stand while she dressed. She also had a tiny bathroom, and in the little, narrow hall between bathroom and bedroom an unexpected panel (which she'd covered herself with half a roll of delicate, beautiful Chinese tea paper, all silver and dragons, which again Aunt Jason had sent her) opened out and became a door behind which there was a very neat and compact and utilitarian little—well, they'd called it a serving pantry when leasing the apartment. It wasn't quite that ; it was really only a cupboard, but a cupboard that had a sink, and a tiny refrigerator and a two-burner electric plate. She prepared her own breakfasts there. And all in all, she'd felt, she did herself rather well. She'd felt very proud of her first efforts to make a home ; she'd loved coming home from the office and sinking down into her own chintz-covered sofa in front of her own fire (which, if she seldom lighted, still was there) with the framed photographs of her mother and father above

—both looking very reserved and elegant, neither of whom
would have dreamed, poor dears, that their daughter would
join, and be glad of the chance, the great army of women
white-collar workers. She'd been extravagant too about
flowers.

As she unlocked and opened the door of her apartment
that night there was a faint scent of violets; she'd got them
the night before on her way home, from one of the flower-
sellers' carts off Dupont Circle and thrust them into a squat
yellow bowl.

It struck her again how greatly life had changed for her
since then.

No one had seen her come into the apartment house.
There was, naturally, no doorman, and no office for the
manager beside the front door. You came directly into a
rather narrow hall and had your choice of a small self-service
elevator and a stairway that, in its first flight, was broad and
gracious and thereafter abruptly narrowed to a steep, narrow
ascent. She took the stairs as a rule rather than wait for the
elevator which was always at another floor, it seemed to her,
and was slow into the bargain. There was only one door
into her apartment and that was the door from the narrow,
third-floor hall with its skillful decoration of white and red-
flowered wallpaper which artfully harmonized with the period
of the house.

As she entered her apartment and closed the door the
telephone began to ring, and it was Steve.

She groped her way to it. "Hello."

"Maida, for heaven's sake what happened to you? I
turned around after I'd finished and you were gone. I hadn't
heard you leave. Nobody knew where you were."

"I came home."

There was a little pause.

"Couldn't you stand it to hear my speech?" said Steve.
"Well, I can't say I blame you . . ."

"No, I had a—a telephone call I'd forgotten; then I came
home. How was the speech?"

"Oh. I don't know. That's not what I telephoned for.
Look, Angela and I are at the Shoreham, dancing. Come
on over."

"No, I . . ."

"Please do, Maida. I want you." His voice had changed;

it was more boyish and at the same time deeper and more
urgent. He really did want her, thought Maida all at once.
    " But . . . "   But it wouldn't take long to slip into a long
skirt and her silver sandals. As she had climbed the stairs,
she'd felt as if she could never move again, she'd been so
tired ; yet to see Steve, perhaps to find out what she could,
and to dance in his arms—yes, she'd go. Why not ?
    As she began to say so there was a blurred sound at the
other end of the wire, then Angela came on. Her voice was
clear, kind and final : " Maida, my dear, I've been scolding
Steve. It's really too bad of him to make you work all day
and then expect you to dance all night. Go straight to bed,
dear, and get your beauty sleep. I'll see that Steve isn't
lonely."
    She paused briefly and then said rather quickly so Maida
had an odd notion that Steve was reaching for the telephone
again, " Good-night. Steve says good-night, too."
    She hung up quickly and finally, without waiting for Maida
to speak.
    So that, thought Maida, presently, settled that. Angela
might or might not know that she, Maida, was in love with
Steve, but in any case she was taking no chances. Why had
she encouraged Walsh Rantoul, then ? Merely because she
enjoyed the romantic idea of rivalry ? It was Steve that
Angela really wanted, and something in the slight telephone
episode convinced Maida of it.
    Probably at that very moment she was leading Steve away
from the telephone, telling him the poor child Maida was
dead on her feet, and swiftly turning Steve's thoughts away,
entertaining him, looking so beautiful that half the crowded
supper room glanced at her now and then and whispered,
" That's Angela Favor over there." " Beautiful, isn't she ? "
" It's Steven Blake with her—the Steve Blake . . . "
    This, Maida decided, was childish thinking, and she called
an abrupt halt upon it ; it was absurd and petty. It had to
do with another world ; something that just now didn't
concern her ; the main and only important question was
what exactly was she going to do ?
    Eventually—about three it must have been—she decided
that the only clue she had to the man Smith was the fact
that he'd said he was Walsh Rantoul's friend and staying in
his house.

It was about that time too that a question came into her mind, so obvious, so salient and so significant a question that she couldn't understand why it had never occurred to her before. If Steve hadn't murdered Walsh either intentionally or accidentally, then who had ?

CHAPTER EIGHT

SHE wanted it to be the big man, Smith. Unfortunately, she was convinced it wasn't ; something in his manner, in his words, in his whole grasp of the situation, all that plus some intangible but instinctively recognised air of truth convinced her.

She realised, thinking it over, that her reasons for believing he was not the murderer were altogether instinctive and not very reasonable. But nevertheless there they were, insurmountable, at least for the present. And there were not many people who could have murdered Walsh : Christine and Angela, and the servants who came and went in the house. Almost no one else. Still there were the open french doors and an easy access from the street to the garden and terrace.

Walsh had said he had an appointment with Angela. But had he ? Certainly when Angela came she gave no indication of it ; she didn't ask for Walsh ; she told where she had been . . . "I looked in at the Slaters'," she'd said, "and then went home to dress." If that was all so, and it was easily proved, there had been literally no time for Angela to come quickly to Christine's house, kill Walsh and leave. Besides, there was no motive for it—none that Maida knew of, at any rate.

She began to see then that the only obvious motive for Walsh's death was that one which Steve might have had. Well, then, she thought, one of the first things to do was to inquire about Walsh Rantoul—very carefully, very quietly, but inquire. Find out who his enemies were ; he must have had them. Find other motives. It was a rather faint hope, for there was all that evidence against Steve ; still it was worth exploring.

Sometime about then, drugged with weariness and shock, she must have gone to sleep.

Around her, Washington lay asleep ; the lovely, gracious Southern city, dignified and curiously simple and charming in the very midst of its ceremony, emerged from the imposed hurly-burly of the day and lay tranquil under the gentle spring stars.

It is a city where anything may happen ; a city of glamour, of intrigue, of cruelty, of kindness and of strange human paradoxes. Cordell Hull, the great and benign statesman, walks quietly, without the fanfare of attendants and car and chauffeur, across the park to his office in the State Department—that office from which go national policies, national decisions, threads in a thousand different directions. Bernard Baruch, who comes down from a former war generation, sits thoughtfully on a bench in the park, feeding the fat squirrels with peanuts, talking quietly to those who come to him, pause, go on.

That perhaps is the real Washington with its lack of ostentation, its true homely dignity. A city where children gather every Easter and roll gaily coloured eggs down the broad lawn of the Executive Mansion, whose gracious lines are typical of the spirit that dwells therein.

There are really few night clubs ; not at any rate the brilliant and sometimes blatant variety that characterise New York. Guests are entertained in one's home, behind drawn curtains. At six the cocktail bars are crowded ; if one is in the mood, there is always dancing somewhere, the Shoreham terrace, perhaps, the Carlton. But it is a city of workers, too. Lights in certain buildings burn all night. Telephone operators on the night shift think nothing of a connection to London, to Rio, to Honolulu—even to Australia. Voices go out over the humming silver wires, deciding human destiny perhaps, in their own measure, for generations to come.

And in the meantime the cars parked along the Tidal Basin leave gradually one at a time. The secluded little corners in Rock Creek Park from where one—or two—may watch the stars become deserted. The shadows grow deeper above the reflecting pool and around the tall, beautiful shaft of the Washington Memorial. The great pillared and domed building on the " Hill " broods and waits for another day. The streets are deserted, echoing emptily to the sound of a belated taxi. Except, perhaps, in the War or Navy or State

Department (and the Executive offices) lights gradually are put out.

Morning was rather chilly and grey with rain squalls threatening.

It was just like any other morning with the horror of the past night dispelled in the clear cold grey of daylight.

At least it seemed so to Maida until, as she struggled into her blue woolly bathrobe and stretched her toes for her scuffs, she saw the folded slip of yellow paper.

It had dropped on the floor as she was undressing. It recalled her with a jolt not only to the terror of the previous night (the shrunken grey heap there behind the sofa with the red blotches on the cornflower-blue tie, and those bright, blank eyes reflecting light blankly), but it recalled her also to the rôle she was going to try to play. It was a difficult and dangerous rôle ; if it went wrong Steve would be lost and she would be lost—and there might be other lives in the balance. There inevitably would be other lives in the balance ; that was the whole object of Smith's attack.

Again she thought of the F.B.I. longingly ; yet if she went to them it meant that the whole story had to come out. It was a vicious circle of thought which always had the same answer.

On the way to the office she snatched a paper and read it swiftly and thoroughly. Impossible though it seemed, there was no mention of Walsh Rantoul. She did see, in the social items, a note to the effect that Miss Angela Favor and Mr. Steven Blake had been seen dancing at the Shoreham the previous night.

The office was exactly as usual—hurried, busy : telephones going constantly, mail being brought, telegrams arriving, the whole department seething with activity. In the outer office there were two girls who typed and made mimeographed copies of orders and coped with callers before (if they had the proper credentials) they were turned over to Maida, whose duty it was to see that only the people Steve wanted to see, and who had a right to see him, got past her and into Steve's large office beyond.

Opening also from the outer office, on the other side of it, was the anteroom to Bill Skeffington's office. The door was open and Bill's own secretary was working busily. Bill Skeffington, a tall, loose-jointed man of about Steve's age, was Steve's assistant. He was red-headed, jovial and possessed of an extremely likeable personality which made him popular among the men with whom he came into daily, personal contact. He often boasted (but with a wide, frank, disarming grin) that he had got into aviation the hard way, first getting his pilot's licence, then barnstorming for a while with his own plane (or planes, for he told of cracking up once or twice, and said he belonged to the early days of the parachute club), and then taking on the difficult job of test pilot for a west coast aircraft company. He was now, he would say with a very wide grin, too old for that sort of thing.

In spite of his engaging and frank grin, his likeableness, his good humour, Maida didn't quite like him. Perhaps his smile was too wide—and his light brown eyes too unsmiling. She felt him to be personally ambitious ; she knew him to be inclined to be slipshod in his work. And certainly he had a tendency to drop everything, when someone he conceived to be important came into the office, and in his own words " rally round." In other, less flattering words, ingratiate himself with someone who had influence.

Steve, so far as she could see, didn't know the meaning of the word " influence " ; he was too busy, he was too selflessly intent upon his job ; anyway, he didn't care. The job was the thing that mattered with Steve—nothing else. He was likely to be brusque, swift, not particularly tactful.

Bill Skeffington always had time for a little talk, a good story, lunch somewhere. She knew, as secretaries do know inter-office politics, that Bill wanted Steve's job.

Once that morning Bill came through her office and stopped to sit, dangling one long leg, on the corner of her desk and tell her—with that disarming grin and those cold eyes—that she was pretty as a picture and he wished she'd work for him and not old Sreve. And she thought with a tightening of nerves what a weapon the thing that had happened would be in Bill's hands. Steve would be out and Bill would be in in almost less time than it took to think it. Only Bill wouldn't do the job as Steve was doing it. Bill couldn't be trusted with planes, with lives, with the very life-blood of a nation in its time of need.

Steve seemed quite as usual too, except for a fresh dressing of gauze and adhesive on his chin. He called Maida, dictated letters swiftly, gave a few orders for telephone calls and then began to see callers. The morning was well-laid out, full, designed to get the most of every moment.

There was no chance to question him, even if just, then she had been able to do so carefully, cautiously, planning her words. Certainly, however, in Steve's bearing there was no suggestion that the night before, he had coolly murdered a man who was his rival in the affections of a woman.

Had he gone back to the library, Maida wondered, when back at her own desk she had a moment's leisure ? Had he gone back to Christine's house during that hour or so when he had disappeared the night before ? Perhaps he—and not Smith—had somehow disposed of the body of Walsh Rantoul.

Well, he hadn't ; she told herself that with firmness and decision. It was something that it was utterly impossible to envision Steve doing. Still he had disappeared for an hour or so, and apparently he hadn't gone for Christine, and he hadn't kept his dinner appointment with Angela. Well, then, where had he gone ?

And what was she going to do about that order—that first command from Smith ? Find out what ocean-flying planes the government is to take over from the Interstate, their size and description, and the date of transfer.

She would have to give them some sort of reply ; she might be able to delay the reply for a day or two, tell them she couldn't get hold of the material they wanted easily and that it would take a little time. But as she thought of the particular kind of inquiry it was, it began to seem to her that it might be a test question. Perhaps they would ask several test questions, whose answers they could easily check and thus discover the accuracy of her own replies.

While naturally it was not widely known that the government was to take over the Interstate's big ocean-flying planes, still the general idea of it was not unexpected and would not be news to the most casual newspaper reader. It was already an accepted fact that anything that was needed from industry or public conveyances by the army or the navy would automatically be turned over to them ; that was expected and accepted. Also it seemed to her that for an organisation of any ability it would not have been impossible to secure, long ago, general but sufficient details of design of many of the big American planes. They were in constant use ; certainly their passengers weren't blindfolded when they flew in the

big passenger planes. Certainly almost anybody could walk
into one of the big airports and watch any plane arrive or
depart which he chose to watch, and a trained observer, such
as an enemy agent organisation would endeavour to employ,
could see as much in five minutes as she could discover in an
hour by going through the files.

There was, however, the date and place of transfer ; they
couldn't know that, and they might presumably have arrived
at some plan for sabotage, the successful execution of which
demanded dates and places.

Well, she didn't know that date. She could falsify it, of
course ; she could and intended to falsify any bit of exact
information that Smith demanded of her, anything in order
to gain time and prevent the success of any enemy project

But she couldn't do it often without being detected.

Time again was the factor that was important ; the boon
indeed that she had to work and pray for. But in the cool
morning light, in the everyday, busy, literal routine of the
office her courage failed completely. The plan that had
seemed last night if not easy, at least practicable, now seemed
utterly childish and futile. To try to pit her own wits
against that of the man Smith and the people he represented
was not only brash and dangerous, it was doomed from the
beginning to failure.

Yet to tell Steve, to turn the whole hideous problem over
to him was literally and actually to turn Steve over to the
police. She always came back to that.

Well—she saw three mistakes in the letter she was typing,
tore it off the roller, got fresh paper and inserted fresh carbons
and began again. She'd have to do the only things that,
just now, she could do.

Steve left the office early for lunch. " Thank God," he
said, stopping for a moment at her desk on his way out, " I
don't have to go anywhere this afternoon or to-night. The
day is clear for work and nothing but."

" What happened to your carnation yesterday ? " she
said. " I thought it looked very handsome. But it was
gone when I saw you later at the broadcasting studio."

He had been toying, boyishly, with the pencils and erasers
on her desk. He didn't look up as she spoke, but it seemed
to her a kind of veil went down over his always rather inscrutable, brown face. " That—oh, I lost it somewhere.

You ordered it for me, didn't you, Maida? I felt very dressed up. Don't know when I've worn a flower in my buttonhole."

"I thought the occasion demanded it." She saw a faint, opening chance and added quickly, although a little diffidently, aware of being the secretary, questioning where she had no right to question: "Did you find Christine? At the Slaters', I mean."

His face still wore an inscrutable, veiled look; if anything it deepened. "No." He paused. "As a matter of fact, I didn't go to the Slaters'."

A really intelligent girl could have gone on from there, thought Maida. She said "Oh," inadequately.

"No," repeated Steve. "I didn't go to the Slaters'. Didn't go to dinner with Angela, either. I met somebody— unexpectedly." He paused again, and then picked up a pencil, examined it as intently as if he had never seen one before and said: "Did you happen to see Walsh—Walsh Rantoul—yesterday?"

After a moment she said: "Yes. He was in the house. At Christine's, I mean. When I came. I talked to him for a few moments before I went to your study."

There was a silence, except her heart beat so loudly it seemed to her that he must hear it. He turned and turned the yellow pencil, watching it, and finally said: "Yes, I saw him, too. After I left you." He put down the pencil and looked squarely at her. "Did you talk to him again, before you left the house?"

So he was questioning her, as she had meant to question him. And however she replied there was danger. She felt like a mountain-climber poised on a narrow foothold, with a rocky abyss on either side; like a swimmer between two swift currents. She answered literally: "No. No, I didn't talk to him." And waited.

Surely he would ask other questions; if he had killed Walsh he must need to know what had happened afterward, why there had been no outcry of murder. No police, no dreadful tumult of ambulance, reporters, inquiry. And the questions he must ask would answer her own question; that one question she could not bring herself to ask. But suddenly, waiting, she wanted to go to him, put her hand upon his own, make him understand that he could count upon her loyalty and her love no matter what he had done—or hadn't done.

Naturally, she didn't ; she couldn't.

He didn't question her further. Instead, he gave a kind of shrug and looked up. "Come on out to lunch with me," he said. "I want you to." He came suddenly around the desk and stood beside her as he had done the night before. "Maida . . ." he said. And then unexpectedly, rather awkwardly, as if he hadn't intended to do it, he put his arm around her shoulders and drew her close against him, and then bent over toward her face. "Maida," he said again, whispering. Looking at her mouth and then, rather soberly, rather gravely into her eyes.

She could feel herself leaning toward him ; she could feel herself waiting for something, something important, something completely and wholly wonderful, something that couldn't be snared into words.

Someone knocked briskly on the door of the outer office.

Steve straightened up, not very quickly, rather as a reluctant concession to necessity. Or perhaps Maida drew away first. She was never sure of that. She was sure, however, that she could have cheerfully throttled the girl who opened the door and stood there—little Jane Somers, a thin, catty, highly efficient filing clerk.

"Oh, Miss Lovell," she said. "I didn't mean to interrupt . . ."

"You're not interrupting," said Maida between her teeth, and thinking longingly of assault and battery. "What is it ? "

It was a question about some correspondence of the previous week. It took some time to straighten out ; eventually, Steve, after waiting and smoking, went on to lunch, telling Maida he'd be back at two.

And shortly after two he telephoned. He was detained, he said.

"I ran into a man I've got to talk to, and it's not about a dog. Who've I got to see this afternoon ? "

She told him, scanning the appointment pad quickly.

"I see. Well—put off Graves and Bennett. I'll telephone Norman myself ; make another date with them. And answer the rest of my mail ; I've made notes on the margins. Leave the letters on my desk and I'll read and sign them some time this evening. Don't wait for me, though, if I'm late. Thanks, my dear."

" All right."

" Oh, and Maida . . ." A thought seemed to strike him. He said quickly : " Look here. You've been working like mad lately. How'd you like to take a holiday ? It won't take you long to. run through the rest of those letters, will it ? After you've finished, leave. Turn things over to the Somers and that other girl. Get outdoors. Mind me, now, will you ? "

Oddly enough, it was in running through the remainder of the mail on Steve's desk that she came upon the thing that settled her first and immediate problem ; and that was a sheet of notes for a press release which included the fact that the government was to take over certain planes from private air carriers. There was no date ; there was no description of the planes. But it was clear that the information, or at least part of the information, that Smith had ordered her to get was very soon to be a matter of public knowledge. There was obviously to be no secrecy about it and, if there had been any way in which it could have been of value to the enemy, there would have been secrecy.

It was like a load off her heart. She could then, without fear of giving—what was the phrase ?—" aid and comfort to the enemy "—put off Smith with half facts, gain more time.

She didn't know the date. The thing to do was to discover the date and then, carefully but convincingly, give them the wrong date. Just to be safe against any attempt at sabotage. She saw then clearly that the date was the important part of the order, the important inquiry. But by telling them, as if they were secret, facts that soon would be no secret at all, she could tell them at the same time the wrong dates ; and they would probably believe it.

Perhaps, and with luck, that would settle the question of that first order, and before any other came she might know better how to defend herself. Time might have come to her aid ; she thought then rather hopelessly of how she was counting upon time—which can be man's enemy as often as it is his friend. Confidential material was kept in a certain locked file in Steve's office ; she didn't have the key but she knew—and she alone knew—where he kept it. It wouldn't be a good idea to discover that date, as she was sure she could from the notes and letters concerning it, just then. There was too much chance of something going wrong; of one of the filing clerks being blamed for it, if anything went wrong; or of someone discovering her in the very act of opening that file.

Better to wait. Better to do it later; if she returned to the office after the others were gone she would not run the risk of interruption. Smith had said he would telephone some time that day, but if he telephoned before she had secured the information he wanted it would give her an excuse for more time.

So she argued with and perhaps convinced herself. Besides, Steve had said to take a holiday, and she would. She would go to Christine's house; she would make some excuse to visit Walsh Rantoul's cottage; she would try to find out everything she could find out about Walsh and about the man who'd said he was Walsh's guest.

Little Jane Somers waved cheerfully as she went through the outer office.

" Off for the day ? " she said. " You look awful pretty, Miss Lovell. But you'd better take your raincoat; it's there in the coat closet."

Her heels clicked lightly along the wide, bare corridor where only the previous night someone had walked and then entered the office which was so homely to-day, so commonplace and noisy and busy, and had typed a message to her on her own machine.

Again, as she had done the day before, she took the bus because it was quicker and then walked across an edge of the park to Christine's house. It was colder than it had been the day before, and by the time she reached the big Georgian house with its mellow pink brick there was a spatter of cold rain on her face.

This time a negro butler instantly answered the bell. But Mr. Blake was out. So there was no way just then to pump Christine, even if Maida had been adept at that somewhat dubious accomplishment.

But she did want to get into the house; it seemed to her that she must see for herself that library—the rug, the tables, the chairs, the sofa behind which Walsh Rantoul had lain. Perhaps there was another clue there, a clue that didn't lead to Steve but to somebody else. If Steve didn't kill him, then who did ?

She said, quite matter-of-factly really and coolly : " I thought I left my gloves somewhere here yesterday. Do you mind if I look ? "

It was not a very good excuse ; it was the same device she had used with Christine. Still, for one who had to learn deception and evasion overnight it wasn't too bad, for it worked. Malcolm, which was the rather stylish name of Christine's elderly butler, knew her well. His face registered clearly a kind of protest to the implication that if she'd dropped a pair of gloves in the house he had been so remiss as not to find them, but he invited her in to look.

" I didn't see no gloves, Miss Maida, Ma'am," he said. " Where'd you think you lost them ? "

" I don't know. Perhaps in Mr. Blake's study. Would you mind looking there, Malcolm, and I'll glance around the library ? "

" Yes'm," he said, and closed the door and waved toward the library. " You know the way, Miss. Somebody dropped a glass there last night, I don't know who. Didn't find the glass either but certainly cut my thumb while I was wiping up the floor." She saw then that he had a strip of plaster on one wrinkled dark thumb. There was, however, so far as she could see, no special significance in his tone ; he was merely disgruntled, doing his little bit of grousing. He started up the stairs and she went quickly to the library.

She stopped at the door, as she had done twice the night before Stopped with the heart pounding suddenly and sickeningly in her throat.

There was, however, nothing there.

Really nothing, she decided after several moments. The room looked as orderly, as undisturbed, as pleasant and everyday with its fresh flowers, its books, its bright cushions as it had ever looked. She found nothing at all to show that a scene of horror had taken place there, of violence and of sudden death, until, just as she heard Malcolm beginning his slow, stately descent of the stairs, she went behind the sofa and bent to look closely at the rug. And it seemed to her that there was a dark, dry spot, a small stain scarcely an inch long. She stared at it, remembering everything that

had happened there too well and too vividly; she would
never be able to forget any detail.

So it was true then; it hadn't been part of a nightmare.
It had all happened, just as she remembered it. That was a
man's blood.

And there were things she had to do.

Malcolm was coming down the hall.

She went quickly to the french doors, opened one and let
herself into the wet garden.

It wasn't raining hard; it was only a slight, dreary kind
of drizzle. Rosy was nowhere to be seen She had an
impression that Malcolm came to the french door and looked
out and saw her walking along the garden path; if so, however, he'd think nothing of it. She crossed the garden, went
through a weigela hedge which was quite tall and saw Walsh
Rantoul's cottage ahead of her.

It was a small house, rather self-consciously charming with
its dormered upper windows, its ivy-entwined chimney, its
leaded casement windows showing blue curtains behind them.
There was a scrap of a lawn and a narrow brick sidewalk.
However, there were masses of shrubs set closely at the sides
of the little house and bordering the lawn to give it, she
supposed, an effect of isolation. The door was blue, too,
with a brass knocker and the house looked already, it seemed
to her, deserted.

But that was because she knew that Walsh was dead.
She took herself and her courage firmly in hand, tried to
recall whether or not Walsh kept a servant who lived in the
house, decided he did not, but anyway she'd have to risk it,
and walked quickly along the wet brick walk.

It was not going to be easy to enter the cottage. Possibly,
even, it was locked.

It wasn't. She stepped over the little porch and opened
the door. The interior was rather dark with the dark day;
a blue mirror ahead of her gave her back a sudden and un-
nerving reflection of herself turned a ghastly blue. As her
eyes adjusted themselves to the dimness of the light she saw
the little drawing-room opening from the hall, done in white
and blue. A rather startling decor, as a matter of fact,
but the thing that concerned her was the leather-covered
desk that stood on a white fur rug across the room.

Well—the thing to do was to go through that desk, minutely,

painstakingly, hunting for every detail she could discover that might give some illuminating fact about Walsh Rantoul, his life and times—and death.

The light was not very good, but she didn't dare turn on the delicate, shell-covered lamp beside her. Sooner or later the fact of Walsh's murder must come out, and then everything concerning him would be thrust into the bold bright searchlight of police and newspaper scrutiny. This would include a visitor to his cottage during the time after Walsh Rantoul was last seen alive. Surely soon someone would inquire for him ; eventually his absence must be reported to the police and a search instituted for the missing man.

She wondered where they would find him, and thrust that hideous half-glimpsed conjecture out of her mind. She didn't dare think of it ; not with the task that lay ahead of her. It was really, she thought suddenly, rather a dangerous thing to do just what she was trying to do, but that other danger loomed greater, and far more menacing. She addressed herself quickly to the contents of the desk—rather untidy and unsorted ; notes of invitation, newspaper clippings, a few business letters. Not a very pleasant task.

It was as she thought that she became aware of the fact she was not alone in the house. Someone was upstairs and walked very softly and quickly, only a few footsteps, across the floor of the bedroom just above her.

And, as she heard it, her hands all at once stiff and cold on the papers before her, there was another louder sound as someone else ran lightly and without any attempt at concealment across the little porch, burst open the door and came in, shaking raindrops from her bright scarlet raincape.

It was Angela, looking perfectly beautiful with her eyes bright and dancing and a clear pink colour in her cheeks.

She said : " Maida, dear, whatever are you doing here ? Malcolm said he thought you'd come to Walsh's cottage, so I followed because . . . ". She took off her raincape and flung it down. She was dressed in pale green wool, thin, so it accentuated her slimness and chicness of figure. She wasted no time, however. She came straight across to the desk, put both lovely white hands upon it and leaned toward Maida.

" I've been wanting to talk to you," she said. " Straight from the shoulder, my dear. I'm like that, you know—direct and frank. Everybody says so. And I like you ; I like you so much, dear, that I don't want you to be hurt. About Steve, I mean. You see . . ." Her words were slower now, more definite. " You see, there's no chance for you there. Steve's in love with me. And I intend to marry Steve."

CHAPTER NINE

HER lovely face, her bright eyes with their hard, bright, black pupils, her crimson mouth looking softer and fuller than it actually was, owing to a skillful use of lipstick, were so close to Maida that the perfume Angela used wafted across the white desk. It was so sweet it was almost cloying to Maida who liked clearer, more astringent scents. At the same time, beautiful and vibrant and full of energy though Angela always was, Maida had never seen her look lovelier than she did then. The scarlet raincape which she had flung down, so it made a vivid patch of colour upon a blue chair near by, had had a hood which Angela had pulled over her curls ; now they were softly and charmingly disarranged. There wasn't any need for Angela to warn her that Steve was her sole and exclusive property, thought Maida rather grimly. Any man Angela had wanted, looking like that, she could almost certainly have had.

Then the spineless surrender of her own thought appalled her—much more than the boldness and certainty of Angela's attack. All Maida's normal, feminine vanity rushed to her aid. Was she going to give up without making a fight ? Besides, Angela wouldn't have made that uninvited assertion if she hadn't had a purpose, and anybody could see with half an eye what that purpose was. She wanted to convince Maida that Steve was in love with her, Angela. So Maida wouldn't interfere ; so Maida would be, in other words, bluffed.

She didn't stop to wonder exactly why Angela had determined upon that rather breezy, to say the least, course. Obviously, some incident, some small event had decided her.

And then Maida realised that the footsteps on the floor of that room overhead had stopped. Angela's voice was very clear and loud ; in all probability it could be heard in every room in the cottage. Who was upstairs ? And why ?

And in another moment the strangeness of Maida's own presence in Walsh's house would strike Angela and she would question her about it.

Later, too, when the fact of Walsh's murder came out, as it must some time, somehow come out, Angela would remember Maida seated at Walsh's desk, calmly going through his papers.

Who was it upstairs ? All at once she thought, *was Walsh really dead ?* And instantly with all her force rejected that question, which was born of the nightmarish, horror-filled events of the past twenty-four hours. Walsh was dead ; she should know that better than anyone. So it wasn't Walsh walking up there—Walsh with his blond hair and delicate, doll-like face.

Angela's expression had changed ; altered and blurred a little, so she looked instead of vibrant and aggressive, merely still. She said suddenly : " What are you listening for ? "

" L-listening ? " said Maida. She'd got to pull herself together, face down Angela and get rid of her as she had done the previous night, as she'd got rid of Nollie Lister.

" Was I listening to something ? " she said. " I thought it was raining again. I thought I could hear it on the—the roof. Do you mean, Angela, that you are announcing your engagement to Steve ? If so, I must congratulate you."

Angela drew back a little and blinked once. Again a kind of blank, immobile look settled over her pretty face. Maida said : " I must congratulate Steve, too. I'll do it right away."

" Oh, my dear, how too sweet of you," said Angela. " I knew you'd be pleased. You are such a dear, conscientious girl and so devoted to Steve's interests." She was no longer blank but smiling and self-possessed and sweet.

Angela went on, purring : " It's still a secret, you know, dear. Steve would be furious if he knew that I'd told even you. And really, it isn't absolutely settled. I mean the date and—and all that. Do understand, darling. And "— she laughed prettily—" and don't give me away, there's a darling. I only told you because—do forgive me, dear—it seemed to me that you rather—well," she laughed again. " Perhaps you like Steve a little. A little more, I mean than

—than—well, you know what I mean." Her hesitation was much more charming than her words.

So she wasn't engaged to Steve at all. And she didn't want Maida to tell Steve what she'd said.

But that didn't mean, reflected Maida rather gloomily, that the engagement might not be true at almost any moment. Then again her thoughts were caught up with the extreme exigency of the moment. She had to get Angela out of the place and search it for whatever she could find. Walsh Rantoul hadn't in life been important, so far as she knew ; it was only in death that he was so horribly important.

Yet—who was it upstairs ? Would she have the sheer physical courage to remain alone in the dreary, haunted, little cottage ?

Again Angela said abruptly : " What *is* the matter with you, Maida ? You keep looking as if—as if you didn't see me at all. What are you listening for ? " She whirled around to follow Maida's own eyes and glanced over her shoulder.

Naturally, no one stood in the tiny hallway ; no one stood at the foot of the narrow little stairway. There were only those ghostly little footsteps beating, beating their way into the cottage.

That was nerves. Nerves and memory. But Maida knew that she couldn't stay in the cottage alone, after Angela went away. She couldn't stay, even to find out whatever she could about Walsh, which would in all probability be nothing, or about Smith—which might be something. It was only a faint chance, of course. It wasn't likely at least that he, Smith, had left a notation in Walsh's cottage to the effect that he was a German spy and there would be found proof of it somewhere, giving number and place.

And Angela turned round. The trend of her thoughts had changed abruptly. She said, her eyes narrow now and shrewd : " What in the world are you doing here, Maida ? Is Walsh upstairs ? Did you come to see him ? "

Well, she'd seen that coming—and she hadn't thought up an answer for it. A fine conspirator she'd make A fine— suddenly the word spy entered her mind, and it struck her as the most fantastic of all fantastic things that she had talked with a spy, that she had been given a command to supply certain information.

Angela Favor was shrewd; she hadn't made herself the place she had made without being shrewd. Maida said: " I was just leaving. I—I came to get a list Walsh asked me to type for him."

She had to explain her presence at that desk, drawers open, notes and letters scattered about. Still she heard with a kind of surprise, the excuse her own lips uttered. Angela glanced at the desk. " A list ? What kind of list ? Couldn't he make it himself ? "

Maida forced herself to give a kind of shrug and started toward the door. " He was to leave a paper on his desk. I imagine it's a—a party of some sort; I don't know. At any rate, it doesn't seem to be here. I'm going now."

Angela looked at the papers on the desk. And Angela was thinking; Maida could see it in her narrowed, self-possessed mouth, her bright, shrewd eyes. She said suddenly: " When did you see Walsh, Maida ? "

" When . . . " said Maida stupidly, caught and pinioned not so much by the question as by the memory it evoked.

Angela waited, drawing her blonde and very lightly penciled eyebrows together. She said: " Is he here now ? "

" No," said Maida. Angela shot a startled and questioning glance at her, struck with that passion of denial. Maida said quickly, in as calm and matter-of-fact a tone as she could command, " No, he isn't here. Shall we go along now, Angela ? I'll "—the word stuck in her throat a little but she got it out—" I'll telephone to him later on and explain."

She was too far gone to retreat now, she thought dismally.

Angela picked up her red raincape. And then went swiftly, swaying her lovely hips a little in a walk that had been much admired, to the stairway. Maida, again, froze to listen and watch.

Angela reached the stairway and put back her lovely blonde head and called, softly at first, in a voice very like Christine's beautifully modulated tones and then more clearly: " Walsh —Walsh. Are you up there ? " She waited a moment.

And Maida's thoughts took their own head again and reiterated the questions: Walsh—where is he? *Where* is he ?

Angela listened and called again and then turned to Maida and opened the door upon the little front step. She gave a little shiver. " How empty the cottage seems ! " she said

unexpectedly. "There's something—queer about it. Desolate and yet—well, I expect it needs to be aired. Anyway,"
she shrugged off the tinge of uneasiness that was in her
manner and her voice and said briskly : " I thought he must
be here. You see, my dear, Walsh is awfully attractive to
women. Everybody grants that. I hope you don't mind
my thinking that perhaps you'd—well, come to see him. Of
course, darling, I didn't mean to hurt your feelings or anything.
Really, it's a compliment to you. You're not—forgive me,
dear—very attractive to men, you know. That is, don't
misunderstand me, Maida, dear, I mean it for the best. I
only thought Walsh had invited you here for a cocktail and
you came. Nothing wrong with that. I was pleased about
it really. I've been afraid you weren't having a very gay
time in Washington. There's no getting around it, a girl's
got to have a certain—oh, a certain something . . . "

" Are you trying to give me an inferiority complex,
Angela ? " said Maida, smiling. They were in the doorway
now ; in another moment they'd be out of the cottage and
gone.

Angela gave her another look that roused Maida suddenly
to a sense of what she'd said and the careless, half-amused
tone in which she'd said it ; not at all the respectful secretary ;
not at all impressed by the famous beauty, Angela Favor.
Angela said rather tartly :

" My dear, if you weren't by way of being a friend of
Steve's, I—and Christine—wouldn't be so kind to you. I
do hope you have the good taste not to impose—oh," she
said, breaking off, " there's Christine."

There was Christine—done up in an old hat and a raincoat
with muddy once-white, gardening gloves and a trowel in her
hand. She was advancing across the garden with a determined tread through the soft rain, not upon them and not
even in their direction but toward the fence that separated
her own garden from the Lister garden. Rosy, a little wet
and disgruntled, was waddling along beside her. And on
the other side of the fence, they had an instant's glimpse of
Nollie Lister, also in raincoat and sodden felt hat, digging
vigorously.

It was only a glimpse through the opening in the weigela
hedge that divided Walsh Rantoul's cottage from Christine's
garden. Christine passed on out of sight. Angela, diverted,

said : " They're at it again. Christine doesn't give a hang for flowers, but every time she sees Nollie digging she hurries into gardening gloves and goes out and digs, too. Digs up so many of her bulbs as a matter of fact that her bi-weekly gardener has to reset them. But she won't let Nollie get ahead of her ; especially when Nollie makes such a fuss over the dog. Some time," said Angela coolly, " he's going to throttle that little fat spaniel, and I can't say I blame him."

She flung the scarlet raincape over her head and started down the path. Maida turned to close the door—and a man coming cat-footed down the stairs stood, a huge bulk in the shadow behind her, and put his finger to his lips.

It was, of course, Smith.

She caught her breath sharply. Angela, going along the path ahead, intent upon keeping her high-heeled red sandals from being caught in the mossy wide cracks of the old sidewalk, didn't turn. Smith beckoned, silently and imperatively.

She made her lips move in an almost soundless whisper : " I can't."

For answer he beckoned again. Quickly, forcefully. He moved his head in a gesture that was a command toward the little white and blue drawing-room she had just left.

She called to Angela : " I'll be along in a moment. I've just remembered—the list. I'd better take another look."

" All right," said Angela, watching the path and holding the cape to shield her face. " Stop in at Christine's when you leave. Malcolm said he'd been looking for something that belonged to you . . . " her voice trailed to a stop carelessly. Probably she felt again sure of herself ; if she wanted to say another word or two to Maida before Maida should see Steve, it was only to clinch Maida's silence. But, again, that didn't matter. Maida moved rather stiffly inside the silent cottage again, staring at the bulk of a man who stood there in the shadow.

" Close the door," he said in a whisper.

She did so.

He turned, sure of her following him, and went into the little drawing-room.

Cottages furnished in dark blue mirrors and cold white chairs and tables, with blue walls and a silver-patterned mantel, need lights to be gay and cheerful. Need lights, and people and warmth. The place was cold, Maida realised then; cold and inexpressibly dismal, with its dark blue and white and the rain slanting against the blue-curtained windows. Anyone would have known, it seemed to her, the instant he walked into the cottage that there was some ugly secret; some peculiar quality of dreariness and silence. Odd that Angela hadn't noticed it, or perhaps she had; certainly, she had. "Perhaps it only needs to be aired," she'd said, and "How desolate and yet . . ." She hadn't finished that.

Smith turned round, and started to unwrap a huge maroon muffler that was around his throat. As much as she had thought of him during the past night and day, she still hadn't really seen his face clearly in her mind, as she saw it now in actuality. It was a big face, and she remembered the strong, sharp downward lines from the corners of his mouth and his nose. His eyes were deep-set and shadowed and at the same time shrewd and guarded. He wore the brimmed hat pulled low again over his massive forehead and he left it there; his brown, long overcoat hung straight down from his broad shoulders. He said, in the most matter-of-fact way in the world: "I've been having a sore throat; have to wear this thing constantly. Gets husky at night and by morning I can hardly talk." And without a change in expression or voice he added: "Well, what's the date?"

"Date . . ." said Maida.

He shot her a quick look. "Don't stall, my girl. The date of the transfer of the planes, of course. I told you to get the material. Well, what about it?"

"I—couldn't to-day. Someone would have seen me; one of the girls in the office. I thought it would be better to—to get it to-night."

He folded up the muffler. "No. That's not what you thought. You thought something would happen to give you a break so you wouldn't have to do it at all. Well, you were wrong. You were only trying to get out of it, you see. Perhaps you didn't know that, but it's true. I've seen it happen before," he went on, almost conversationally. "It's a question of the first step being the one that costs. After a time you won't mind. But just now you are grasping at excuses to put off doing it. That's very dangerous, Miss Lovell. When I say get some fact or some date or some figure for me, that's what I mean.

The trouble was that he was right; she could easily have

got the date he wanted then and there and she knew it ; if one of the other girls had come into the office, even if Steve had returned unexpectedly, none of them would question her presence there. Smith was quite right ; it was part of his job to know people, to outwit them psychologically, as much as it was to be ruthless, without mercy, and intelligent. She said : " I will get it to-night."

" See that you do. I've got some other little chores for you, by the way, and I want prompter service from you hereafter. In fact, I intend to have it. You understand that, do you ? I've no time to waste with your little scruples and indecisions. Either you do what I tell you to do, promptly and accurately, or you don't. It's up to you. You know what will happen if you don't."

Oh, yes, she knew what would happen. But she said abruptly, with a strong angry hatred of the great man before her and all that he stood for that gave her the courage of faith and of defiance : " I understand. But I'm not going to do it. Steve didn't murder Walsh. I know he didn't. He wouldn't have been such a fool."

Smith looked, for the first time, a little surprised. His eyes opened wider ; his hands stopped folding the muffler. She had to avert her glance from those strong, brutal hands. She said : " He wouldn't have been such a fool as to murder a man and then leave him there in the library at Christine's to be found. He wouldn't have been such a fool as to shoot him with his own revolver. And leave that, too. To be found and traced to him." Tears were suddenly in her eyes ; an angry stifling throb in her throat. " He wouldn't have been such a fool," she cried unsteadily, beating her hands together.

CHAPTER TEN

HE LOOKED down again at the maroon woollen folds of the muffler, and began again to fold it into a neat, smooth roll. His great hands were steady and calm, his face utterly without expression. He said in a matter-of-fact way : " I expected that."

" But it's true. Steve didn't . . . "

" Don't raise your voice. I meant I expected you to make that kind of outburst. Nerves," he said. " I knew it would come sooner or later."

" I'm going to tell Steve. . . . "

" Oh, no, you won't. You don't want to put a rope around his neck, do you? And he can't report me and my "—he smiled, the deeply indented corners of his rapacious mouth curving inward a little, still eyeing the muffler solicitously—" my nefarious practices because he'd have to admit his own guilt at the same time. And even allowing for his being willing to do that and give himself up, I don't think you'd really like to see it, would you? Now, now, my dear, be calm. It gets you nowhere to make a scene like this. It's hysterical," he said disapprovingly. " I must say, up to now, you've behaved rather well. I thought you were intelligent when I first talked to you. But just in case you do have any doubts as to the authenticity of my claims—don't. I've taken the trouble to have the fingerprints on the revolver developed and—there are places where one can get that kind of thing done, you know—I've compared them with a fine set of Blake's fingerprints which were obtained for me last night. By a very efficient person who left my message to you, typed on your machine. The fingerprints are the same, and there are no others on the revolver.

" You would say that in any case."

He shrugged his shoulders and lifted his eyebrows. " It's really a waste of time to have to tell you all over again that you haven't a chance against me," he said, still in that conversational, unperturbed way which alone was convincing, for it showed his certainty of his own ground. " I saw the murder, remember."

" You couldn't have! He didn't . . . "

" Look, Miss Lovell. Listen. Use your good sense. I told you last night that I had seen to it that I was in the clear. There is nothing about my life that anyone could possibly know about—any investigator, I mean—that won't bear scrutiny. I could be called as a witness ; I could testify in a court of law ; my whole life could be bared to the scrutiny and examination of a defence attorney and I'm willing to swear to you now and here that nothing—nothing, mind you—could be brought against me."

It sounded convincing ; yet he must be bluffing.

" That can't be true ! You are working in the pay of an enemy government. You can't do that without leaving some trace, some proof. And once that was known, do you think your bare word would convince anybody ? "

He held up one big, muscular hand.

" You underestimate my intelligence again," he said rather sadly. " You are constantly doing that. When you know more of this—this profession that I follow—you'll know that one lives only so long as one leaves no traces. And I would do just what I've said I'd do. I know what happened in that library, and I'm not going to waste the time I'm wasting now, convincing you over and over again that it's very much to your interest and to Blake's to—follow my advice."

And as he said that a very terrifying thing entered Maida's mind. He had the revolver and what he said of it might or might not be true. He had the carnation, and the material evidence in his possession plus his accusation would almost certainly bring about Steve's arrest. *But he was the only one who knew.*

The little cottage was very cold ; as cold as if death had entered it and cast its breath upon those cold, blank, blue mirrors. He knew ; but no one else knew.

And he looked at her suddenly and a queer, quick light came into his eyes, and he said abruptly : " Well, well. I underrated you. I'm intuitive, you know ; that's part of my job, too. Being intuitive has saved my life once or twice. But I'm really surprised, Miss Lovell. I didn't think you would let anything like that enter your own calculations." His eyes narrowed thoughtfully. He tipped his head a little on one side to watch her for a moment ; then he said blandly : " Aren't you ashamed of yourself ? Really, now ! To be thinking in terms of violence. You, a nice girl, I'm sure, to let yourself wish that something would happen to me. Something violent—eh ? Something sudden ? "

His look was no longer bland ; it was vulpine again, and certain of himself. " Put that thought out of your mind," he snapped. " Now, then—find out for me these things. Listen carefully. I may be away for a few days, but someone will telephone to you or give you an opportunity to get these facts to me. All you have to do is to get them and remember them. Now, then—first find out how many planes are expected to come off the assembly line at the "—he named

one of the large military aircraft plants in New England—
" during this month. Get the descriptions—fighter, pursuit,
bomber-fighter, bomber, you know exactly what items I want.
Get them. Next find out when "—again he named a pro-
minent name ; a high official in the army, one associated
with military aeronautics—" find out when or if he intends
to fly to the coast and if so on what plane, leaving when."

" I can't," she whispered in horrified revulsion. " I can't
—this is impossible. I can't do this. . . . "

" You can and you will," he said. , " To-night I'll get in
touch with you somehow. Meantime get the date of the
release of those Interstate planes to the government. That's
all now. I advise you to take a hold on yourself before you
go across to Mrs. Blake's, if that's where you are going. By
the way "—he was unfolding the maroon woollen muffler—
" by the way, why did you come here ? "

She was still too shocked by the hideous vistas of treachery,
of traitorism, of sabotage and swift death, to reply. He said :
" Never mind. I know why. You hoped to get some kind
of line on me. Well, don't, my dear. There was only one
link that joined me and Walsh. And that "—he put the
muffler around his fat neck again and patted it comfortably
into shape—" that was my razor. I'd brought it in my
pocket and left it on the shelf in the bathroom upstairs."
He patted his pocket. " I've got that now. Probably
nobody could ever have traced it to me ; one razor is very
like another. Still it is not my policy to take chances. And,
before I leave, in case that very naughty little thought that
I caught a glimpse of a moment ago in your eyes, returns, I
might tell you that I am not the only one who knows that
Steve Blake was in the house, in the library, and fought with
Walsh last night. Ask your little friend who digs in the
tulips. What's his name ? He saw the fight, too. I've
already made certain of that. Good-night, my dear. Until
I telephone to you."

He gave a final tuck to the muffler and went without
another word, quietly, yet boldly, out of the door. Instead
of going along the brick sidewalk toward Christine's, he
turned the other way. She could see his dark bulk vanish
around the corner of the porch. She moved somehow, went
to a window. There he was, turning into the street rather
quickly, probably with a swift glance up and down to see if

he were observed, but with nothing surreptitious, nothing sly in his attitude.

There was only the sound of the rain against the windows, a soft, chill little whisper. Nothing else.

She sat down presently, nervelessly, in one of the great soft chairs Walsh Rantoul had selected and bought. It was a blue chair with a table beside it whose top was blue, too, with mirror-covered cigarette boxes and match boxes.

Smith hadn't mentioned the monstrous thing he'd done the night before.

She couldn't do the things he asked her to do. They were impossibilities. She couldn't make herself, not for Steve, not for anything, give such information to the enemy.

The demand about the Interstate planes had been, literally, she thought a test question, designed to see if she meant to give the right answers or to try to trick them.

Well, the question about the number of planes being finished that month might be such a question, too, she thought suddenly. She reached absently toward the little mirrored cigarette box and stopped before her fingers touched it, thinking again of fingerprints. But then she'd touched other things—the door, the desk, the letters upon it. She took out a cigarette and lighted it with a nervous jerk of her fingers.

She began again to think, feverishly; turning and twisting her thoughts as a fox driven to earth turns and twists to find a way out.

No; the number of planes might not be really important. It was nothing that would (like the Interstate transfer) be released to the press. Still, there were ways to get an estimate of those things, and even so, an exact estimate was not important. It was the aggregate estimate of plane production that the enemy would want to discover.

The kernel of it all, the question he really wanted an answer to, was the last one. Did General X plan to go to the coast? Was he going to fly? When and from what airport would he leave and what plane would take him?

That was for sabotage. For a skilfully arranged trick, accomplished perhaps very simply, very quietly, at some airport where the plane stopped for refueling which would, in a few moments, crash the plane, and thereby eliminate a man who was one of their foes.

Well, she would fight, too. Suppose she found out the
time and circumstances of the scheduled trip (and it was by
no means certain that she could discover it ; even if Steve
knew he could be extraordinarily tight-lipped about a thing
like that) ; but suppose she discovered it, and then privately,
but very urgently warned Steve. No, she couldn't do that.
He'd say : " How do you know it's unsafe for the General to
make this flight ? " He'd have the whole story out of her in
a moment. But she could warn the General, secretly, not
telling him who she was.

But then she wasn't going to do that either ! It simply
wasn't possible that she was sitting in this dreadful, desolate,
chill little cottage—Walsh Rantoul's cottage—planning to
give any kind of information to the enemy.

No—she wouldn't do it.

But she'd still work for time. She had to do that. And
the purpose of her visit to the cottage now was to search for
clues—clues to Smith, clues to anything.

She put out the cigarette and rose. It wasn't going to be
easy. Not with that last sight of Walsh's delicate little face
with the great bruise upon it always in her mind. Not with
a memory of Walsh himself at her elbow, smiling, saying :
" Won't you come to my cottage, Miss Lovell ? Or may I
say Maida ? "

Well, she had come. She was there. And she must hurry.
The cottage was small. It didn't really take long. She
made herself search it rapidly but rather thoroughly.
Upstairs, where there were two tiny bedrooms done in chintz
with dormered windows ; downstairs, where there was only
the tiny hall, almost as small a dining-room and kitchen, and
the gloomy, blue and white drawing-room. Indeed, it
seemed rather remarkable that Walsh Rantoul had accumu-
lated so little. Nothing—not even his letters—seemed to
date back more than three or four months. He must have
come to Washington, she thought idly, at about the same
time she came—and Steve.

And he had apparently had the habit of destroying all his
personal letters.

In fact, there was a rather singular absence of those small
but natural and inevitable indications of personal friends, of
family and relatives and background. There were no photographs, no letters, not even any pieces of furniture which

looked as if they pre-dated, say, the previous summer. To all intents and purposes Walsh Rantoul had dropped out of the sky, whole and complete but with no previous and mortal existence.

It began to seem definitely sinister. He had no job either. She had supposed vaguely that he lived on an inherited income. Everybody probably had supposed that, for he was always well-dressed, he lived in a moderately luxurious way, he always had money to spend. She'd seen bills, lavish bills, really, for one man, showing that he did not limit himself as to money. The bills had been paid, too; she had seen no balances left unpaid from previous months. Thinking of that, she looked for but did not find bank statements or a bank deposit book. Still he must have had money. She wondered exactly where it came from.

There were, of course, explanations. The obvious one was that he had deliberately cut himself off from the family he must have had somewhere; possibly he had quarrelled with them, more likely he had simply drifted away from them. Still, it was a curiously complete separation. Perhaps it had been a question of leading his own life, using inherited money to lead the kind of life he liked to live. and that might have been a few layers above what, a generation ago, would have been called his station in life. There were young men like that; born snobs, working their way upward by their wits, cutting themselves off from those who had been stepping-stones on the way up, receiving their somewhat questionable reward in a precarious, occasional association with the great and the near great. Not that Walsh had achieved a particularly exalted position. Indeed, the only ground for considering such a theory was the marked and unusual lack of clues to his past which had certainly been intentional on Walsh's part; and it might be due to petty snobbery and it might not. But where that led her was exactly nowhere.

She'd ask Christine what she knew of him. Surely he'd had to give Christine some sort of bank and social reference when he had leased the cottage. In any case, if there was more to be found in the cottage, she couldn't find it. It was still raining and growing darker; it was with relief that Maida decided she could do no more there.

The cottage itself seemed to watch her cross the room to the tiny hall; seemed to listen as she opened the blue door;

seemed to wait, breathlessly, for her to close it. Along the
wet brick path it seemed to her that the sightless windows
watched her retreat.

She hurried through the weigela hedge. There were lights
in the library in Christine's house. There below the terrace
in the massed shrubbery Smith had stood the previous night.
On an impulse she left the walk and crossed the wet lawn,
looking young and green under the rain, and walked along
the line of shrubbery. Yes, here was a place from which
one could see almost the entire room through the french
door—if one were fairly tall, that is, as she made herself by
standing on tiptoes. She could see lights, and the table and
people moving about and talking. Christine was sitting
behind a tea table, the firelight making rosy gleams upon the
silver and china and Christine's bright hair and moving,
pretty white hands. Angela was standing by the fireplace,
talking to Steve. His tall figure and black head were un-
mistakable. Bill Skeffington was there, too ; handing cups
for Christine, smiling and talking. And on the other side of
Christine sat Nollie Lister, holding his knees together to
balance a plate upon them and apparently listening to Bill
Skeffington. It seemed to Maida she could hear his always
breezy, loud voice, even where she stood.

She'd better go in. Presently Angela would remember
that she'd left her at Walsh's cottage and begin to wonder
why she didn't return. She walked around along the hedge
again and across the terrace. Malcolm came in with a dish
of muffins just as she reached the french door, saw her, and
opened the door for her. Everyone turned as she came in.

"Oh, there you are," said Christine, comfortably and
kindly as always. "I was about to send for you. Angela
said you were at Walsh's. Good Heavens, Maida, you look
as if you'd been walking in the rain. Take off your hat and
let it dry. And your jacket."

Bill Skeffington said : "Hello, Maida. Want some tea ?
Here, I'll get it for you. Sit down here, darling."

Steve from the fireplace beside Angela only looked at her,
a cigarette halfway to his mouth. Angela, her slim figure
outlined handsomely against the flames, said : "Why didn't
you bring Walsh with you, darling ? "

And at that point Nollie Lister, sitting uneasily beside
Christine made a slight, convulsive motion, and his plate slid

with a crash from his knees to the floor. Everyone else probably looked at the shattered plate and the scraps of muffins. Maida looked at Nollie and saw the direct way his eyes went to the gauze and adhesive on Steve's chin, and then as quickly avoided it. The way his uneasy fingers went to the collar that was always too big for his scraggly little neck and pushed at it agitatedly.

Then Steve said quietly : It seems to me somebody said Walsh was out of town. Get Mr. Lister another plate, Malcolm. And how about some hot muffins ? ''

Rosy came waddling in from the hall and sat down in front of the tea table and begged. Bill Skeffington, who was pouring tea for Maida, stopped for a fractional second. He had rather large, outstanding ears, and it seemed to Maida that they moved, became alert and rigid like a dog's at the sound of Walsh's name. But then Bill knew that Steve and Walsh had quarrelled the week before ; everybody knew it ; possibly Bill would rather have liked to make capital of it if he could have discovered a way to do so. He didn't look up ; and Nollie Lister said with a nervous little cough : " I'm afraid I've broken one of your plates, Mrs. Blake. It's always difficult for a man at a tea party. If one only had a lap," he said, and gave a little nervous laugh and everyone else laughed a little too politely. Everyone but Steve, who put his cigarette to his lips and took a deep breath. Christine sat back and got out her knitting and a cigarette. People began to talk ; the broken plate was apparently forgotten. But Nollie Lister moved to the sofa and placed the plate Malcolm brought him on the table beside him and presently Bill Skeffington wandered over to sit beside him and to engage him, Maida saw with a kind of chill, in conversation.

CHAPTER ELEVEN

CHRISTINE was talking about her knitting. " I dropped a stitch somewhere about here." She was hunting methodically along the brown loops.

Maida got up. She moved quickly across the room and sat down beside Bill on the sofa with Nollie Lister on the other side of Bill's big, athletic-looking figure.

Nollie was saying something, replying apparently to something Bill had said. She heard only the end of his sentence. " . . . I don't think so. I'm not sure when I saw him last."

Him ? Walsh ?

Christine was frowning over her knitting and didn't hear it. Angela from the fire, beside Steve, glanced across at Christine and said : " Darling, I'm inviting myself to dinner. Is that all right ? "

" I suppose so," said Christine. She added childishly and a little petulantly : " You only want to stay because Steve will be here. You never used to want to dine with me."

Angela said : " Nonsense, darling. I dance attendance upon you. You are outrageously spoiled." She came across, slender and lovely in her soft green frock, put her hand on her sister's plump shoulder and gave it a little squeeze. Christine said shortly : " Well, you needn't pinch ! Go and tell Malcolm you're staying."

" All right." She went to the bell. Nollie Lister swallowed some apparently very hot tea rather loudly, put the cup down nervously and reached for a muffin. Bill turned to Maida, swinging one long leg over the other and smiled. " So you couldn't resist me. My charm over women. Hey, Steve, what have I got that you haven't got ? "

Steve put his cigarette in the fire. Christine scrabbled over her knitting. Malcolm came to the door and Angela spoke to him. Bill said to Maida : " I was just asking Nollie if he'd seen Walsh Rantoul lately. Have you ? "

" Walsh ? " said Maida. " Why—yes, I think so." She lifted her cup to her lips.

" When ? " said Bill.

Nollie leaned forward again so she could see his pale, rather wizened face and the look of uneasiness it wore. Uneasiness and knowledge. Smith was right ; Nollie did know something. Smith obviously had managed to extract something of that knowledge—and perhaps in doing so had sharpened Nollie's suspicions. In all likelihood nothing would suit Nollie better than to tell it—publicly, as a witness, getting his hitherto remarkably undistinguished name in the papers, posing importantly for photographs. Important witness in Blake murder trial.

She hoped she wronged him. She replied to Bill in as

casual a tone as she could command : " Not long ago. I'm not sure. He's always around somewhere, isn't he ? "

Bill swung his foot, looked at the toe of his brown Oxford, ran one hand over his curly, vigorous red hair and said : " Oh, always. Ubiquitous, that's the word for Walsh. That's why I asked. Did you say he was out of town, Steve ? "

Nollie Lister cleared his throat nervously and dug his hand worriedly down in the little space around the upholstered cushion below him and looked at nobody. Steve turned around, shoving his hands in his pockets and meeting Bill's alert, light-brown eyes.

" I said I thought he might be," said Steve. " I don't know." His face was unmoved. Angela, crossing the room toward Steve again, paused to take a cigarette from a box on the table which had a drawer below it. Steve's revolver had been in that drawer. Angela said, rather archly : " Now you're talking about my very special beau. That is, not as special as you, Steve. Only more devoted. Although, as a matter of fact, he didn't telephone to-day, and he usually does."

" Well, then," said Bill, " where in the world is he, Angela ? Nollie here says he didn't see him about the cottage to-day at all."

Nollie cleared his throat again and mumbled : " I was working in the garden, you know. Working—tulips are coming along very well indeed. I—er—just happened to notice that there weren't any lights in the cottage and no smoke from the chimney."

Bill said : " The mystery of the missing Walsh. How long's it been since you saw him, Angela ? "

Angela moved to Steve and bent her head toward him, pursing up her lips to accept the light he held for her cigarette. " M—m, I don't know," she said. " Yesterday, I think. Yes. I had lunch with him."

Christine glanced up, her fair forehead wrinkled. " Why on earth do you want to know, Bill ? " she said. " Does it matter ? For my part I rather dislike Walsh. I'm glad he didn't come to tea."

Angela laughed. " That is a surprise. Christine never dislikes anybody. Why don't you like him, Christine ? "

" I don't know exactly," said Christine, whirling the brown

yarn around. And added unexpectedly : "Except he's like a—a nosey, idle kind of woman, always poking around into something that—that isn't his business."

Steve said : "By the way, Bill, you got that office memorandum I sent around ? "

"Oh, yes," said Bill, his eyes still watchful. Nollie Lister set his cup down with a clatter. And Maida got up again. "Thanks so much for tea, Christine," she said. "Let me find the stitch for you before I go."

"No, I've got it now," said Christine, still pettish. "I had to ravel out a quarter of an inch."

Steve started toward Maida, but suddenly Angela's white hand was on his arm, and Bill was springing to his feet, all joviality. "I'll take you home, dearie," he said. "I've got my car outside with tyres that will still run if I keep my fingers crossed. Good-bye, Angela, beautiful. Good-bye, Christine, my pet."

Nollie Lister had a look of queer speculation on his face— speculation and, it seemed to Maida, knowledge. He was digging nervously into the cushions of the sofa again and, only as they left, got to his feet and said good-bye uneasily and awkwardly. Steve came to the door with them and Angela, her hand still thrust lightly but determinedly through his arm, came to. At the door Malcolm gave Maida something.

"I found 'em, Miss," he said. "Only they're not brown."

She scarcely heard what he said, but took the soft object he thrust into her hand and said good-night to Steve and Angela. The wide door closed behind her and Bill, leaving a picture of the two in the lighted hallway, with Angela's yellow hair close to Steve's shoulder. It was twilight again ; soft and damp, with the air fresh and clean-smelling. It was still cloudy, but the rain had stopped. Bill was suddenly rather silent and thoughtful ; he steered her down the street toward his small car which was parked, as it happened, directly across the sidewalk from the cottage.

The little gate to the cottage was closed ; the shrubs all around looked misty in the dusk. The cottage was, naturally, dark. Bill opened the door for her and paused. "Wait a minute," he said. "I'll just see if Walsh *is* at home."

"But . . ." she began and caught her breath and stopped.

"But what ? "

"But it doesn't really matter, does it ? "

It was the wrong thing to say. For he reached out suddenly across her knees and switched on the little dashlight and, as it spread a soft glow upward upon her face, he said softly : " Doesn't it ? "

So she hadn't been mistaken. She hadn't been misled and frightened by her own sense of guilty knowledge. Bill really was on the hunt. Some word, some look, some inflection that was wrong, not quite normal, not quite consistent had started up a train of speculation in his alert, ever-seeking mind. Or something Nollie had said before she reached them. She said lightly : " Not to me. Go and see if he's at home. I'm not in a hurry."

She thought he wouldn't go, but he did. The little gate slammed softly through the misty dusk, and she could hear his quick footsteps on the brick walk that ran around the cottage to the door at the rear—which was, really, the main entrance to the cottage and the door she had entered from Christine's garden. She could see Bill's tall, raincoated figure showing dimly light among the misty shrubs until he turned the corner of the cottage wall. Looking for Walsh.

She didn't dare think of that. Indeed, at almost that exact moment she stopped the vacillation, the arguments with herself, the constant weighing of this course against that one, that had dogged her up to then. Thinking, questioning, weighing the chances of this or that possible course, was of no help ; there was really only one thing she could do.

In a few moments Bill came back, got in beside her, and started the car He turned on the lights of the car The pale golden rays glimmered on the wet pavement He said briefly : " He's not there."

They drew away from the kerb, passed Christine's lighted house and turned through the park. Presently Bill said, watching the road ahead : " And I don't think he's been there for a—for awhile. . . . It's funny back there The cottage, I mean It's . . . " He paused for a long time, turned a corner into the busy street and said again, thoughtfully : " It's funny. It's—as if there's something wrong with the cottage."

She knew what he meant. It was what Angela had meant too.

" Dear me, Bill. How mysterious you sound ! What's the matter with you ? "

" It's not me. It's the cottage. And I "—again he seemed to travel some rather long and elaborate path of thought before he finished the sentence he'd begun—" and I'm not sure just why."

" Bill," she said, " let me out at the corner below my apartment, will you ? I want to . . . " To what ? Wasn't there a florist's shop at that corner ? " I want to get some flowers," she said.

" I'll buy your flowers for you, baby. Then I'll take you to dinner. What do you say ? And after dinner there's a good film over on Connecticut Avenue. They say "—he seemed to pause longer than it was necessary in order to turn a corner—" they say it's a good spy film. Some say the stories of espionage are overdrawn, but I always say anything's possible after what we know of Norway."

It was coincidence ; it had to be coincidence. *But what exactly did Bill suspect ?* And what was he going to do about it ?

She knew the answer to the second question. Bill was Bill. He had good qualities certainly ; but he was also hard, selfish, and ambitious. He wouldn't rob a bank or he wouldn't lie if he thought he was going to be found out ; perhaps he wouldn't exactly lie, anyway. But he'd serve himself and his own interests first and above everything and without any question as to the rightness of the means he grasped at with which to advance himself.

" Come on," he said. " You haven't got another date, have you ? Besides, Steve's having dinner at home with Angela and Christine," said Bill smoothly. " So you may as well come out with me."

The lights of the little florist's shop loomed up ahead. It was perfectly possible to keep one's temper for the space of half a block. And when they reached the corner in another few seconds, she had a little luck, for the light changed to red suddenly and Bill stopped his car and she opened the door quickly and slid out before he could grasp her wrist as he tried to do—laughing again with a flash of white teeth.

" Thank you, Bill," she said. " And the next time Steve asks me to dinner I'll be sure to let you know." She turned quickly toward the florist's bright little store. She watched through the windows as the light changed, and Bill's car disappeared down the street. Of course he might be curious enough to circle a block or two and come back. She bought a bunch of violets and, as she paid for them, she saw, for the first time, the soft objects Malcolm had thrust into her hand and she had clutched tightly ever since, along with her handbag. They were gloves but not her gloves, naturally, since she hadn't lost any gloves in Christine's house. They were very soft wash leather and rather large and loose : they were earthstained and spotted with water. Definitely not her gloves ; they belonged to Christine.

She put them into her handbag, pinned her violets on her shoulder and looked again through the wide glass windows along the street. So far as she could discover Bill had really gone on. On the street she was lucky again and got a taxi at once. She gave, as she had done the night before, the address of Steve's office.

An hour later she left the office building.

She stopped at a little restaurant and had dinner ; she walked home through the misty spring night. Her small apartment wasn't, though, the haven of refuge it had always seemed, because the moment she reached it and closed the door behind her she began to expect the telephone to ring.

And it did ring, twice. The first time it was Hortense. She lived just below and she and Maida were on rather casually friendly terms—eating together occasionally, going to a movie, joining in a protest about insufficient hot water.

" Why didn't you answer before ? " said Hortense.

" I just got here."

" Just got here, my eye ! I heard you walking around up there an hour ago and telephoned and you wouldn't answer. Of course, if you don't want to answer the telephone it's your business, but I heard you ! " Hortense's voice was teasing. " Anyway, I want to know about a movie to-night. Care to go out ? "

After she had hung up she looked carefully around the small apartment. And presently was convinced. Hortense was right and someone had been there. Searching for something ? But what, then ? And why ? Things were put back but not quite as they had been—a stack of stationery awry here, a handkerchief case at the right instead of at the left, a favourite blue Lalique perfume bottle pushed behind the mirror instead of standing in its usual place on the little glass tray. But she found nothing missing, except a half-written letter to Aunt Jason, begun and interrupted the previous Sunday, which she'd left on the open secretaire. At least she thought she'd left it there. She knew she hadn't finished and mailed it. Still, there was nothing of even the slightest importance in the letter ; there was no conceivable reason for anyone to take it anyway.

How had Smith got into the place—for it must have been Smith. And again, why ? As she was trying to find an answer to that the telephone rang again.

It was Smith. She told him, quite coolly really, everything she had planned to tell him. The Interstate planes were to be turned over to the government on the third of April, which was the following week, Friday. She gave him an approximate number of planes and an approximate description.

" Have you got the thing I asked you for this afternoon ? "

" The number off the assembly line . . . "

" Don't talk so much. Have you got it ? "

" But that's production. He has nothing to do with that."

" Get it. And get that other date."

He hung up.

She caught a glimpse of herself in the mirror and thought briefly that it was curious that there was no change in her face or the look in her eyes. She only looked rather white. In the middle of the night she wondered what Smith would do when he found out that the fact that the Interstate planes were to be turned over to the government, the approximate number and approximate description was to be in a news release in only a day or two and thus public knowledge. And that the date was not the third of April, as she had told him, but five days earlier—the twenty-ninth of March, Sunday. But he would discover that later ; the date would not be in the news release, and when he had discovered the real date it would be too late to do any damage to the planes. It was then Tuesday night.

Wednesday morning again the office seemed to be just as usual. Except that Steve sent for her at once.

He was standing by the window when she came into the office, his back turned toward her. He turned a little and said : " Hello, Maida," and looked back again—out the window toward, she knew, the dome of the great white building that stood for so much in Steve's life.

She waited, a slender young figure in her soft blue dress,

her eyes dark suddenly with alarm. Something was different about Steve—something in his voice ; he seemed to find it difficult to say whatever he'd sent for her to tell her. Her brown, smooth hair caught a gleam from the sun. Her chin lifted a little, unconsciously. Steve said, over his shoulder, rather gruffly : " Oh, by the way, that news release I gave you—or did I ?—about the Interstate planes, do you remember ? "

She must have nodded, although he didn't turn to see it and apparently took her silence for assent. He said : " Cancel it. The order for the news release has been rescinded. The idea is not to let it get out to anybody for fear of sabotage. But that's not what I sent for you to ask. Maida, were you here last night ? Here in the office, I mean ? "

CHAPTER TWELVE

THE OFFICE was perfectly quiet. It was a sunny clear day with a few buoyant, heaped-up white clouds and one of them drifted lightly across a corner of the sky visible through the window above Steve's shoulder before either of them spoke again. Here was a danger she hadn't foreseen. And it was an obvious danger ; one that ought to have been self-evident. Steve wasn't blind ; on the contrary, every sense he had was alert and strung to a high pitch of concentration on his job. He would, naturally, detect almost at once anything that wasn't quite right ; anything that was a little, inexplicably, wrong. Still, the danger of Steve himself discovering what she had done and putting the obvious interpretation upon it was one that had not occurred to her. And she must answer.

" Yes," she said.

He turned around then from the window. He was smiling a little and somehow, intangibly but definitely, too, the atmosphere of the room changed. He said in his usual, matter-of-fact voice : " Don't mind my asking. They made me."

" They ? "

" Never mind. It's a new rule that goes into effect to-night. Anybody visiting the office building has to sign in with the night porter and sign out again when he leaves. It's nothing unusual ; most office buildings have such a rule. It just happens that we haven't here, up to now. And it happened that the night man and the elevator boy told the Federal man who was here this morning that, among several people, you had been here in the building both nights. I was here last night about ten, myself. And Bill came in just as I left. But anyway—just as a matter of routine—the Federal man who came to suggest and apply the new rule—well, wanted me to put it up to you and see if you admitted it. You see there's a general tightening up of precautions all along the line. They mean to stop every possible chance of leaks of information through the office staff. Not just our office staff, but every one. I tried to tell him I knew you and you would as soon "—he laughed—" shoot yourself as give information to an enemy agent—sooner. But he said, okay, if you're so sure of this girl put it up to her without explanation. Ask her point blank if she was here and see if she admits it. It made me feel like an awful fool just now, questioning you like that."

He looked a little embarrassed and a little apologetic but mainly just matter-of-fact and natural. He said : " It's always this way. Rules apply to everybody. Only thing I hated was asking you without explaining why ; but I wanted to, too, after I'd had my little altercation with the Federal man. If everybody was as loyal as you . . ." He sobered suddenly and came quickly toward her. " Why, Maida, I didn't hurt you, did I ? I never meant—you know how I feel about you. Why, you are . . ." He broke off and took her hand. " I'd trust you with anything I knew."

If her knees hadn't turned to jelly she could have moved ; as it was she didn't dare. She just stood there, trying to look composed and natural, gripping her stenographer's tablet and pencil with one hand, trying not to clutch at Steve's warm fingers with the other which he held.

He said : " Why, Maida, I didn't mean—you look so white and . . . " He was rather white himself ; troubled and sorry for the wound he thought he had given her. What would she have said if the circumstances were what Steve thought they were ? She said it quickly : " Steve, how could I be hurt ! I think it's a very good plan." (And only she knew how necessary just then ! No more mysterious messages left on her typewriter !) " You know me too well, surely, to think a mere, everyday, office-routine question would upset me. Are you ready for me to take your letters ? "

He wasn't satisfied. " You looked upset."

" Oh, Steve ! " She moved nearer and put her hand on his shoulder, looking up into his face. " Haven't I worked for you for three years ? Don't you think I'm a sensible young woman ? Do you have to be afraid of hurting my feelings ! "

He looked down into her eyes for a moment and then said : " No. No, Maida. Not you." He paused again for a moment ; so long a moment that she heard dimly the little, muffled clang of a typewriter bell in the outer office and the honking of a car in the street below. Yet the everyday sounds seemed distant, as if they were outside a wall that suddenly surrounded her and Steve. Then he put his hands toward her ; slowly he drew her nearer and took her in his arms.

For an instant or two they stood like that, strongly aware of each other. Then Steve bent his dark head ; his cheek was warm and hard against her own : he turned her face a little like that, by pressing his cheek against it, and kissed her lips.

Something beat in her heart that was like little waves beating upon a sunny shore. The strangest part of that swift moment was its simple, clear happiness. Sun and wind and rain—and life itself for a moment had no mystery and no dark quality of threat.

As unexpectedly then they were standing apart, looking at each other—a little questioning, a little uncertain, both afraid of words.

The buzzer at the desk sounded. Steve took a breath, glanced at it impatiently, swung around toward it, came back to Maida and took her hands, the stenographer's pad between them. He leaned over and kissed her again but very gently on the mouth. She smiled a little and so did he. Then he went quickly to the desk.

As he talked into the little box from which, when he pressed the button, Jane Somers spoke urgently and metallically about a caller. Maida walked to the window. She heard him making an engagement with whoever it was in the outer office for later in the day. It gave her a breathing space.

At the same time the memory of Smith returned. The

situation was unchanged unless it was more difficult. Steve
cut off Jane Somers, and looked at the stack of papers on his
desk indecisively, as if his thoughts were not on the work
ahead of him.   Maida walked back to the desk and sat down
in her usual chair beside it, the stenographer's pad on her
knee.   Steve glanced at her and smiled a little again ; there
was a spark of laughter and of something less definable in
his grey eyes.   She said, her voice uneven : " Letters ? "
He looked at her for a moment, still with that little spark
dancing deep in his eyes ; then he said : " I suppose so.
Yes."   He turned to the papers before him.   " All right . . . "
As he began to dictate the first letter, his face changed to
the mask of concentration she knew so well.   She glanced
idly down at the wastebasket which stood almost at her feet.
It was empty, except for a withered small, purple violet.   A
violet that must have dropped from the cluster she'd bought
and pinned on her jacket the night before.
Where had he found it ?   He'd known then that she'd
returned to the office that night.   He knew her fondness
for violets ; a few times he'd sent her violets.   Had she lost
the betraying little flower somewhere in the filing cabinet,
caught it in the drawer, dropped it on the desk as she bent
over it, reading and searching for the information she'd given
Smith ?
The information that, now, was not to be public knowledge
and therefore harmless !   She'd forgotten that.
Steve had known all along that she'd visited the office the
previous night and he hadn't asked her why.   He had almost
found her there.   He'd returned at ten, he'd said—no, there
was a large margin of safety.   And Bill Skeffington had come
back to the office, too (so he hadn't gone to the spy movie),
later, just as Steve left.
Steve had known and hadn't asked her why she had come.
And now, she might have done incalculable damage by
telling Smith what she had told him, and there was no way
she could undo it.
Well, at any rate she'd given him the wrong date.   Perhaps
—she stumbled over a phrase and had to ask Steve to repeat
it.
Somehow she got through the rest of the letters.   By that
time Steve was caught in the busy, hard-driven routine of
work and scarcely noticed when she left the room and went

into her own small office. It was an exceptionally busy day and gave her no time to think. She had lunch sent up, a glass of milk and sandwiches. She worked till five-thirty— till six, and Steve was still working and people were still coming and the girls in the outer office were beginning to look over-thin with fatigue and pale. In the morning they looked merely slender and young and fresh ; nights, when it was late and it had been a hard day, they looked all at once pinched and white and their bones stuck out.

Steve left about seven ; he was with Jim Bennet, manager of one of the civilian air lines ; Jim Bennet was talking busily as they went through Maida's office. Steve stopped.

" For God's sake go home and get some rest."

" I will. I'm almost finished."

" Go now. Good-night, Maida."

" . . . and if we can get hold of those two-engined jobs," boomed Jim Bennet from the doorway.

" Good-night, Steve," she said. The door closed behind them. Had Steve meant what, that morning, he had seemed to mean ? Or was it just impulse and a girl he liked ? He hadn't said anything ; he hadn't even looked as if he re-membered it all that day. Well, then how could you tell ? The obviously sensible thing to do was forget it—at least just then. And go back to work. The outer office was empty by that time, for she'd sent the other two girls home a half hour before. At ten minutes after seven, just as she was straightening up her desk and yawning, Smith telephoned.

The ring of the telephone seemed inordinately loud in the empty office. Before she picked up the receiver she knew who it was and she was right.

" Got it ? "

" Got—no, not yet. I'm not sure I can get it."

" You'll have to. Hurry up about it. What about the date for that "—he must have been talking from a pay station somewhere, for he hesitated and said guardedly—" for that westward journey ? "

An airplane hurtling through the night, carrying a man who was important to America, crashing ; again as so many times that ugly vision passed through her tired mind. It was always the same ; the airplane lighted, going steadily through the starry sky—and suddenly lurching, diving, a little flame arising from somewhere, a sudden, horridly plummeting streak downward, a crash and a dreadful burst of flame and smoke. She shut her eyes and saw it against her eyelids. She said: " I'm not sure. Not yet."

There was a silence, one which took on an ominous, threatening quality. Then he said with the utmost certainty and confidence in his voice : " You're not going to give up, you know. You don't dare."

Again quickly, not letting her say anything more he hung up. She put down the telephone slowly, and Bill Skeffington from the doorway said suddenly : " What's the matter, Maida ? "

She hadn't heard the door open, and she wondered how long he had stood there. And what he had heard.

But then she hadn't said anything that would mean anything to him—had she ?

" What's the matter ? " she repeated. " Why, nothing. Why ? "

He hesitated, even his curly, thick red hair looked somehow alert and inquiring and his light eyes were very still. " You looked scared, if you want to know. Who's the big bad wolf ? "

" I don't know what you mean. I'm tired. . . . " She got up, and reached for her typewriter cover and yawned painstakingly. " It's been a horrible day."

And it had—except for a blindingly happy moment and its memory. She thought that rather wryly as Bill came forward. He was very spruce and smart in his grey tweed and green tie, and he carried a roll of newspapers under one arm. The newspaper caught her eye. Was there, yet, any outcry about a man—a missing man—a murdered man ? Stop that, she told herself, and forced herself to smile as Bill sat on the corner of her desk and grinned at her. " I don't know who it was over the telephone, but you looked as if it was Frankenstein's monster come to life. Who on earth was it ? "

She went to the locker for her coat and hat—and to turn her face away from Bill. " Nobody much," she said. " What's in the papers to-night ? " She pulled the little mirror to a better angle and put her small, smart blue hat on top of her head and pushed her hair up so her pompadour was smooth and neat. Steve had told her once, in an unusual moment of compliment, that he liked her hair like that, high, away

from her slender neck and ears, smooth and shining. Steve . . .
Well, she wasn't going to ask herself again what he'd felt that
moment, early in the morning. Bill said, as she had said :
" Nothing much. That is, except the war news. Of course
here in Washington you—hear things. Before they get into
the newspapers."

She pulled the gossamer blue veil as far as the tip of her
nose.

" Things ? "

" Yes, things." There was no mistaking it ; a note of
some special significance was in his voice. Suddenly, as she
turned her head to adjust the hat, she caught sight of his
face in the mirror, and the way he was watching her. It was
exactly like a cat at a mouse hole.

Bill Skeffington was somebody to reckon with. She
reached for her short blue coat. " What do you mean,
Bill ? "

He smiled suddenly ; not his usual, public smile but a
thin, secretive one—unless the little mirror and her own
imaginings were deceiving her. " I don't know whether
you've missed it or not. But it—or rather he—is certainly
missing. And there's talk."

Her heart quite literally and actually missed a beat. She
fastened her jacket ; she took out her handbag ; she put on
her gloves—seeing the yellow gloves that belonged to Christine
as she did so and, incredibly, noting them and telling herself
to remember to return them. She closed the locker, shutting
out that sharp, secretly smiling reflection of a tall man,
rangy, with blazing, curly red hair. She started to put on her
gloves and turned around. " There's always talk. What is
it this time ? I'm leaving now, Bill. Shall I lock the outer
office ? "

" I will. I'm leaving, too. I stopped to ask you to dinner.
Don't turn me down this time." He was smiling his public
smile now, wide, boyish, disarming. He got up and took her
unwilling arm and drew it through his own. " Come on, my
pretty child. I will a tale unfold. Over dinner."

He locked the office. The corridor was wide and echoing
with emptiness. One or two belated workers were in the
elevator ; she tried to get a look at the headlines and the
news items of the paper under his arm and he caught her at
it and said archly : " Naughty, naughty. I'll give you the

paper as soon as we get to dinner," while his eyes coldly marked her interest.

It was nearing dusk as they emerged into the street. She went to dinner with him ; she ate and smiled and listened to him talk. It was only over coffee and cigarettes that he leaned confidentially, but with those cold eyes very sharp, over the table.

"I got you here under false pretences," he said, smiling. "The only bit of news I really have is something that isn't really news. In fact, it's dearth of news. But a rather startling dearth."

"Oh, Bill, don't try to rouse my curiosity over nothing important," she said—voice light and lips stiff.

For a fractional instant his smile was as fixed upon his lips as if it had been nailed there. "I'm afraid it may be rather too important. To Steve at least. You see, Walsh Rantoul has disappeared. And there are some ugly whispers."

He waited, watching her. After a moment she said : "Whispers ? "

"Naturally. I—managed to establish a few facts. I haven't talked to Steve. I thought it better to talk to you."

"What facts ? " she said, and pretended to drink.

"Well—a few. For one thing Walsh hasn't been seen by anybody for over forty-eight hours. Yet he hasn't gone on a trip. At least if he did he didn't tell Angela he was going, and he took no clothes with him; and his trunk and hand luggage are still in the cottage. He's got a man, a coloured boy, who comes in by the day. He says Walsh hasn't been in the house since the day before yesterday."

"Why did you inquire about him, Bill ? It's not really your business, is it, if Walsh Rantoul chooses to . . ." She swallowed some of the hot coffee and made herself say : " To leave town for a few days ? "

"My business ? Well, perhaps not. On the other hand— well, that's where the ugly little rumour comes into it, Maida. You see, Steve had one very public row with Walsh last week. And it seems that on Monday he had another row with him. At about dusk that night. And Walsh hasn't been seen since."

CHAPTER THIRTEEN

SOME WOMAN, leaving the restaurant, brushed closely past them, her handbag swinging against Maida. It gave a necessary and welcome diversion which was long enough for Maida to decide what to say. She said it, not too boldly, but laughingly a little : " Exactly what desperate implication do you suggest, Bill ? " She held her breath, literally, for his reply.

It didn't come at once. He frowned, his thick sandy eyebrows drawing close together over the thin but marked bridge of his nose. Finally he said, making a pattern on the tablecloth with his long, square forefinger : " I'm not implying anything. Steve is my friend and, as it happens, my boss. I only want to know the truth. Did he threaten Walsh and why ? What did they quarrel about ? I thought you could tell me."

" No, I can't. I don't know. And I don't think it's your business or mine. You said there were whispers. What kind of whispers? It all seems very "—she had to swallow hard before she could get the word out—" very silly to me. Do you mean that people are saying that Steve—well, as you say, threatened Walsh ? Frightened him so he left town like that, at once ? Without letting anyone know ? "

He didn't answer for a moment. Then he said, still frowning : " I don't know, In any case, I'm not going to say anything of this to Steve. Not yet. As to the talk—it's going the rounds, or beginning to. I've heard a word here and there. Walsh is ubiquitous, you know. Always turns up everywhere. So when he doesn't turn up and isn't seen around, naturally there's a little talk."

" Obviously you went to his cottage again and inquired about him. Why did you do that, Bill ? You were not on particularly friendly terms with him, were you ? "

" I told you why. It's on account of my—loyalty to Steve. Everybody knows about Walsh and Steve. I don't want them saying anything that would—would damage Steve."

" How did you know that he and Steve had a row Monday evening ? "

" From an eyewitness, darling. But that's all I'm going
to tell you now."

" Oh, Bill, don't be so silly and—and mysterious. Tell
me."

" Nope."

" I think you're making it up."

" Do you, really ? " He beckoned to the waiter. " Check,
please. I'll tell you what I know, Maida, when you're ready
to trade. Tell me what you know, and I'll tell you what I
know. Think it over, darling. Ready to go ? "

Outside the restaurant she refused a taxi, saying she
wanted to walk home. He didn't, that night, invite her to
a moving picture. He said good-night in an absent-minded
way and walked briskly in the other direction.

It was a balmy, spring night, soft and gentle as only a
Washington night can be. No air raids yet, she thought,
looking up at the stars. There were fewer lights though ;
and once or twice she had an uneasy sense of being followed.
That, however, was mere nerves. So Bill had got his nose
to the trail ? It further complicated an already difficult
situation. Difficult ? She smiled a little at her own word
and its understatement, and wished that Nollie Lister had
been at the bottom of the Red Sea before, in Christine's
lighted, small library he had let the plate of muffins slide off
his nervous knees and crash to the floor—and thereby set
Bill Skeffington to thinking. Obviously Nollie was the eyewitness he meant ; obviously, too, however, he couldn't have
seen everything. And she already knew from Smith that he
had seen something, while standing there on the terrace
perhaps (or behind Smith, so he didn't see into the lighted
library), while Steve and Walsh quarrelled.

What had they quarrelled about ? And how could she
undo the damage she had done ? The press release is rescinded, Steve had said.

When she got to her apartment she tried to telephone to
Smith and in some way put him off, make him believe her
information was inaccurate. She tried several times but no
one answered. It was in fact three days before she talked to
Smith again or had any communication from him.

It was a very strange three days, mainly and paradoxically
because things swerved unexpectedly back into their usual
and accustomed orbit.

Spring came fully and rather early. The air was soft, the skies clear and blue, the sun was gentle and warm. All at once small green leaves masked the shrubs; overnight Rock Creek Park turned green and lovely and the cherry blossoms along the broad, serene Potomac burst, here and there, into bloom.

Every train brought hordes of people into Washington. Every train took fewer away than it had brought. There was a victory in the South Pacific and it lightened people's hearts a little. There were smiles, and a quick-running contagion of strengthened cheer and determination which was like wine. Like a promise; there would be more to come and ever more. In the streets, in the cocktail bars, at stately dinner parties, in the offices, everywhere there was rejoicing. It added to the naturalness of those warm, spring days.

And it had the headlines in the papers. Every day Maida searched the local items, buying the paper eagerly, then afraid to open it, then taking the plunge and searching it for some mention of Walsh Rantoul. She found nothing.

That in itself began to seem wrong. There must have been inquiries, even if there had been less talk, really, than Bill had said in his effort to induce her confidence. Surely someone would wonder why Walsh hadn't replied to some written invitation to dinner, or some card, or some telephone call. Surely soon, some inquiry, some remark would start itself and, like a snowball rolling downhill, suddenly accumulate comment, until it reached everybody's ears; until it got in the newspapers. She tried several times to telephone to Smith and never succeeded in reaching him. · She received, however, during those days, no further orders.

There was luckily a pressure of work in the office. She saw Steve constantly but only in the office, and there was such a mass of detail, so many people, so many letters, so many departmental meetings which might last thirty minutes and might last six hours that there was no time to talk to him. Anyway, there was nothing that, just then, she could say. The period of vacillation was in the past; her thoughts were completely now engrossed with ways and means out of the ugly tangle in which she was enmeshed. Ways and means, however, which existed only to be considered, found weak and impossible of performance and discarded.

Yet there was undoubtedly a kind of false security in those days—part of it due to the necessary concentration for long hours every day upon work that had to be done well and quickly, part of it due to the wave of optimism over the city, and the spring, and (to Maida) the fact that as yet there was nothing about Walsh in the papers.

Except for something in a column ; it was only a line to the effect that Walsh Rantoul had not been at some dinner. " Where," queried the columnist, " is Walsh Rantoul ? Now that we think of it we've not seen him for several days. Walsh is one of our most delightful and entertaining diners-out. By the way, expect an important announcement soon regarding a marriage in military circles. We are informed that the lovely young daughter of General so-and-so——" Maida read no more. The name Walsh Rantoul had leaped out of the column as if it had been in large block letters.

But that was all.

Angela did not come near the office during those days, except once when she came in unexpectedly about five, looking very lovely in a cream woollen suit and smart red hat and sables, to invite Steve to take her to a cocktail party. She had her car downstairs, she told him, and it had been ages since he'd been away from the office. Steve good-naturedly refused ; he couldn't go, he told her ; there was a late conference coming up. Angela had pouted prettily, patted his lapel and finally departed.

After she was gone it struck Maida suddenly, typing up some reports, that Angela had looked a little pale and fine-drawn. Nervous would be a better word. Instantly she thought of Walsh. Everything led back to that, but the question was, had Angela become curious too—as Bill had done ? If so, what then ?

She heard no more from Bill. Indeed he kept rather ominously out of the way and didn't come in once to loiter at her desk as it had been his habit to do. Several times, naturally, she saw him, but it was always in the way of business and always in a hurry.

The second day something unexpected happened that further gave her a queer sense of recovered security. That was when she took a letter at Steve's dictation which indicated that Major-General X had already, starting the day before, arrived at the coast by airplane. So she was safe there.

And so was Major-General X. Again that haunting vision of a falling, flaming airplane crossed her mind. She shivered in spite of herself and Steve saw it, and she had a bad moment then (there were other bad moments during those days, too) when he stopped dictating and leaned across toward her.

" What's the matter, Maida ? "

" I—nothing, really, Steve."

He was unconvinced ; his eyes so dark and urgent with question that she avoided their look. " Shall I go on ? " she said.

And after a moment Steve said, in a different voice : " Yes. Where was I . . . ? "

She told him and continued automatically making the right marks in her shorthand tablet. By the time he finished it was almost dark.

So far as anything in Steve's words or manner was concerned the little scene that had taken place so unexpectedly and so abruptly the morning after her visit to Walsh's cottage might never have happened. He was engrossed in work ; so was she. It was not, however, a satisfying explanation.

However, in spite of her queer, almost paralyzing sense of lulled security she did do two things. The afternoon of the third day she finished her work unexpectedly early (due to Steve's being caught in a protracted conference) and went to see Christine, leaving Jane Somers to carry on in the office.

It was Saturday and the streets were full, many offices having closed early. Walsh had been killed on Monday and there was still no outcry, no news of it, no horror of discovery. Again, she refused to think of what, that dusky evening, Smith had done. She walked through a corner of the park and found Christine at home.

She was in the library, reading and eating chocolates, looking very bored. " My dear," she said, shoving her spectacles up across her lovely white forehead. " I'm so glad you've come. How nice of you ! Sit down and I'll tell Malcolm to bring us tea. No, come out on the terrace. We'll have tea there. I'm simply delighted to see you. Steve stays at the office all hours, and Angela has come in only once in the last three days, and then she only stayed a moment and went across to Walsh's cottage and then went away. He wasn't at home. I've nothing to do and—come along, my dear. What a pretty suit! That shade of pink becomes you—petal pink, isn't that what they call it? Though how you can wear it at the office and still look so immaculate. . . . ?"

" I didn't," said Maida, helplessly trying to get an oar into the conversation. She recognised with dismay one of Christine's talkative moods; still perhaps she'd talk with equal facility about Walsh. She said: " I went home and changed to this. Aunt Jason sent it to me from Peck and Peck's. I do think it's pretty." She had rather wished Steve could see her in it; the soft pink wool, with her white blouse and the twisted pink wool turban were rather becoming. However, he hadn't and in all probability wouldn't. She let Christine install her in a greenish metal chair and looked out over the stone balustrade and the shrubs, where a man had stood and watched the scene in the library behind her. And where—somewhere—Nollie Lister had stood and seen a little of the same scene. He was as usual digging in his garden, on the other side of the fence with Rosy sitting on Christine's side, watching him sluggishly. Christine saw the direction of her look and said pettishly: " That Nollie Lister! His bulbs aren't coming up any better than mine in spite of his bringing them home with him from Holland, all wrapped in cotton wool, if I know Nollie. Besides, he's quite capable of going out and buying tulips and passing them off as his own at the flower show. Of course, they're supposed to be at their best the second year, but I don't see anything marvellous about them so far. And with the war and all there may not be a flower show, anyway! Oh, Malcolm, put the tea here, please. What *are* you looking at, Maida?"

Maida realised she was staring through the new green halo of the hedge toward Walsh's cottage and looked away.

But at the end of an hour's conversation with Christine she was little wiser. She knew a great deal about Christine's other neighbours, for she had led up to inquiries about Walsh in a roundabout way, asking about the people across the street, about Nollie Lister (and she really wanted to know more of him because certainly he came within the rather short list—unless you counted people like Jane Somers or Malcolm or the other servants, or people whom Walsh and

Angela knew but the rest of them did not know—who might conceivably be familiar with Christine's house to enter it almost at will), and about the corner house, on the other side of the wall which marked Christine's property, beyond the cottage. That house, Christine told her, was vacant and had been vacant for some time. It was a gloomy old house, built in her childhood by some people by the name of Prey. " He was a retired brewer," said Christine with a giggle. " And they all drank beer like water, I remember. But they were very generous people and always had marvellous Christmas parties with quantities of little decorated cakes and such Christmas trees! Little angels all over them! I don't know what happened to them. They moved away a long time ago, and the house has been empty ever since ; once in a while somebody goes through it and cleans and airs it." Her blue eyes clouded. " I suppose they were German," she said. " I never thought of that till now. Well, there are lots of fine, loyal German-Americans! But there's nothing very interesting about the house across the street."

Nevertheless she told Maida of it in chatty detail. It simmered down to an army family as its present tenants, with two girls of college age and the probability that they would give up the house at any moment, for they had insisted on the army clause in the lease (how did Christine know all this, thought Maida with a kind of wonder that was mixed with admiration) and the major was likely to be transferred any day. And as to Nollie Lister, the Listers had lived there forever, too, as she, Christine had done. The old people had died many years before and Nollie was the only one left. " He should have married," she said, and looked suddenly rather pink, and sparkly. " He sort of likes me, you know. He always did when he was a kid—and a thin and scraggly child he was, too, always having indigestion. He's got over that somehow ; so much for travel. The Listers were quite nice people in an old-fashioned, solid sort of way. He'd been a sugar planter somewhere in the East, I remember. Nollie's father, I mean. Nollie doesn't like women much— at least, I've never known him to, although I don't suppose I would have known. Still," she sparkled again mischievously, " still, there's a look in his eye, if you understand me, and I think you do. A pretty girl like you! What did you say, Maida ? Oh, Walsh. Well, Walsh is a different kettle of fish. He's a newcomer, and I'm not very fond of him really. . . ."

So in the end, if she knew really startling details of Christine's other neighbours ("Do you know the Major has the oddest habit of walking in his garden in his pyjamas! Don't you think that's funny? He's not very pretty either. Well, he'll get more exercise now he's in active service again.") she discovered very little concerning Walsh.

Christine only knew—or at least only said—that Walsh had heard that her cottage was to let; had come and leased it; had given her some references, which she hadn't bothered to look up, and had been a good tenant and that was all. "Except that he's underfoot a lot," said Christine with a yawn. "Although, I must say," she added, "I haven't seen Walsh around for "—she stopped and thought and frowned— "why, for almost a week! How very odd! I must go over to the cottage and see what's wrong."

Finally, convinced that Christine knew no more of Walsh than she had told her (and that she had already aroused Christine's curiosity about his absence which certainly was a dubious accomplishment), Maida went away.

She did learn definitely that Angela had been inquiring about Walsh.

On the way home, opening her bag to pay for the taxi, she discovered Christine's gloves. She'd intended to return them; well, she would the next time she saw Christine.

As always since she knew her apartment had been searched she entered it rather hesitatingly, nerving herself to do so, yet there was never anything there, or anyone. It was due to the same impulse, however, which she had now and then on the street—the highly unpleasant sensation of being followed. She made opportunities to look behind her in store windows, in the mirror of her handbag—and every so often her own fancy insisted that she saw someone she knew. Once a tall man with bright red hair was just disappearing around a corner; once she was sure she saw Nollie Lister, dressed up in city clothes, scuttling unobtrusively along behind her—although when she went back he had disappeared, and a man about his size was buying tooth paste in a drug store along the street. But it wasn't Nollie. Once she remembered that she was only a couple of blocks from a club where Angela was a member, at the time she saw her.

Never, when she let herself turn around, was there anybody who seemed particularly interested in her—with the exception, that is, of the time when she looked so hard at the man coming just behind her that he stopped, smiled and lifted his hat and invited her to have a cocktail with him. They were just passing the Carlton with its comfortable yellow and mirrored bar and it was about time for cocktails. Yet, in spite of the absurdity of the incident, half an hour later she was caught again by the same feeling of being under close observation.

In the apartment the sense of that previous mysterious visit lingered like an ugly perfume. Besides, the telephone was in the apartment.

She hated and feared the telephone. It was a black symbol of horror and treachery; it was an ever-present threat. Nights, several times, she dreamed it had rung and she awakened sick with fear to find that it was only a dream and no one answered when she took it up and spoke into it.

She was trying to write another letter to Aunt Jason (what *had* happened to the first one?) and staring at the paper, digging holes into it with her pen when, actually, the telephone did ring.

Smith at last? Smith with a new order? Smith demanding the answers to that other order and answers she could not give him? She hadn't tried to discover the number and description of planes expected off the assembly line at the New England plant; and she didn't intend to tell him that the Major-General had already and safely reached his destination. She took up the telephone.

But it was Steve, suddenly and jubilantly in a holiday mood. "There's news of another sea victory," he said joyously. "Come and have dinner with me. The conference is over and it's Saturday night. Let's go out on the town. I'll get a table somewhere and call for you in half an hour. Right?"

"Right," she said. And hoped after she hung up the telephone that she hadn't really sung it.

She hunted for her prettiest dress and decided on a pale, pearl grey, slim and graceful and plain except for the dark crimson slippers and exaggeratedly long, dark crimson gloves. She fumbled over her little tray of lipsticks and found one to match. She thanked her stars again for Aunt Jason when

she put on her one evening wrap—ermine—made over
successfully from the old enormous and tailed cape Aunt
Jason used to wear to the opera.   There were points in having
a rich aunt.

Steve arrived in twenty-eight minutes. She opened the
door for him, and he gave her a look and then a quick hug.
Too quick, as a matter of fact, and altogether too matter-of-
fact ; however, it was a hug.

" You look sweet," he said.   " Reminds me, I'm hungry.
Come on."

They went to the Shoreham.   Since it was Saturday
night, the night on which office workers and civil service
employees can stay up late without thinking of working
hours the next day, it was unusually crowded. But there
was also the usual sprinkling of names ; a famous fighting
Senator sat next to them with his pleasant, quiet wife.   An
equally famous but unpopular Senator sat at another table
not far from them and ate as if he never expected to get
another meal.   The youthful president of an airline company
was gallant with the smiling pretty daughter of another
famous statesman.   Uniforms were everywhere on slim
young figures—and some not so slim or young.   " Let's see
how many titles we can bag," said Steve watching the dancers
floating past them.   " I've got three generals and an admiral
already, and I must say," he added critically, " their dancing
needs revision.   There's a waltz, though," he sighed a little
enviously, watching the men in uniform.   " Now it'll be
different.   All navy officers can waltz like crazy.   Well, so
can I.   Shall we ? "

So they waltzed.   His arm tight around her ; quite tight,
really, for the floor was crowded.   There was, however, in
spite of all the people around them, nothing in the world but
Steve's arms, his brown face above the black and white of
his dinner clothes (which he so longed to exchange for a
uniform, any uniform), his nearness and the lilting, wistful
measures of the waltz.   It was a Strauss waltz, heartbreaking,
lovely, nostalgic.   Reminding one of tragedy, of gaiety and
hope, of life and love and happiness.

Steve put his cheek lightly against her own for an instant.

It was the smallest, gentlest caress—as warm and as sweet
as the waltz itself.   And as fleeting.   The Vienna of those
gay and tender waltz times was no more ; and the unfathom-

able future was there, upon them, upon America. What things could be saved, unchanged? What lovely memories would be only memories? Victory lay ahead—but how far ahead and over what path of blood and sacrifice no one knew. When would they waltz again?

Perhaps all Washington (all New York, all the civilised world) felt something of that question and consequently that wistful clinging to the small bits of beauty and gentleness, the little fragrant symbols of a chosen way of living. Perhaps, too, nerves were already feeling the battering pain of war, and saying, " Live *now*—live *now*," like the beating of a warning drum. Certainly there was the need for gaiety, for laughter. For waltzing. The lights dimmed a little, blue and soft rose, and then too soon the music stopped, except that it still went on in her heart.

They went past the dancers, not speaking, Steve's hand on her arm, guiding her to their little table.

Bill Skeffington was there waiting for them. His face looked ashy ; his eyes were gleaming. " I thought I'd better come. They don't want it known publicly yet. Steve "— he leaned toward them, pitching his voice low—" they've just got word. Half an hour ago, there was a fire at the Interstate hangars. The seaplanes they were to transfer to the government to-morrow were burned to ashes."

CHAPTER FOURTEEN

THE LIGHTS changed softly again ; they dimmed over the packed tables, and a spot of light fell upon the suddenly vacant dance floor—vacant except for a microphone and a smiling master of ceremonies who was talking into the microphone. Maida heard only vaguely what he was saying, but ever afterward remembered, nevertheless, the flourish of music from the orchestra as it gave a salute to the army, a salute to the navy, a salute to the marines. " Anchors aweigh, aweigh. Anchors aweigh . . . "

She must have sat down, for she was looking up at the two men. She couldn't hear what they said ; she couldn't hear anything but music and blurred words in her own mind: *But I told him the third ; this is only the twenty-eighth.*

The men sat down too ; they were now directly across the table with its flowers and silver and Steve's flat leather cigarette case with its initial catching the light in a wide gold B. She said, her voice strained and harsh : " Were any lives lost ? "

For a second both men looked at her, caught by her voice, her eyes, something in her face. With another surge of music from the orchestra a dancer ran out on the floor and the spotlight began to follow her and someone at the microphone sang : " You're everything to me."

Then Bill, eyes narrowed, face still weirdly pale, said : " No."

Steve said quietly (but there was something new in his face, too, something anxious and questioning, that was quite aside from its stricken gravity) : " Maida, you'd better have a drink."

He half turned to beckon to a waiter, but she shook her head and he pushed the goblet of water toward her. As she took it he said to Bill : " Keep it out of the papers. Telephone to . . . " She didn't hear the name. " Then meet me at— oh, Christine's. Later."

Bill nodded and slipped away, past the packed tables. She put down the goblet.

She leaned over toward Steve, as someone sang and sang, and the dancer whirled in rainbow lights near them and dipped and turned, and she said : " Steve, I've got to talk to you. Alone. Now."

He looked at her across the table. His face was pale and hard too ; his eyes very dark. After that one look he didn't question. " All right. Now's a good time to leave."

He got a waiter's eyes ; the check came, a round of applause broke out and the dancer bowed. Applause stopped and waves of music submerged the packed and dim room again, and Steve was standing beside her. " All right, Maida," he said, and slipped her coat around her bare shoulders ; her long crimson gloves caught a flash of light as she rose, and she thought with heartsick horror that she had dipped her hands in the blood of her country to save the man she loved— who would hate her when he knew.

Steve was going ahead, making a lane through the tables and people, his broad shoulders and tall body sharply clear against the blurr of white tablecloths and women's light

dresses and bare shoulders. There were people crowded in
the doorway, too ; the head waiter bowed and smiled ; they
emerged into the wide lounge, dotted with chairs and groups
of people, talking and smoking. Somehow she moved and
walked beside Steve up the stairs to the lobby level. She
stood beside a pillar while Steve stopped briefly at the check-
room, and a girl in pink with a rose in her hair ran past her
and down the stairs, hand in hand with a young ensign ;
both were laughing.

When they were moving again toward the door, she realised
that Steve was inducing her to walk rather slowly and deliberately. The car was near. A doorman saw Steve and
brought it around and said, smiling as Steve's hand conveyed
a tip to his own : " Good-night, Mr. Blake ; good-night, sir."

The window was down in the car and the balmy, fresh
night air touched her face. But she was back in the world
of nightmare.

" We'll go home," said Steve, turning into the street.
" Christine's at a party ; we can talk there."

After that one look at her face he had accepted the importance of whatever it was she had to say. That struck her as
curious—but only vaguely, through her terrible preoccupation. Her vision of flaming, burning planes had become
a terrible reality. Six seaplanes, big planes, important
planes that took time to build when time was of such
tremendous value.

Bill had looked at her when she had asked if any lives were
lost. Then Steve had sent him away.

Before she realised it, they were on Christine's street ;
they had stopped ; they were getting out, her long skirt
catching under her heel so she stumbled and Steve caught
her and she leaned against him for an instant, and saw beyond
his shoulder the low light outlines of Walsh's cottage behind
the dark shrubbery.

He had a latchkey ; here was the hall with its winding
stairway and its crystal-hung candelabra reflecting themselves
in a hundred lights in the gilt-framed mirror. She had a
quick, blurred view of a girl with a chalk-white face and
enormous eyes walking past the mirror. Steve said : " I
think Malcolm's out for the night. We'll go into the
library. . . ."

" *Oh, no !* " cried Maida.

Steve stopped. " Why "

" Because . . . " She caught her breath, and said : " All right."

Then they were in the library ; she was on the sofa. The french doors were closed ; the lights were on, and the room was quite ordinary and pleasant with its flowers and its cushioned chairs. Steve was at the table where the glasses and bottles stood on a tray, pouring something into a glass. " Here," he said, coming to her. " Drink this." He put it in her hand and turned in a matter-of-fact way to pour a drink for himself. Then he came and sat beside her on the sofa, turning the glass in his hands, and said very quietly : " Why not the library, Maida ? Because of Walsh ? "

" *Walsh ?* "

Steve put down his glass. " Tell me, Maida, what you know. I wondered if you'd heard or seen anything. But I thought you would have told me."

" Steve, I found him."

" Found Walsh ? Here ? That night ? "

" Here, Steve. On the floor—there. That's the way it began, you see. That's the way it began. And now those planes. Only I said the third of April, I tried to deceive them ; I tried to . . . "

" Maida ! " His face was exactly the colour of ashes. He took the glass out of her shaking hands and put it down. " *Maida, what do you mean ?* "

" Oh, Steve, Steve. It was your revolver ! And they knew it ! Smith knew it. . . . "

He gripped her shoulders. " *Maida, what are you saying ? What revolver ?* "

" But he was dead," she said, half-sobbing, moving against his hands. " He was dead, Steve."

The room was hushed and listening. His hands were hard upon her shoulders. " Dead," he said at last, whispering. " So that was it ? He died then. And someone—someone must have—*Maida, what happened ? What do you mean ?* "

" Steve, did you kill him ? "

" Did I . . . ? " he stopped. His face changed ; his hands were less hard and demanding. He put one hand gently under her chin and, looking straight into her eyes, he said : " No, Maida, I don't think I killed him. I met him here as I was leaving. We had a—silly kind of fight. He got home to my chin and I hit him and then I left. He's not been around since, and I didn't know what had happened. I didn't want another silly story of a fight to get out so I said I thought he was out of town. I did think so, too, except— once I thought perhaps I had killed him without knowing it, you see, but if I had they'd have found him here. Or somewhere. Maida, *what* revolver ? "

" You didn't . . . " she stopped.

He repeated it : " I hit him and I think knocked him down. I was furious because I'd let myself be drawn into another fight with him. I left without looking back at him."

" But you didn't get your revolver out of the drawer ? You didn't touch it ? "

" No. I don't understand what you . . . but the answer is, no, I didn't. . . . " He stopped and said quickly : " He was shot, then ! He was dead and you came down and . . . "

" And Smith was there ; almost at once Smith was there ! But I told him the wrong date. . . . "

" Maida," he said. He put his arm tight around her so she leaned against him. " Now then," he said. " Tell me."

So she told him—slowly, and in a consecutive and detailed way, as things had happened. She told everything ; she thought she omitted nothing, but there were actually at least two things she didn't tell because they seemed unimportant, merely details. But she told of the evidence against him— the red carnation, the revolver, the eyewitness.

Once he got up and went to the door, opening it to glance into the hall. Once he went to the french doors, too, and made sure they were fastened and glanced out through those winking black window panes. " He was out there, then ? "

" Yes. Behind the shrubbery ; behind the balustrade of the terrace."

He pulled the thick blackout curtains with which the doors were newly equipped—that week, she thought dully—and came back and took her in his arms again. " Go on." His face was strained and white ; his voice very gentle.

When at last she finished with the deception with which she had tried and so horribly failed to defeat Smith, he got up and walked across the room and back again. She watched him move back and forth against the pleasant room, and the long blackout curtains, but she didn't really see him, for instead she saw planes burning. It was an unendurable sight.

"Oh, Steve, Steve," she whispered. "I've done a terrible thing. I've been so wrong, so . . ."

"*Don't.*" He came quickly to her again. He knelt down beside her. He put his arms around her. "Darling, darling, you did it for me. Don't you *know* that I know? Don't you. . . .?" he stopped and held her for a moment. "It's been hell for you. You are the bravest, loveliest . . ."

"I did it, though, Steve. I gave information to the enemy."

"You didn't intend to. I—listen, my darling, *don't think of that now*. Think of what we've got to do. Think. . . . Did you ever see Smith anywhere before?"

"No. I'm sure of it."

"And he hasn't telephoned to you for three days?"

"No."

He thought for a moment. "I didn't kill him, Maida. That is, I didn't shoot him. If he died from a bullet wound, it had nothing to do with me. When he disappeared, you see, I got worried about it. I've heard of men dying from a blow. I didn't think I'd hit that hard, but every so often that very thing happens. It's been known to happen even in a—well, friendly kind of wrestle; accidentally you strike over the heart, knock somebody against a table edge or something like that. But of course if he died like that, he'd have been found, I thought. So I really thought he'd left town. I think I hit the side of his face—yes, that's right; you said there was a bruise there. Well, I suppose there might have been a concussion if I knocked him against something. The only way we can be sure is to have an autopsy made."

"Oh, no, Steve! That would mean . . ."

"Where was he—that is, what did Smith do with him?"

"I don't know."

There was a longish pause. She said suddenly: "I was in the office that night, you know. I . . ."

"Yes, you told me, Maida. I knew anyway. A violet, wilted, was caught over the lock of a filing cabinet. I didn't suspect you. I was only to ask you—that doesn't matter now, dear, believe me."

He went to the telephone. She got up, too, moving as stiffly as a doll. "*Steve, you can't* . . ."

He was beginning to dial. "That's what they're for, Maida. There's nothing else to do."

" There's all that evidence against you ! "

He said slowly : " I don't see how I could have hit hard enough to hurt him much. I'm pretty sure it couldn't have been that that killed him. Therefore it must have been the revolver shot . . . "

" It was your revolver."

" But I didn't shoot him and somebody did. I've got to report the murder. If I don't, I'm an accessory after the fact—that is . . . "

" Am I that ? An accessory after the fact ? "

" Maida . . . "

" Of course I am. I concealed the murder. That's— serious, isn't it, Steve ? "

He said slowly : " There were unusual circumstances. Threat . . . "

" If I hadn't believed his threats, if I hadn't believed and told him about those planes . . . "

" Please don't, Maida. I'll do something. I'll . . . " He stared at the rug for a moment and then abruptly put the telephone down upon its cradle. " The point is now to get Smith. I'm not in any real danger. At least, I don't think I am. Even if I am, I'll get out of it. Besides—I don't mean to be a hero, but I really don't count. Smith and the organisation he's got is the important thing."

She caught at his arm rather desperately : " Steve, what did you do that night ? Where did you go ? Isn't there some sort of alibi you can give them ? "

" It's just as I told you, Maida. I came downstairs from the study and heard somebody moving about here in the library and thought it might be Christine. It would save me a trip to get her to the party. So I came back, but it was Walsh. And he—well, for the second time he simply walked up to me, made some kind of a crack, I don't re-member what, and before I knew it took a swing at me. The same thing had happened before—publicly, and so it didn't exactly embarrass me as a person but definitely was embarrassing to the job I'm responsible for. We've got to give people confidence in the men who are trying to do this job, who represent them, who—well, in a way, who lead them through the war. A public brawl isn't likely to inspire confidence ! I hated it from that angle and was resolved never to let it occur again."

"What was your quarrel about?" she said, thinking of Angela. And thinking of Bill.

But Steve looked suddenly and honestly puzzled. "That was the crazy part of it," he said. "We didn't quarrel about anything. He may have got worked up about my taking Angela out, but somehow I didn't think that was it. It was just"—he spread his brown hands—"it was just about nothing! I didn't *have* a quarrel with Walsh. I don't know why he attacked me, like that. The only explanation that occurred to me was—well, a kind of crazy one maybe. But you know how he was. He seemed to have nothing to do but run around to parties, and he seemed to get quite a kick out of any scrap of attention—newspaper attention, I mean. He was inordinately vain and rather fancied himself, I think, as a ladies' man."

"Yes," said Maida, remembering Walsh's fatuous smile, his soft caressing hands.

"Well, I thought afterward, wondering what in the world had got into him (and after I saw the various items, veiled far too lightly, in the columns), I thought maybe it was only a way Walsh had thought up to get a certain amount of attention focused upon himself. Particularly as a—well, a rival of mine and a suitor of Angela's. Angela is so well known, you know, and so handsome. I suppose in a way it reflected a kind of glory upon Walsh. At least that's the only explanation I could discover for it at the time. I put it out of my mind, except I had decided to see to it that it didn't happen again. Then just as unexpectedly it did happen again, the same way. Except it was right here; it wasn't so public; I was mad at myself then, more really than at Walsh. I left as quickly as I could, telephoned to the Slaters' and left a message for Christine to take a taxi home and walked over into the park. Then my chin was bleeding, so I walked until I got to a drug store and the clerk dressed it for me. I told him I'd fallen. . . ."

"Did he know you?" she asked tersely.

"I'm not sure. I didn't think of it at the time. It's not an alibi anyway. It was at least twenty minutes or half an hour after I'd left the house. I'd held my handkerchief to it, hoping it would stop bleeding."

"I didn't mean an alibi. It's—oh, Steve, Steve, he would be still another witness against you. They'll find it. They'll find him. They find everything." She stopped. A bell was ringing somewhere, muffled yet sharply insistent. It was the doorbell; it was repeated and repeated.

"Servants must be all out," said Steve, "or asleep. I'll go. . . ."

The sound of the bell made the house seem empty, as it had seemed the night Walsh Rantoul was killed. So there was something rather ominous and even premonitory about the repeated distant peals. Steve went out and she got up and followed him into the hall and was there in time to see two men enter as Steve held the door back. They were two policemen.

Steve closed the door behind them. One said: "Mr. Blake?"

Steve said: "Yes," inquiringly.

The policeman who had spoken gave Steve a hard, measuring look. The other one put his cap down upon the table beside the glittering candelabra and stared down into it for an instant. The first one said: "We'd like to see you, Mr. Blake. Alone."

"Why, certainly, officer. What's gone wrong?"

Maida had her hand tight upon the newel post. The policeman glanced along the hall, over Steve's black shoulder and his gaze encountered her own. He didn't blink or change his expression but he seemed to register her, standing there, as a camera registers a picture. He said, shifting his eye to Steve again: "Well, it's the man next door, Mr. Blake. We had a tip. . . . I think we'd better talk to you alone."

"The man next door?" said Steve. "What's he done?"

"Seems to have got himself murdered," said the policeman.

CHAPTER FIFTEEN

EVERY so often in life something that cannot happen, does happen quite simply, quietly and matter-of-factly. The matter-of-factness of it is almost as surprising as the fact that it has happened. The sky doesn't change its colour; the earth doesn't rock. There is no crash of cymbals offstage.

Instead a policeman (two policemen) come to the door, ring and say in a matter-of-fact way that they've come to inquire about the man next door who seems to have got himself murdered.

"This," Steve had said, "is my secretary. You can talk before her. Will you sit down ? How about a drink ? "

They sat down and refused drinks, saying they were on duty. One of them said it was a warm night and he guessed spring had come all right.

Maida sat in the corner of the sofa and, mainly, wished they had had more time to talk, she and Steve—so as to arrange a programme. Steve was being very guarded and yet very cool and unconcernedly pleasant. But he hadn't said at once : " Yes, I was about to call you. I know about Walsh Rantoul." So that meant he had determined in a split second, literally, upon some course of which she knew only that it included concealment. For the moment at least.

Steve offered the policemen cigarettes and took one himself. The dark panes of glass in the french doors opposite winked and showed piecemeal and rather eerie reflections : a glimpse of a girl in a long grey dress and a toe of a crimson sandal ; Steve's black head and the flash of white shirt front and black tie as he moved his hand toward an ash tray, the solid bulk of blue in the chair where Christine liked to sit and knit (her knitting bag was hanging over the arm of it then) ; and nearer another bulk of blue whose profile looked just like any profile, nothing threatening about it, nothing sinister. Its owner was saying, however, that Walsh Rantoul had been murdered and that they had found the body.

"Body ? " cried Steve. "Where ? Who killed him ? "

"Well, it's a kind of funny story, Mr. Blake. Him living right next to you, you see, we thought you might know something about him."

"Walsh Rantoul ! " Steve leaned forward. "Look here, are you sure of this ? It's hard to believe. . . . "

The other policeman pursed up his mouth in a wry look that was rather horribly convincing. Maida looked away from him quickly. The policeman next her said : " Oh, yes, we're sure, Mr. Blake. You see, we got a tip that he'd disappeared and there might be something screwy about it. We came around this morning and looked the place over. Found nothing except evidence that he hadn't been there for several days. We inquired around and nobody knew anything about where he'd gone. No milk bottles on the steps, though, and no newspapers, or mail. So we decided we'd got a bum steer—you know, somebody got curious and worked up and called us up ; they're always doing it."

" Women," said Steve, and smiled. It was rather adroit, the slight smile of sympathy and deprecation, below his guarded eyes, but it didn't succeed. The policeman did not say it was a woman or a man or who it was who had telephoned and given them the tip. He said instead : " We came back to the cottage just to give it the once over again before we made the report and checked it off. And—well," he cleared his throat. " As a matter of fact, Mr. Blake, it was that little spaniel dog. It seems he belongs to Mrs. Blake, your sister-in-law."

Rosy. Unlucky, fated Rosy ! What had she done ? Moreover, they had taken pains to discover some facts about the household ; they knew Steve was Christine's husband's brother ; they knew the spaniel belonged to Christine.

The other policeman had the wry look on his mouth again and glanced at the bottle of Scotch on the tray longingly. Steve's face was a brown, hard blank. " What do you mean, officer ? Yes, Rosy belongs here."

" Well," the policeman who was doing the talking glanced apologetically at Maida. " It's not very pretty, Mr. Blake. It seems—not to make a long story of it—that this Rantoul had been killed, shot. About a week ago I should say, maybe not that long. Anyway he was just—well, buried. And the dog found him."

Now surely the room would rock ; the cymbals would crash offstage. Neither did, There was a small silence. The policeman with the wry look coughed a little. Steve looked at the policeman who was nearer her. The pattern of the slip cover on the sofa was of yellow and blue flowers on a cream background ; Christine's knitting bag looked homely and everyday. Nothing had changed.

" Found him ? " said Steve finally.

The policeman shifted in his chair, put one leg over the other. " Yes, Mr. Blake. He was buried in a pretty shallow kind of grave. Over there . . ." He jerked his head toward the cottage. " We were there, you see, and we saw the dog digging. I'm a flower grower myself, and I just went down along that line of shrubs between the cottage and your place here, intending to stop the little dog. Thought she was

digging up spring bulbs, you know. And then I saw a "—
he cleared his throat—" saw a scrap of something that looked
like cloth. Grey cloth," he said thoughtfully.

"Good God!" said Steve.

"Yes," said the policeman as if Steve had asked a question.
"It's a kind of a bad business."

"But, look here—when . . . ? "

"I was about to explain that, Mr. Blake. You see, we
thought we'd better do things pretty quietly. Didn't want
a mob of sightseers messing up the place before we had a real
chance of things. Nobody was about ; we telephoned headquarters from the cottage ; the medical examiner, photo-
graphers and all came without anybody around here knowing
anything about it. It was early afternoon ; your sister-in-
law had gone out, and I guess the shrubs have enough leaves
to screen what went on. Anyway, the servants here didn't
seem to notice anything, or at least didn't come to inquire
if they did ; and there's a wall and an empty house on the
other side ; we waited till dusk to remove the body. It's a
nice residential neighbourhood, you know. We don't want
to make it tough for the taxpayers around here. Of course,
we'll have to do a certain amount of questioning, and we'll
have to give a story to the papers. But the way it broke
we've got a chance to do what we want to do in the way of
fingerprinting and photographs, and searching the cottage
and grounds before we let anybody know about it. It'll be
in the papers to-morrow, I think. Depends on what the
Chief decides. Well, Mr. Blake ? "

He stopped, waiting. Steve said : " I suppose you want
to know what I knew of him. This is really a kind of shock,
lieutenant. He's been here at the house frequently. The
cottage belongs to my sister-in-law, you know ; she leased it
to him a few months ago."

"Yes, I know. When did you last see him, Mr. Blake ? "

It was a lucky thing that Maida's body didn't seem to
belong to her, didn't belong to anybody, was just a thing
sitting there on a sofa. Steve said at once : " Sometime this
week. Wait a minute—I think it was the first of the week.
Anyway, it was the same day as the reception at the Brazilian
embassy. Whenever that was. Monday, I think."

"Where did you see him ? "

"Right here," said Steve.

" Here ? "

" Yes, exactly. Here in this room, I mean. I'm pretty sure I haven't seen him anywhere since."

There was a rather long silence. The policeman looked at Steve and Steve looked at the policeman. The other policeman got up and went to the french doors and with an effect of absentmindedness that still came in the boundaries of investigation, opened one of the french doors, looked prolongedly out on to the terrace and closed the door again.

" Where is the dog ? " said Steve. " I haven't seen her around. . . . "

" Oh, she's here somewhere. Bloson took her up through the garden to the kitchen door. A coloured man took her in and thanked him. What about this meeting with Rantoul, Mr. Blake ? Tell me about it."

" All right," said Steve. " There's not much to tell, though. He was here, waiting for somebody. . . . "

" Who ? "

" Why, I don't know, really. I assumed he was waiting for Mrs. Blake to come home. I'm not sure I asked. I came to the house to get some papers I wanted from my study. I noticed there was a light in here—it was about dusk—and I came back to see who it was. It was Walsh Rantoul, obviously waiting and having himself a drink." He motioned toward the tray and glasses. The policeman's eyes did not follow his gesture, but remained on his face. Steve went on : " We said a few words—not much ; hello, and how's everything—that kind of thing. That was all, really. I was in a hurry and left."

" He was still here when you left ? "

" Yes," said Steve. Something had shut down very tight upon his face. Suddenly Maida saw that he was letting Christine and perhaps Maida, herself, in for questioning and knew it and didn't like it. She wished, but not for that reason, that he had not made that admission. But Steve was a lawyer ; and obviously he was thinking hard and had been thinking hard from the moment the bell rang.

" What papers ? " said the policeman.

Steve lifted his eyebrows a little. " Why, some notes for a business letter, as a matter of fact. Why ? "

" Anybody else here at the time ? " asked the policeman.

" No," said Steve.

That was to keep her out of it; but Christine knew she had been there—Angela knew it, Malcolm knew it. Besides, it was not she who was in danger; it was Steve with all that clinching evidence against him. She let herself glance at him and saw the stubborn curve his mouth had taken, the straightness of his black eyebrows and the level look in his eyes. She knew that look. It was rare, it was unpredictable, and it was as fixed as concrete. He looked like that when he'd made up his mind to follow some course, willy-nilly, right or wrong, to hell with the consequences, full steam ahead.

The policeman said: "Mr. Blake, I don't like to ask this, but I guess it's common knowledge. Do you mind telling me what you and Rantoul fought about the week before? It was in the papers, you know, and . . ."

"That's all right," said Steve briskly, still with that level, damn-the-torpedoes look in his eyes. "Everybody knows about it. Except me. We just had a little bout, very publicly, and there *wasn't* any reason for it."

The policeman waited and Steve smiled a little and waited too. Finally the policeman said: "But, Mr. Blake, there must have been some reason."

"None."

"But—well, now look here, Mr. Blake. He hit you and you hit him . . ."

"And apparently half of Washington saw it. All right. But the fact is, lieutenant, there was no reason for it."

There was another short silence. Then the lieutenant said: "Well, Mr. Blake, if that's your answer, it's your answer."

Steve got up with a kind of spring, walked around and leaned against the back of the chair he'd been sitting in, his hands locked together, his face grave. "It's the truth. I had no quarrel with Rantoul. I don't know why that happened; he said something—I don't even remember what; the kind of thing a drunk might say, if he happened to meet somebody he didn't like and wanted to say so. Only he wasn't tight. Then he hit me and that surprised me too. I hit back, naturally, and walked away. It was an absurd incident which so far as I am concerned meant nothing."

"Did you speak of it when you saw him here last Monday night?"

" No."

" What happened ? "

" Just what I've told you. He didn't apologise, if that's what you mean. All I wanted to do was get out. So I did."

" You didn't have another quarrel ? "

" No," said Steve. Maida took a long breath.

" What'd you do after you left him ? "

Steve waited a moment, his face sober, his hands clasped. The lamp-shade made a rim of shadow that began just about at his shoulders. Then he said : " Lieutenant—by the way, may I ask your name ? "

" Morrissey."

" Lieutenant Morrissey, why are you questioning me like this ? If this is a murder . . . "

" It is," said Lieutenant Morrissey with simple force.

" Well, then, I can only suppose that there's a suspicion of me back of your inquiries. Now it's your job to inquire. But I don't want to get involved in this thing." Something in Lieutenant Morrissey's face said that nobody ever wanted to be involved in murder. Steve went on : " I didn't shoot him. I expect you'll find whoever did kill him. But in the meantime I don't propose to be haled into the papers as a suspect. Are you proposing to do that ? "

Lieutenant Morrissey exchanged a perfectly immobile look with the other policeman who then scratched his ear with an air of decision, wholly, so far as Maida could see, unjustifiable. Lieutenant Morrissey said : " Naturally, Mr. Blake, you've got any citizen's right to be protected. I don't want to make unnecessary trouble for anybody, In fact, I haven't ques-tioned more than a few people so far, and those were very general questions."

" Do you mind telling me who ? " interrupted Steve.

" Not at all," said Lieutenant Morrissey. " I just came from the apartment—that is, the penthouse apartment of Miss Favor." He stopped there and eyed Steve rather closely.

" Oh, I suppose because she saw something of Rantoul. As we all did."

" H'm'm," said Lieutenant Morrissey. " You didn't quarrel over the young lady, did you, Mr. Blake ? "

" *Miss Favor ?* "

" Yes, Miss Angela Favor. Seems there was some com-ment to that effect."

"Well," said Steve. "We didn't quarrel over her. Of course, I expect I'd say that anyway, but it happens to be true. What did Miss Favor say? I expect the news of his death was a shock to her."

Lieutenant Morrissey looked at the floor and the other policeman scratched his ear again and looked into space. "So she said," said Lieutenant Morrissey. "You say you don't know who it was Rantoul expected to meet here?"

"I haven't the faintest idea!"

"Well," said Lieutenant Morrissey, pungently, "it wasn't likely a stranger. I mean there aren't many people that he'd be likely to arrange to meet right here in Mrs. Blake's house."

"Probably not. Still, it's hard to say what he would do."

"M'm. I asked Miss Favor when she'd seen him last. She said lunch on Monday. She didn't mention having a date to meet him here later in the day." Again he eyed Steve closely. And Maida remembered what Walsh had said. "I'm waiting for Angela—she's late." Yet, later, Angela had not seemed to know that Walsh was there.

"Have you told Mrs. Blake?" said Steve suddenly.

"Well, no. She was out all afternoon, you see. Then she came in and it seems her room is on the other side of the house, so I don't expect she saw anything. Besides, as I've said, we were very careful not to attract any attention. Mr. Blake, can you suggest any reason for this murder?"

"No," said Steve flatly. (And truthfully; why *had* Walsh been murdered? It was—at least it might be—an important question.)

"Isn't there anything you can tell me that might be of some assistance to us?" said Lieutenant Morrissey.

"I don't know very much about him. He came here early in the winter . . ."

"Oh, I know when he came, and when he leased the house. I know something of his friends in Washington and where he went and the people he knew. Trouble is, I don't know just where he came from, and, it's rather odd, Mr. Blake, but there's nothing in the cottage that gives me any information along that line. He seems to have just dropped out of the blue, so to speak. No background, no former life. No past."

Steve frowned. "That's queer. It's queerer when you think of Washington. Why, he must have known somebody.

He must have had letters of introduction. He must have had some sort of access to—well, to people."

"Yes, Mr. Blake," said Lieutenant Morrissey. And turned to Maida. "Did you know him?" he asked her directly.

She couldn't trust her voice. She nodded.

"When did you last see him?" asked the lieutenant. At the same instant, the front door swung open and a wave of voices and footsteps came down the hall. Someone said clearly: "But that's too ridiculous, to think of them questioning you!"

Steve took quick advantage of the interruption. "That's Christine," he said. "That's Mrs. Blake, my sister-in-law. She . . ."

"Ah," said Lieutenant Morrissey. "I expect that Miss Favor is with her. She must have told her about Rantoul's death."

"Look here," said Steve, going to the door and saying it somehow rather casually, as if he didn't particularly want to know, "don't you work with the F.B.I.?"

"It depends," said Lieutenant Morrissey, getting to his feet. "We're District of Columbia police; the murder's in our jurisdiction. But if we want them to use their laboratories for us, or to use any of their records, they always oblige. Why, Mr. Blake?"

"I just wondered," said Steve from the doorway. "Everybody thinks of the F.B.I. first; because their headquarters are here, I suppose. But of course, this is a city affair . . . Hello, Christine, dear. Hello, Angela. Christine, I'm afraid . . ." He disappeared. Maida sat quite still. Lieutenant Morrissey and the policeman exchanged another perfectly silent, expressionless look. The voices in the hall and the footsteps reached the door in a swirl of silk and perfume and flowers. Angela and Christine came in. Christine was jabbering with excitement, her eyes bright, darting from one policeman to the other. Angela, in white satin and a long mink coat, her beautiful blonde head high and her eyes startlingly hard and jewel-like in her lovely white face, stopped beside Christine.

Bill Skeffington's curly red hair came into sight too; but what made Maida's heart really stand still was the sight of Nollie Lister, coming in the doorway, just ahead of Steve. He was dressed in white tie and tails. His eager, thin little face darting this way and that, his hair plastered down wetly, and his neck just as scraggly and ill-fitted in evening clothes as in sweater and flannel shirt. Nollie, who had seen that second fight between Steve and Walsh Rantoul ! Nollie, who would be a star witness, telling all he knew and getting the resultant attention !

Maybe she was wrong. Maybe he got a vicarious drama out of watching his neighbours' lives, yet had not only discretion, but the milk of human kindness somewhere in his flat little breast.

Bill's flaming hair and resonant voice filled the room. " What's all this about Walsh ? I met Christine and Angela on the doorstep. I was coming to talk to you and Steve. I can't believe it ! Who killed him ? My God, Steve, have you heard ? "

Angela looked at Lieutenant Morrissey and said : " Well, Lieutenant, you here too ? "

He said : " Good-evening again, Miss Favor." Angela's eyes went to Maida. Against the little jerky tapestry of voices and exclamations (" Murder ! " cried Christine shrilly, " Walsh—oh, how horrible ! ") Angela looked Maida up and down, saw how she was dressed, let her eyes flicker once toward Steve, long enough to note that he, too, was in evening clothes, and then she came closer to Maida. She said : " Dear me ! You and Steve dancing somewhere ? Or at a party ? So that's why Steve couldn't go with Christine and me to the Fowlers' to-night."

Her eyes were bright and hard. Maida saw, however, with a kind of absent, surface surprise that Angela was trembling and trying not to.

CHAPTER SIXTEEN

AND all at once in the middle of the talk, the questions, the exclamations, Christine and Angela had settled down to a long wrangle as to Walsh Rantoul's introductions to them and to the other people he knew. Christine had leased her cottage to him ; it kept coming back to that. Angela kept saying, " But people can't do that in Washington ! It just simply can't be done."

" What can't be done ? " said Lieutenant Morrissey, breaking away from Bill Skeffington's questions. Where had they
found Walsh ? What had killed him ? Was it murder ?
Were they certain it couldn't be suicide ? Or accident ?
Where had he been buried ? Oh, in the garden ? " Garden,"
squealed Nollie Lister, and sucked in his breath and pushed
down his collar agitatedly. " *My* garden ? *My* tulips ? "
He was reassured on that point. And then Lieutenant
Morrissey turned abruptly to Angela with his question.

" What can't be done ? " repeated Angela, drawing her
slender shining eyebrows together. " Why, getting—well,"
she hesitated briefly and said in a deprecating way, " to know
people. Like that, I mean. Washington is not like other
cities."

" It's changed lately," wailed Christine. She had sat
down in her favourite chair. The policeman who had been
sitting there was standing in the shadow behind her.
Christine's pretty, plump face was screwed up with distress
and a kind of incredulous petulance. " It's changed lately !
All these people ! It's not like it used to be. Anybody can
go anywhere now. . . ."

" Not at all," said Angela. She reached for a cigarette,
lighted it and sat down near Maida on the sofa, and her hands
were still trembling despite her cool voice and decisive manner.
" Not at all. Really, Christine, didn't you know anything
about him ? "

" He gave me bank references and one or two names."

" Who ? " said Lieutenant Morrissey.

" Why, I . . . " Christine stared blankly at the carpet,
twisted her hands so the jewels glittered and said helplessly :
" I don't remember."

" Didn't you do anything about it ? " demanded Angela.
" Didn't you write to them or telephone or anything ? "

Christine bridled and flushed. " No. One never really
does things like that when one—well, just rents a house.
I could see that he was a . . . " She stopped. A very
peculiar look came over her face, for Christine, as she rarely
did, was really thinking.

" Do you mean he wasn't quite a gentleman ? " said Angela,
smiling coolly and watching Christine, and yet very much
aware of everyone else in the room—of Steve, leaning an
elbow on the mantel, his face inscrutable ; of Nollie Lister,

on the edge of a straight chair, listening nervously; of Bill
Skeffington, lounging upon the arm of a chair, the light
gleaming on his red hair, his face hatchet-sharp; of the two
non-committal, quiet policemen.

"What a silly thing to say, Angela!" snapped Christine.
"You do manage to seem so very vulgar. You . . ." She
collapsed like a little pink balloon done in black tulle ruffles.
"Yes," she said, shutting her lips firmly. She cast a spark-
ling, defiant look about the room and opened them again.
"That's just what I thought. Just now. I'd never thought
of it before."

Angela laughed shortly. And her long white hand with
its gleaming crimson nails pressed itself unsteadily down into
the folds of her sleekly-fitting, white satin gown as if trying
to hide. Steve said to Christine: "Can you remember any
of the names he gave you?"

Christine glanced helplessly at her writing desk against the
wall. Her house was perfectly kept; but accounts, letters,
dates, confused themselves irremediably in her mind, although
every so often she was able to pluck from that confusion some
shrewd and salient fact. She did so now.

"I don't remember the names, except that I knew them.
Familiar names, you know. I think I threw the scrap of
paper away. But I do remember thinking—not then but
later, when he came over through the hedge and I was having
tea and I asked him, of course, to have some—naturally, I
would. He looked a little lonesome and anyway . . ."

"Do get on, Christine," said Angela.

"All I wanted to say was I do remember thinking that
he didn't seem, for all he said, ever to have lived anywhere."

"What an odd thing to say!" said Angela, and put out
her cigarette.

"You mean," said Steve gently to Christine, "he didn't
talk of other places or people?"

"Yes, of course. He was interested enough in Washington,
and in you, Steve, and me and Angela and everybody I
mentioned. That is, naturally," said Christine, becoming
more and more flustered and more and more angry. "Naturally
I didn't sit there and talk of my acquaintances. But if I
said a name, no matter how casually, I do remember Walsh
sort of—sort of fastened on it. Like a fish."

There was a short and rather baffled silence. Lieutenant

Morrissey cleared his throat and Bill Skeffington said wheed-
lingly : " Fish, Christine, darling ? "

" Certainly," said Christine thoroughly ruffled. " I should
think you could see that yourself. And now he's murdered
and in my very garden. . . . " She looked around, reached
for her knitting bag, snatched out yarn and was on the very
verge of tears.

" Octopus," said Steve quietly, smiling a little at her.

" Yes, of course ! " said Christine and sniffed. " That's
what I meant. And besides, Angela, you know very well
that you introduced him to a lot of people. What are you
going to say now ? "

" I had no idea you knew so little of him ! "

" I told you ! "

" No, darling. You really didn't say anything that.you've
said to-night."

" But he wasn't murdered then," said Christine, as if that
clinched it. Steve said : " Lieutenant, are there any further
questions you'd like to ask any of us now ? Anything we
know . . ."

" Why, yes, Mr. Blake. Did you give Rantoul anything
the night you met him here ? "

There was a very full and electric and instantaneous kind
of silence. " The night you met him here." Everyone there
heard it, and it seemed to Maida that there was an almost
palpable question in every face there. Christine's hands
clutched her knitting tightly while she looked at Steve and
said : " *You met him* . . . " and stopped.

" Yes, I saw Walsh here. Monday night."

" *Here !* " cried Christine.

" Yes. Here in this room, just for a moment or two."·

Angela was listening so hard she wasn't breathing. In
another moment she was going to say, " Why, he wasn't
here when I came that night ; only Maida was here ! " She
didn't say it though, and Lieutenant Morrissey said : " Did
you have an engagement to meet Rantoul here, Miss Favor ? "

" No." She smoothed her satin dress over her slender
knees. " I would have told you if I had."

Steve said : " He seemed to be waiting for someone. I
supposed it was you, Christine. We didn't say much, and I
went away."

Christine's face was deepening until her face looked swollen with pinkness. " The impertinence ! Walking right in here, of all things ! "

" You weren't expecting him, then, Mrs. Blake ? " asked the lieutenant.

" Certainly not ! Let me see. Monday night. Monday— why, I was out till after seven, I'm sure. I didn't expect him. I didn't invite him. He never came into my house like that. How *could* he have come in ! The servants were out, I remember. I've shifted days around. They take their day out, all together, on Monday, and we get it over with for the week. No one was here to let him in. . . . "

The lieutenant made a kind of gesture toward the french door. Christine saw it and said : " Why, yes, I suppose he could have come in that way. Nobody ever comes through the gárden. It is so protected—walls and the fence. Oh, somebody *could* get over the fence, but I never lock the french doors. I shall, of course, after this. Murder ! And Walsh ! But how really preposterous ! How. . .? "

Bill Skeffington said : " When was he last seen alive, lieutenant ? "

" We aren't quite sure," said Lieutenant Morrissey. " I was about to ask you, Mr. Blake, if you had given him any-thing that night ? "

He'd given him a paste in the jaw, thought Maida, un-expectedly. Steve said : " No."

" Ah," Lieutenant Morrissey got up slowly. " There was some notes for a radio speech that you delivered that night in one of his pockets, you see, Mr. Blake."

" *My* speech ? "

" Yes," said the lieutenant. The other policeman seemed to drift toward him. He said : " Possibly he picked it up from somewhere here. We'll find out perhaps when the fingerprint tests come in. There's a lot of that kind of thing yet to do, you know. Bullet is being extracted . . . "

" *Bullet !* " squeaked Christine. Angela looked milk white, and rigid as marble.

Nollie Lister gave his collar a downward shove and seemed to be struggling for speech that didn't come out. Bill got up and he and Steve walked toward the two policemen who were suddenly in the course of leaving. " Thank you," said Lieutenant Morrissey. " Thank you. . . ." His calm, busi-nesslike gaze went around the room. The two policemen disappeared in the hall, Bill and Steve after them. They were talking; voices and the sound of motion drifted back into the library. Nollie Lister watched the door, fidgeted, and got up; he put his overcoat across his arm and took up his hat.

"I'd better go," he said. "I guess I'd better go. Dear me, to think of it. . . . Good-night, Christine, and thank you for asking me to-night   It was very pleasant indeed, very pleasant. Good-night, Angela." He got to the french doors and glanced back at Maida unexpectedly, so he caught her looking at him. Was he thinking of Monday night—of a struggling little dog, and Maida's anxiety to get rid of him? He said : " Good-night, Miss Lovell."

The french door closed behind him. They could hear his footsteps across the terrace.

"What a jerk!" said Angela forcibly. "Why did you invite him to take us to-night?"

"Nollie?" said Christine. "Really, you're impossible, Angela! I invited him because I—because he . . . "

"Because Steve was out and you wanted a man to take you," said Angela and got up and went to the hall door and frankly listened, her golden hair shining, the deep V in her dress showing her soft white back almost to the waist. "I really think they are leaving. My God, what a mess! I've taken Walsh Rantoul around to half of . . ." She stopped suddenly. Christine finished : "To half of Washington. Well, you would do it, Angela. Besides, I don't know that there's anything really disgraceful about being murdered. It's the people who are questioned about it that don't like it."

Angela bit her lip. "Naturally, Christine! You don't think it's Walsh I'm worrying about, do you? It's what may . . ." Again she seemed to check herself abruptly and again Christine said it placidly : "It's what may come out about him. After all, there's got to be a reason for a person being murdered. And you did go about with him a lot, Angela. Several people have asked me pointblank whether it's him or Steve you're going to marry."

Maida got up. "Good-night, Christine," she said.

"Good-night. You haven't said a word, Maida, dear."

"No, that's right," said Angela, meeting Maida's eyes. "Maida hasn't said a word. Look here, Maida, I've got my car outside. I'll take you home."

Bill and Steve were coming back along the hall, and Maida wanted to finish her talk with Steve. They must plan and plot and arrange. " No, thanks," she said. " Don't bother."

" Nonsense," said Angela. " It's not a bother." Steve and Bill came into the room again and Angela said, " I'm just taking Maida home. Then I'll go on home, too. There's really nothing we can do about this. I suppose somebody came out of Walsh's mysterious past and took a shot at him and that's that. Will you come now, Maida ? '

Surely Steve would intervene ; he didn't, however. He said : " That's good of you, Angela. No, you're right. There's nothing really we can do about the murder."

He and Bill walked out through the soft spring night to where Angela's long car and chauffeur waited. The chauffeur, standing behind the car, smoking, put out his cigarette quickly and got in the car. It pulled away from the kerb and Maida had a glimpse of the two men standing silhouetted in the light from the open door behind them. Bill, big and powerful in his tweed suit with his sharp face lifted, and his hands shoved in his pockets and his head high in the air. Steve, just Steve ; tall in his black dinner clothes, his face in the shadow, inscrutable.

It was never easy to know what Steve was thinking. Bill was frankly excited. But he hadn't, yet, told the thing that Nollie had told him. The police did not know that Steve and Walsh had fought, briefly, again, and they would not know it unless Bill told them. Or Nollie. But how long could they count on Bill ? And Nollie ?

Then she became aware of the fact that Angela intended to say something. First she leaned forward and gave the chauffeur Maida's address (rather to Maida's surprise she remembered it accurately). Then she rolled up the glass window between them and the driver's seat, turned to Maida with an air of resolution, waited a moment and said nothing.

Said literally, absolutely nothing. They rode quickly along through the park, turned on to a through street, went smoothly on amid the occasional, glancing lights of other cars. The dusk in the car was scented with gardenias. What did Steve intend to do ?

She all but forgot Angela's presence. They reached her apartment house, stopped, and Angela said unexpectedly : " I've been a God damned fool."

Maida turned with a jerk. Angela said : " Good-night, Maida. I thought I could . . . " she paused.

" Could what, Angela ? "

She didn't reply. Instead, she said : " Maida, what were you doing in Walsh's cottage that afternoon ? Did you know then that he was dead ? "

Maida's heart was pounding again. Somebody had said the best defence is offence. She said (a little too quickly, she knew) : " Why were you there, Angela ? "

There was another silence. Then Angela said with a short laugh : " That gets neither of us anywhere. Good-night, Maida."

The car rolled away as she went up the steps. She remembered her own happiness (in spite of what she knew ; in spite of everything) when she'd run down those steps, arm in arm with Steve, only a few hours before.

She walked up the narrow stairs to her own apartment and let herself in. The light was on. She'd left it on, hadn't she ? The little yellow lamp was like a beacon ; it drew her to the table and in the downward glow of light a paper lay. It was torn off her own yellow memorandum pad and some-one had written on it in a queer backhand : " Three transport planes will leave for the coast within the next three days, each carrying a full load of ferry pilots, expected to pilot bombers east. Find out exactly dates and planes."

She was still sitting there, on the footstool beside the table, her head in her arms, her long crimson gloves falling like a stain across her knees and down to a pool of crimson on the floor when Steve came.

CHAPTER SEVENTEEN

STEVE SAID, walking up and down the floor, that they had to find Smith. That was the first thing to do. That was the important thing. Smith—and with luck the people behind him, or who took his orders. And the next thing was to find out who murdered Walsh Rantoul and why. That was important, too. But Smith came first.

" There must be some sort of organisation," said Steve, stopping to light another cigarette. " We know that there must be at least two people directly concerned, perhaps more."

That was obvious, of course. Smith, no matter how talented he was in diverse and questionable ways, couldn't be in two places at once. "He couldn't," said Steve, "be burying Walsh under the hedge, and breaking into my office to type out that first message to you, at the same time. It's got to be somebody who's accessible to Smith by telephone and somebody who has skeleton keys, or knows how to work a lock—criminal knowledge, but not exactly exclusive to burglars. That person or Smith himself came here, obviously, since you left." He glanced around the little apartment and back at the paper that lay on the table.

A tray with coffee and empty cups stood on the table, too. The air was thick with smoke and it was very late. Steve started to pace again; and Maida got up from the sofa and went to open the window. It was lucky it was only Hortense below to hear Steve's pacing footsteps. She drew the thick curtains aside and lifted the window. The night was cool and very clear with the starlight almost as bright as moonlight, and the indefinable stir of spring even in the night. Behind her Steve said : " Is there *anything*, Maida, *anything* you've forgotten ? "

She cast her thoughts back over their long talk. " I don't think so. Perhaps if there is I'll think of it ; there must be, of course, details I've not remembered."

" This," Steve nodded at the paper on the table, " isn't the first time he's been here. He'll come again. We'll have to do something about that, you know."

" There wasn't any point to his first visit here. The only thing gone was a letter of mine to Aunt Jason . . . " She broke off at the look in Steve's eyes. He said : " He could have taken some of your writing paper—easily proved to be yours, perhaps with your fingerprints on it. He could probably get somebody to copy your handwriting."

" But . . . "

" Never mind. It's only a guess. Forget it. Probably you only lost the letter. What it still boils down to is, find Smith. There's a telephone number to go on, and the fact that he knew Walsh. But then Walsh knew so many people, curiously many, really, considering the length of time he lived in Washington. And your description of him."

She turned around. The apartment had grown chilly as it grew later. She had changed quickly, while the coffee was cooking, into a soft, warm housecoat, primrose yellow, so long that it touched her toes. Steve said suddenly : " You're looking awfully pretty."

She laughed a little. " Am I ? I feel as if I were part of a nightmare. But not so much, Steve, as I did before I told you."

He didn't say : " You ought to have told me before " ; he didn't say : " If you'd told me, if you hadn't in your heart been afraid that maybe (just maybe) I had murdered Walsh, we could have done something to stop Smith sooner. We might have saved six precious, ocean-flying planes." He didn't even look it out of his eyes. That was, however, one of the nice things about Steve ; he almost always accepted any given situation as it was ; he never wasted time talking, or even thinking, of how it might have been.

Part of that was his lawyer's mind and training ; part of it was Steve.

He said : " Clues to Smith : almost none. But we can find him." He didn't say how. " Now, then, he wants you to get the number of planes off the assembly line at the plant he names ; I don't know anything about that, and you can tell him that you're sure I don't ; the date General X flies to the coast ; well, that's settled anyway, since he's already there. And now this . . ." He glanced down at the slip of paper on the table ; something implacable, a terrible anger, looked out of his eyes, as if for a dreadful instant he shared the vision that had haunted her. " I'll fix this," he said. " The transports are supposed to leave Monday night, from the city airport. I'll have to . . ." he paused, eyes narrowed, mouth tight. " Yes, I'll fix that. It means . . . God, if there were only more *time* ! Well, there isn't. But I can stop any attempt at sabotage in this case."

She came back to the sofa and sat down, leaning her head back wearily against the cushion to look up at him. " Steve, I tried to put them off about the six planes that were burned. I planned ; I thought if I pushed up the date (in case they planned to destroy the planes before they were transferred) then the planes would be safely transferred before they acted."

" Don't." `

" But I failed . . . "

" It doesn't help to feel sorry for yourself."

" Sorry for myself ! " She set her lips hard so as to hide their unsteadiness.

" Oh, Maida, don't look like that. I only—you see, I know you. We're in this together. Don't give up the ship."

Sympathy, of course, would have been her undoing; knowing her, Steve knew that. Besides, he was right. The task before them was infinitely more important than her own futile self-reproach. " All right, Steve." She poured herself another cup of coffee. " Smith will call me, you know. He may call at any moment."

" Yes, I know."

" Can't he be traced by the telephone number ? "

" Maybe. If he's not gone—found another hiding place. He sounds pretty smart."

" He is."

" Maida, *think*," said Steve suddenly. " Maybe we can bag the lot of them ! *Think* what it would mean ! "

" Steve, are you sure they won't charge you with murder ? There's your revolver . . . Smith has it; if the bullet is really from that revolver it will give them what I've heard you call ' jury ' evidence. And you were in the house and admitted it to the police; and you said you saw Walsh . . . "

" Yes, I thought it was better."

" Already they're questioning you. Steve, who gave them the tip about Walsh ? "

They'd been over that before ; they'd been over everything before.

" I don't know. It could have been Smith himself. . . . "

" But why ? "

He shrugged. " I don't know. But he knew of Walsh's death. It could be Nollie Lister. He's a kind of a busy-body, and if he actually saw me with Walsh that night, as Bill said he did, and then Walsh disappeared, he might have grown curious enough to do just that. Might have put two and two together. Decided it was his duty as a citizen. As it was," added Steve with rueful truth.

" Could Bill have done it ? "

" No, not Bill."

" But he was so curious, Steve. He went and sat beside Nollie . . . "

" Yes, I remember."

" He said somebody had seen you and Walsh fight that night ; it must have been Nollie."

" But he didn't tell the police, to-night. That shows he's loyal."

" He can do it later."

" He won't. Nollie Lister may tell, later, but not Bill. I rather expected Nollie to blurt it out to the police then. But he's a cautious soul ; probably wanted to think it over. Besides, Christine's known him forever. He wouldn't go out of his way to get me into trouble."

She hoped Steve was right, and reluctantly went back to Bill. " But Bill told me, said there was talk ; he asked questions. I told you everything he said."

" Yes, I know. But I just don't think Bill would do it, if he really suspected me of having had anything to do with Walsh's disappearance. Particularly if he suspected murder. Bill's my friend. He's loyal to me."

" Bill," said Maida, because she had to say it, " wants your job."

" Why, naturally, I suppose he does. I know Bill. If I were in his place, and if he were in mine, I should want his job. Basically, Bill's all right. And I can count on him."

She gave up. " Then if Bill didn't tip them off—or Nollie, or Smith, then who did ? Who knew that something was wrong ? "

" A curious neighbour could have done it—well, that's not likely either. I forgot the wall on the other side of the cottage and the street in front ; the people across the street wouldn't be likely to notice Walsh's absence. Perhaps it was somebody who telephoned to him, some merely social acquaintance, and received no answer ; or somebody who invited him somewhere and received no answer. Somebody made curious by the little note in the gossip column—I saw that, too, you know. Anybody, really, could have done it. Even," said Steve, " the murderer."

The murderer ! The phantom figure which was so important.

" I wonder who killed him," she said slowly, " and why ? "

" Yes," said Steve. " It would help to know."

"Christine's house," she whispered. "The revolver out of that drawer."

"Lots of people could have known that," said Steve quickly. Too quickly.

"*Steve!*"

"All right, Maida. The answer is, yes. Somebody we know, and know well *could* have murdered Walsh—Christine, or one of the servants, or Nollie Lister—especially if Walsh trod on his garden. Or *I* could have done it. Or—who else was familiar with the house? Angela . . ."

"He said he was waiting for her."

"She didn't admit it. Probably she wouldn't, though, to the police. None of us admitted the whole truth. I didn't ; you didn't, thank Heaven."

Someone they knew—someone very familiar with Christine's house. It was a terribly short list—on murder—and there was only Christine and Angela and the servants who, as far as she knew, could come and go in Christine's home. And Nollie Lister. "And Bill," she said aloud.

"No motive," said Steve tersely.

"Steve, what are you planning?"

"Only what I told you. I'm going to try to find Smith, and give the police all possible help in trying to find the murderer. Except I'm not going to put my own neck in a noose. Or yours. But you see, Maida, this is part of the war. This is part of the path ahead. This is the enemy, Maida."

He was right, of course ; and she'd been terribly, fatally wrong. Culpable in the truest and gravest sense of a crime against her country. She tried to check that course of thinking as Steve had made her do before. She couldn't undo what she'd done ; the only restitution she could make was to help find Smith. (With luck we might bag the whole organisation, Steve had said.) She said : "But *you* are important. Your job's important."

He gave her a quick look, and came to sit beside her and put his arms around her. "Why, Maida, don't you see that I—I understood ! I thought it was . . . I think you're . . ." he stopped. Steve, the fluent, Steve, who was never at a loss for words. Steve who was never thrown off his guard. He tightened his arms around her so she lay against his shoulder, and couldn't say anything.

There was only the sound of the tiny French clock on the mantel above them. Steve's shoulder was warm and hard; his arms more comforting than she would have thought anything in the world could be.

But the little French clock was measuring time and time meant everything. She drew away from him so as to meet his eyes directly, and let her hands slip up to his shoulders.

" Steve, we've got to call the F.B.I."

" Yes, I know. It's—yes."

He didn't move, however, and the circle of his arms was still firm and like a barrier shutting out terror.

It didn't actually shut it out, though. Six planes burned already because of her, she thought with horror again. Three transports in danger; transports carrying ferry pilots, skilled and expert men, brave and confident, going to fly bombers to harried battlelines.

" Call them now, Steve. You always said that was the thing to do. You always said one never knew where there were enemy ears and enemy eyes; you said they were in the most unlikely places—among people you thought were friends; within the very walls of the city. Even the—the girl at the next desk, the woman in the next apartment, the man next door . . . " she stopped. Steve's eyes leaped to her own.

" Why, yes—Walsh Rantoul ! " He waited as if to test it and sprang up and cried softly : " Why, yes ! He came out of nowhere ; he made friends as if that was his job. He had plenty of money and no visible means of getting it. He—why, yes ! He could have been an enemy agent ! He . . . " He stopped again, thought hard, spun around on a suddenly exultant heel and caught up her hands. " Maida, my lamb, you are a bright girl. You're beautiful and I love you and you've got the sweetest mouth that God ever made, but, my pet, my prize, you have just had a brain wave. Walsh Rantoul, by golly, that's it ! He knew Smith, too. They were in it together. That's it and—now then : did his murderer know it ? There's something : did whoever it was that killed Walsh know that Walsh was a spy ? It alters everything. Who *could* have entered Christine's house ? Obviously only someone accustomed to do so. Who knew where my gun was kept ? That narrows the field, too. *Who knew he was a spy ?* "

A small memory caught at her, vanished, returned; she plucked it out of the whole fabric of the evening when Walsh was murdered, and it was something she hadn't told Steve. "Someone was at an upstairs window, when I rang. At least, I felt someone was looking at me; as I looked up I thought the curtain moved. I didn't actually see anyone. It was only an impression. I saw nobody at all when I went into the house, except Walsh."

"It could have been Walsh at the window. He could have been trying to get into my desk—if he was an enemy agent."

"Your desk was unlocked."

"There was nothing much in it. Nothing at all of. importance. I usually lock it; I might not have locked it that day. The thing against this theory is Walsh's lack of— oh, brains. He was shrewd in a way, but not really forceful. He struck me as inept, likely to make mistakes, and too assured of his own ability to be safely trusted. That would have been my opinion, I mean, if I'd been, say, considering him in relation to work. However, certainly a large share of the spies we know of have been anything but master minds. Besides," he swerved abruptly, " it needn't have been Walsh at the window. It could have been the murderer—hiding in the house, waiting his chance. Did you hear the shot?"

"I heard, as I told you, something I took to be an automobile backfiring. The doors were closed and the library quite a long way from your study."

"You didn't hear me leave?"

She shook her head, wishing miserably that she had, for if the shot had occurred after Steve's departure her own testimony to that effect would serve to clear him. Wouldn't it? It wouldn't; Steve said: "Not that that matters. First, I must—I mean I'd rather not bring you into it. Not . . ." Steve was suddenly and elaborately casual. "Not just yet anyway," he said, and hurried on before she questioned that casualness. "And second, if you only heard the front door close you couldn't possibly say who went out of it. I—look, my emerald, my woman above rubies, I'm going. Dawn cometh. I've got things to do. I—what the hell did I do with my topcoat? Oh, I didn't wear one. I dashed out of the house as soon as I could leave Christine. Didn't want to arouse Angela's queries by insisting on a talk with you while

she was listening. I'm going. I think you're a nice girl."
He bent over her, kissed her briefly on the mouth and went
to the door. And then he came back to take up the piece of
paper on the table. Again his brown face hardened as he
glanced at it, but his eyes were intent and bright with purpose.
He swung around to the door again and stopped. "I forgot,
Maida. We've got to fix it so you—so Smith—so they can't
get at you."

"Steve, you are going to call the F.B.I., aren't you?"

Something flickered like a veil over his face. "No, not
now. I—not now; trust me. They are already in it from
the other end, the Interstate end of it. They were on the job
the instant the fire began, practically—hunting down the
causes, the leak, the loophole, the man inside the plant, the
ways and means. This—no," he said again. "I'm not
going to them right now. Please trust me, Maida; it's
important. And don't under any circumstances let anyone
come in the apartment. Put a chair under the doorknob
to-night. Have the lock changed Monday. Get a big bolt
and have it put on the door. And take no chances. Understand me. Now, then—I suppose I ought to leave rather
quietly, considering everything. What a wanton woman
you are, having a man in your apartment at this hour!"
He opened the door, grinned a little and vanished.

Silence, except for the ticking of the little clock. But it
was a different kind of silence, now Steve was gone. It
became presently more than she could bear. She got up,
propped a chair under the doorknob as Steve had told her
to do, and moved absently about the room for a moment or
two, emptying ash trays, straightening cushions, removing
the coffee tray.

But suppose Walsh had been an enemy agent, where
would it get them, really? There was still that evidence in
Smith's hands.

Why hadn't Steve been willing to call the F.B.I.? It was
the reason she had determined her course in the first place—
because she had thought that Steve would send for them
and for the police instantly. Yet he hadn't.

She'd put out all the lights and the sky was growing pale,
and she was almost asleep when two other thoughts occurred
suddenly to her. Steve had said she was in danger from
them, meaning from Smith and the men working with him;

yet she couldn't be unless they knew she had told Steve the truth, and that Steve consequently would do everything he could do to find and put a stop to their whole organisation. And even then an attack upon her would be mere revenge ; it would endanger themselves to no purpose. Or, wait— sleepily she reached for some knowledge, some comprehension that was on the very edge of her consciousness.

And then she grasped it. Why, of course, she alone could identify Smith.

The other thought came much later, exactly as she went to sleep, for she thought she'd been dreaming and that Steve had said he loved her.

CHAPTER EIGHTEEN

In the morning, strangely enough, she didn't look like a warlock, a hag or even a woman with a secret. Steve knew the whole truth now ; Steve understood ; Steve was going to do something. ·And Steve had said he loved her.

She was quite sure he had said it.

Of course, he'd been talking a lot of nonsense in his relief at getting what he'd felt was a clue and a substantial line of investigation. Something that could conceivably give them a solid step ahead along a hidden and treacherous path, as one finds a rock in the middle of a swamp. If rocks, she thought, turning off the shower, ever get into a swamp. The point was, Steve had clutched that one chance with both hands and hurried away. But he'd said he loved her.

He'd said it lightly ; not to be taken in earnest, naturally. People·used love like that ; a word that covered everything.

It wasn't right, either, she decided indignantly. When you talked of loving anything at all you ought to mean it ! At least when Steve did ; it was only when it was Steve that you wished he meant what he said. She saw her own face in the mirror ; it was amused, yet rueful. She said a couple of words with some force and reached for a blue blouse and the telephone rang sharply. Smith.

The silly little mood of gaiety vanished like a small ray of sunlight. Smith hadn't telephoned and she hadn't seen him for days, yet she was perfectly sure it was Smith then, waiting at the other end of the wire.

She hadn't talked to Steve about what to say to Smith ; perhaps it was just as well ; her replies would show no effect of planning. The telephone rang again and again and again and at last she made herself go to it.

" I've seen the papers," said Smith abruptly.

" Papers . . . Oh, about . . . "

He cut in. " So he was found. What happened ? Quick . . . "

" The police were told to investigate. . . . "

" Who told them ? "

" I don't know. I didn't. I don't know who it was."

" Go on."

" They came to his house. They were about to leave when Rosy . . . "

" Rosy ? "

" The little dog. The spaniel."

" Oh. I see. I didn't have time to do a better job of it. So the dog is responsible for it . . . " There was something in his voice that gave her a swift kind of pang of concern for a fat and spoiled little dog. She felt as if she ought to tell Christine to put the dog in some safe place for awhile. He said : " Well, it's all right. They've questioned Blake, I see. And all the suspects. After all, it's a limited field. I've got the revolver, you know. I've got the remains of a red carnation to be planted at an interesting place for the police to find ; not that that would be more than a corroborative detail. Still, police are more or less sensitive to corroborative details. And I've got a beautiful letter from you, on your stationery, in handwriting any expert would swear was yours, which involves you up to your very charming little throat. What about those figures I asked for ? "

Steve was right, then. The letter to Aunt Jason in her own handwriting which a passably good forger could copy. On paper Smith had taken at the same time—easily proved to belong to her ! She said unsteadily : " The general had already gone."

" I know that. Somebody slipped. What of the planes off the assembly line . . . ? "

" I don't know ; he doesn't know. There's no way for me to find out."

" Get him to inquire ; use your head. Do it at once. Now then—you got the message last night ? "

She changed her mind and wished she had talked to Steve about what to say. Suddenly she saw that she must find out where to reach Smith. She said slowly: " Yes. But I—I've got to have time. . . ."

There was a long pause at the other end of the wire. So long that her pulses began to pound hard again and her throat felt dry. What was he thinking—that big man, whose intuition seemed to have tentacles, groping out over the air, over the wire, testing her, feeling out the meaning behind something in her voice that she herself couldn't hear.

But he couldn't see her eyes. He couldn't tell by some change in her face, some subtle look about her mouth, some difference in her breathing or in her attitude what she really knew or thought. He had only her voice to use for a reckoning rod. He said: " You're not telling the truth."

She caught herself on the verge of protesting. " All right," she said, " you don't have to believe me."

Again there was a probing, measuring silence. She waited and finally he said: " I believe that you know exactly when they are to leave."

She said nothing. And suddenly, out of that black instrument she held in her hand, came opportunity. " I'll see you," he said, " or telephone to you and tell you where to see me, sometime to-day," and hung up.

It was that sudden and that quiet. But her hand was trembling when she put down the telephone. As somebody else's hand had trembled. Why, Angela's, of course, in the folds of her white dress. That seemed to carry with it some other small memory, but she couldn't think then what it was. She did think, why was Angela like that? Why did she start to talk to me, and stop? Why did she seem, for an instant when she'd called herself a fool, a different Angela? And what did she mean—if she meant anything beyond exasperation at herself and embarrassment because she had, in a way, sponsored Walsh? Certainly she had gone about with him constantly. But was it something more? In any case, it was a problem that would have to wait.

Smith. Exactly the same; exactly as if no interval had intervened between his telephone calls. As if those Interstate planes had not been burned.

For an instant, it seemed to her that it was queer that he

hadn't spoken of that at all ; it was somehow, an ominous omission.

Her knees were shaking, too. She sat down. She looked very odd, half-dressed like that, the blue silk blouse on over her little white petticoat. What had she been doing when the telephone rang ? Why, getting ready to go to the office, of course. She'd forgotten it was Sunday until Smith mentioned the papers. Sunday.

She would know where to find Smith ; she would tell Steve.

She reached for her skirt, with its full blue and grey plaid pleats, and her jacket. She had finished dressing when Steve telephoned.

There was relief in his voice when she answered. " You're all right, then ? "

" Yes, of course."

" I thought after I'd gone that I ought to have brought you back to Christine's. It's just as well that I didn't though, for the police have been there again. Better not to get you into it any more than . . . "

" Steve, where are you ? I mean is there an extension . . . ? "

" I'm at the drug store. Drove over ostensibly to get cigarettes while they question the servants. Nobody followed me—at least I don't think so. I'm not under arrest. Maida, I've been thinking : If Smith telephones to you . . . "

" He did. Just now." She told him quickly. " So," she finished, " he'll telephone again. Or he'll come here or tell me where to meet him and I thought . . . "

" You thought I'd use you for bait. My God ! "

" But if you were here with some policemen, I'd be perfectly safe. It's a perfect way to get him. . . . " He interrupted. " Maida, you really are a little fool. Don't you suppose that I thought of that last night and instantly discarded it ? It's so obvious that . . . Why, it wouldn't even take him in for an instant ! So does that settle it ? "

" No. You're saying that because you're afraid I'd be hurt somehow. I'm sure that he believes that you know nothing about him. Besides, he wouldn't have to see me at all. I can tell him to come here. You can—can stop him when he arrives at the apartment house. Even before he comes in. I've described him to you. It's so simple. . . . "

There was a pause. She had almost convinced him, she

thought; at least, he was thinking it over. Then he said: "Too simple."

"But it can't hurt just to try. . . ."

Again there was a pause. Finally he said: "That telephone number, you know, has been disconnected. By exerting a certain amount of pressure I got the street address and went around there, early this morning. Smith had been there. It's a rooming house. He had one room and a telephone, and the woman who runs the place described him as you did. But he only had it for a month, was very seldom there, and she knew nothing about him. Maybe I'm just a bad detective, but I think she really didn't know anything more of him. The room was taken instantly by somebody else when he gave it up three days ago. She's nearly beside herself with business; has to turn people away and induce them to double up and all that kind of thing. Tracing somebody in Washington these days when it's so fantastically crowded is like tracing a needle in a haystack. Anyway, that's that; unless to-morrow I can get some information out of the telephone company, but I doubt that."

"Steve," she said, "he wants to know the time when the transports leave."

"You don't have to remind me." She knew him so well that she knew by a change in his voice exactly how he was looking, intent and frowning. "All right," he said suddenly. "Listen. When he telephones tell him to come to your apartment. He'll duck that; it's Sunday and people are around and he won't want to be seen. Besides, if you suggest it he'll think it's a trap. He won't be perfectly sure, you see, that you've not told me all about it. So then if he refuses that as he will, tell him . . ."

"Yes?"

He said reluctantly: "Tell him you're going to take a walk about four o'clock, and you'll stop—where are there always tourists?—I know, on the steps of the monument. He can come to you there and speak to you. I'll be somewhere and—yes, it may work."

"All right."

"And pay no attention to the newspapers. I don't think any one of us is seriously considered as a suspect. They still don't know where he was when he was killed." There was a click and an operator's voice said: "Three minutes are up;

another nickel, please." He said : " Wait a minute." The
nickel jangled into the box. " Maida, I think it's a lousy
plan ! I've changed my mind ! It's . . . "
    " I'm not afraid. There are always people there. Besides,
I'm his source of information, don't forget that. I'm his
lever. . . ."
    He said, rather dryly : " Don't try too hard to be sensible.
We're both fools . . . "
    She said firmly : " It's all right. Good-bye, Steve."
    But after she'd hung up she wasn't so brave. Smith was
unpredictable. Smith was intuitive. Smith was dangerous.
    She tucked a red scarf around her throat and picked up
her red flat handbag. Thinking of Smith and her talk with
Steve, she transferred her powder box and small silver and
bills, her gold pencil, her tiny blue engagement book ; her
St. Christopher medal, Christine's gloves which she must
return, her cigarette case—all the small articles one carries
in a handbag, from her brown bag to the red one. She walked
to the little newspaper stand. The headlines were not of the
murder as they would have been before the war. Instead,
they told of another victory ; she read that first avidly and
with a great gratitude for the men who had made it possible.
    But the murder was on the front page. Well-known
resident murdered. Walsh Rantoul. She read it quickly,
read it again slowly and thoughtfully. There was no mention
of the notes for the radio speech that Smith (obviously to
give the police a lead toward Steve—yet that was again only
for revenge in case she herself reneged on her bargain) had
tucked in a pocket of the grey coat Walsh was wearing.
There was no mention of the fact that, so far, Steve was the
last one known to have seen him alive. There were, however,
certain facts. He had been living in a cottage which belonged
to Mrs. Harcourt Blake, which, in fact, adjoined her own
garden. The place where· he was buried was overlooked
(except for a hedge which as yet was not thick with foliage),
by the windows of Mrs. Blake's house. The residents of the
Blake house were Mrs. Blake herself and her brother-in-law,
Mr. Steven Blake. There followed here a short resume of
Steve's career. Rather as a footnote there was a mention
of Miss Angela Favor, Mrs. Blake's sister, who was also
frequently at the house, having her own latchkey.
    It was an ominous note. The statement that Angela has

a latchkey to the Blake house indicated that they had been very interested in latchkeys or, in other words, in the number of people who came and went freely in the Blake house.

It finished with a very general and rather vague paragraph about Walsh, which did not say that his life previous to his residence in Washington was a blank but by the very absence of any facts regarding it, made it clear. There were in all several columns ; how and where he was found, a theory of burglary, the absence of a revolver, and the fact that he had been hastily buried by the murderer.

There was no mention of the fact that Angela had come to the house when she had come. She had, then, kept her own counsel about that. If Christine or Malcolm remembered that Maida herself had been there, neither of them mentioned it ; she thought it likely that neither of them remembered it. Not yet, at least. And, still, neither Nollie nor Bill had told of Steve's fight with Walsh in Christine's house ; at least, if it was known by the police there was no mention of it in the papers. There was no mention either of the already famous fight the previous week.

It was a queer day. Sunday is always outwardly quiet in Washington. Even in wartime the city reverted with a kind of sigh of relief to itself, became quiet and leisurely and gracious. People poured out of town on Saturday, and poured back by the trainload on Monday morning. But Sunday was quiet. Washington had always been a city where people invite their friends to their homes. The real hospitality of the city is offered behind drawn curtains, at one's own table, before one's own hearth fires. Perhaps that fact contributes to the grace and the charm, the dignity, the effect of a pleasant, ceremonious little bow to the amenities of life. On Sundays when the frantic hum of work has lulled for a little, the old Washington, the heart of a gracious and in a sense majestic city (because of its place in the world), can be felt. The serenity of the broad Potomac, the blue hills of Virginia across it, blend perfectly with something tranquil and lovely in the very air.

There are quiet but gay supper parties, some of them institutions, never changing except in the brilliant inflow and outflow of Washington residents and visitors, for all the world, some time, comes to Washington. There are circles and circles and circles, all of which, almost, seemed to Maida to touch and revolve upon each other. Maida herself, an office secretary, working hard at her job, had no place whatever in the silken social fabric of the world's most important and most interesting city. Still—because of Aunt Jason's letters to friends in Washington, introducing her niece (Aunt Jason always knew somebody, everywhere, and usually important somebodies), because of an old school friend or two of Maida's, even because of Christine's kindness—Maida had had more than glimpses of many of those interweaving, interdependable circles which in the end made a kind of hierarchy.

Consequently, she had always looked forward to Sundays. A trip to the country and lunch at somebody's house and a walk over the hills ; tea or cocktails around somebody's drawing-room fire ; small, candlelit supper parties. And talk, always talk.

That Sunday was so different, she might have been in a different world. She sat by the telephone, waiting for Smith. Noon came and went ; two o'clock, three o'clock. Hortense came up once from her apartment directly below, set for a leisurely gossip. It was then after three, and she had barely got there when Angela came. Both times Maida asked who it was before she opened the door. The second time Hortense lifted her eyebrows. "Dear me," she said. "Are you expecting public enemy number one, or a Nazi ? " She left when she saw Angela. And Angela, dressed in riding clothes, stayed only a moment and didn't mince words.

"Look here, Maida," she said. "Sometime we've got to have a talk. Right now—I've come to propose a bargain."

"Have a cigarette ? "

"Thanks. See here. If you'll not tell the police that I came to Christine's last Monday night when they—at about the time when they seem to think Walsh was killed (at least they've not found anyone who saw him later than that), I'll not tell you were there."

"All right," said Maida after a moment. "If I can avoid it."

Questions flickered in Angela's eyes. Something hard and sharp and cold was there, too. She stood for a moment, smoking nervously and striking her polished boot with her riding crop. She looked as if she hadn't slept ; but there was colour in her cheeks and she looked handsome with the net smooth over her blonde hair, below her black hat. Her white stock and black coat and beige breeches set off by their severity her handsome figure. She went away, however, as abruptly as she came, saying her car was waiting, that she'd been riding in the country and then driven back to town, and had to change to go somewhere for cocktails. Maida did not ask her to linger. It was nearing four o'clock ; in another hour or two you couldn't count on visitors at the monument.

And just then Smith telephoned again. Almost at once, when she heard his voice, she knew that something was different, something had happened. He was terse, definite, powerful, yet there was something else in his voice, too, something as coldly inimical as the thin edge of a knife. He refused both her offered meeting places instantly and finally, and proposed another. She was to go to a motion-picture theatre on Massachusetts Avenue ; she was to sit at a certain place ; she was to wait for him there, or a messenger from him. That was all.

A motion-picture theatre. Well, there were people there, she thought, but it would be hard to follow him if that was what Steve proposed to do. She tried to demur, and got nowhere.

" You tried to deceive us about the date of the Interstate plane transfer," he said. " You have told Blake the whole story. You are trying to trap me. You are a very silly girl."

There was such cold, poised anger in his voice that it, as much as the truth he spoke, held her suddenly silent. He said : " It will be better for you if it doesn't happen again. Do as you're told."

She got Steve at once at Christine's. Eventually, speaking guardedly because of the possibility of someone listening on the extensions, they agreed upon a course. She was to go to the theatre ; Steve couldn't then tell her what exactly he planned to do.

So she went. It was a curious two hours. No one came near her, and she saw no one she recognised except once, as she turned to look toward the entrance of the aisle along which she'd been told to sit, she thought she saw Bill Skeffington move away out of sight, behind the partition between the audience and the foyer. She wasn't sure ; there was only something about his walk or a half-glimpse of red hair that made her think of Bill. She didn't see Steve at all, and she didn't see Smith. She left finally, emerging with a crowd of soldiers and their girls, all giggling. She took a taxi back to her own apartment. Obviously something had gone wrong. But where was Steve?

It was night by that time, a soft, warm spring night again. Quiet had settled down over the apartment house ; she saw no one and heard nothing but her own footsteps on the carpeted stairs.

The light on her landing was out ; burned out, probably, as sometimes it did. She had to grope her way to her own door. Her keys made a little jingling noise. She found the key of her apartment and opened the door. It was dark in the room ; she closed the door behind her.

When she turned she realised that someone was there.

There was no motion and no sound, but there was a difference. She took a step forward into the silence and the very thick darkness.

She stumbled and flung out her hands and pushed herself frantically backward. For the thing she had stumbled over didn't move, and it ought to have moved.

It was in fact the total absence of all sound or motion near her that was so horribly convincing. There ought to have been something ; the flutter of breathing, the intangible quality of life and sentience. There was nothing.

Her shoulder was pressing back against the edge of the little table. She thought of a light and was reaching toward it when there was a sound.

Only it came not from beside her, but from somewhere in the black pocket across the room. It was a whisper, clear and thin and indescribably matter-of-fact : " *Don't turn on the light,*" it said out of the black space. " *Don't move.*"

She thought with queer, sharp lucidity : why, it's a woman ! There was no mistaking the businesslike sincerity about it. She sank back, away from the table. The whisper said : " That's Smith down there. I killed him. Listen : when do the three transports leave ? I want the right date this time, remember. Don't lie again."

CHAPTER NINETEEN

" I DON'T KNOW, I tell you.   I don't know."
  " Not so loud.   What is it, quick ? "
  " I don't know."
  " Hurry . . . "
  " I don't know."
She'd said it, it seemed to her, a thousand times, into this
dark nightmare come true.   Blackness everywhere and that
thin whisper out of it, indescribably certain of itself, indescribably cold and indescribably determined.
  " When ? "
  " I don't know."
Where was Steve ?   She had a diminishing hope that he
would come, making a noise on the stairs, knocking at the
door.   Except it might be dangerous.   It would be dangerous,
of course.   Steve flinging open the door ; Steve outlined
against the light from the hall.   Then she remembered that
he couldn't open the door, it had locked as she closed it.
And there was no light in the hall to be silhouetted against ;
it hadn't burned out, though ; it had been turned out intentionally.
  When the whisper came again she thought it had moved,
toward the inner wall, so it floated eerily from the thick
darkness at the end of the sofa.   The curtains had been
drawn over the windows ; she realised that, and that was
why the room was so dark.   She herself had moved too—
a fractional inch at a time, but not because she had any plan
for escape, for that would be hopeless and she knew it.   The
bulky, silent thing in the darkness there on the floor convinced
her of that ; Smith was dead and whoever it was whispering
out of the blackness had killed him, mercilessly, and would
just as soon kill her.   Once that whisper had said so, but so
matter-of-factly that it was not as if it had been intended as
a threat.   So it was more impressive.   She had drawn backward though, toward the fireplace and the windows, a little
at a time, not because she thought she could escape but
because she couldn't bear to be so near that thing on the
floor.   Once the whisper warned her sharply not to move, so
she must have made some sort of rustle.

She had been afraid of Smith ; it was nothing like the
terror that was now in the dark, small room, that floated out
of the darkness whispering to her.

" When ? "

" I don't know." How many times had she said it ?

After a second or two the whisper said something different.
It had moved again, it was definitely nearer, yet she could
still sense nothing of the whisperer's identity. He—she ?—
was nearer ; that was all. She could see nothing. She had
thought at first that it was a woman ; now she wasn't sure.
She felt a slight jar, as if whoever was there had touched the
other end of the sofa, the end opposite her. Why was he
coming nearer ? Very stealthily Maida moved backward
again a little ; she was doubled up on the floor, knees under
her and scraping the woollen fabric of the rug. The whisper
said, changing its question : " You told "—there was a slight
but quick pause—" you told Blake, didn't you ? You told
him."

The pause was just before the name, Blake. Was that
because whoever was there had almost said Steve ? No, no,
it couldn't be. A murderer and a spy—double infamy—
but the second was the worst. Angela—no. Christine—no.
Who else ? Her flying, frightened thoughts touched even
Jane Somers in the office and rejected that name at once.
Then it must not be a woman, in spite of some indefinable
quality in that whisper that had made her think that it was.
Well, then, who ? But then she might be mistaken ; that
sudden hesitation before saying " Blake " might be for some
other reason altogether.

" You did tell him." The whisper drifted with unearthly
clearness over the length of the sofa, through the darkness,
above the body of Smith.

" No."

" That's another lie. Listen ; you tried to lie about those
Interstate planes. When do the transports . . . ? " the
whisper stopped.

There was a listening quality in the silence ; Maida listened
too, and heard nothing, except it seemed to her that something was sliding softly over the rug somewhere. Only the
atavistic sense of the nearness or the distance of another being,
that humans share with animals, told her that whoever was
there was at least no nearer to her. At least she thought not.

And then all at once she knew, for there was the softest click and a faintly twilight section appeared in the direction of the door. The door had opened, then, only a little. But the light drifting upward from the hall of the landing below barely sufficed to outline that rectangular, thin opening—and suddenly a swift movement across it. At the same time she heard what probably that other person had heard, and it was the deep hum of the elevator. The dark flicker at the door vanished; it had so little substance and solidity, it went so fast, that there was only one thing she thought she saw, and she wasn't sure of that. But it did look as if that fleeing figure wore a hat—a black, hard hat, like a derby. She was leaning forward, both hands spread outward on the rug, hunched over like a child, staring at blackness, trying to retain the barest flicker of an outline on the retinas of her eyes—and failing. She thought she had seen the hard outline of a derby hat—she couldn't be sure. And that was all. The movement at the door had been so swift, too fleeting; the hall outside too dark. The door was closed too quickly.

But someone was coming!

She managed to get to the lamp on the little table, without stumbling again and without touching that dead hand; she was certain that whoever had been there had gone. The elevator stopped at her floor.

She was afraid to open the door until she heard some voice, something that was safe and identifiable. There was a slight delay; the little elevator was a self-service elevator; somehow the wrong button was pushed, it started down again, and back up, and stopped again; eventually both doors were opened; there were voices at last in the hall. When Steve's voice said "Maida" loudly, and when he knocked on the door, she opened it.

"It's dark in the hall," said Steve. "We couldn't . . . What's the matter? My God!" He went quickly into the room.

Then she saw why there'd been some slight confusion in the tiny elevator, for two men followed him. The little elevator would scarcely hold more than two people. Both of the men looked at her and then past her into the room.

She closed the door. She looked down.

It was Smith. He wasn't wearing his red muffler; his

throat must have got well, she thought queerly. He was looking at them, sleepy yet bright-eyed. Only they weren't sleepy, they were merely half-closed ; they weren't bright, they merely reflected the light from the small yellow lamp. She was swaying ; no, it was the wall. One of the men who was kneeling beside Smith—all three of them were doing that—got up swiftly and came to her and said : " Look out ! Sit down."

But she had to tell them something very important. " He's gone—she's gone. Down the stairs. Quick—just before you came. He heard the elevator. He was here when I came . . ."

It wasn't possible for any of them to understand her ; she knew she was gibbering and she tried to explain, but both of the men who had come with Steve were moving quickly, like extraordinarily lithe shadows past her again and out the door and down the stairs.

Steve got up. " Smith ? "

She nodded. He said : " Here—quick . . ." He took her into the little bedroom and turned on the light and put her down on the bed. He took the pillows out from under her head and stuffed them quickly under her feet. His face was extremely white ; she had one glimpse of it and closed her eyes again.

" When ? " he said.

She forced herself to speak clearly, in a funny-sounding voice, but still a voice. Not a whisper. She must have been fairly comprehensive too, for all at once Steve was gone. He hadn't gone far, though ; she felt sure of that because she felt safe. Who were those two men ? She kept her eyes shut tight. And after a while there were voices in the sitting-room. They were talking of covering something. They were talking of the streets and the darkness and the traffic on the next street. They were talking of searching the apartment house, too. She heard words : " Not a soul that shouldn't be here ; bad luck." " There'll be another time. Whose revolver ? "

" Mine," said Steve's voice.

" Through the heart, I should say," said another voice.

Steve came into the bedroom. She waited until he was beside her so when she opened her eyes she'd be sure to see him. Not anything else ; not anything that whispered and whispered, from a black and nameless mouth in the darkness. He put his hand on hers and then she opened her eyes.

Steve said : " You look better."

She was better, too ; she was, in fact (incredibly, miraculously), Maida Lovell again, lying on her own bed, able to see the pale yellow curtains and the reflections of perfume bottles on the ruffled dressing-table. She wasn't just a thing, crouching in the dark, crawling away from a bulky presence that she couldn't see but knew was there.

She swung her feet around and sat up.

" Go easy." Steve looked very queer. Much queerer than she ; she stood up and went to the dressing-table. She touched her hair ; she picked up a powder puff and put it down. Steve said : " Maida," questioningly.

She said : " I think I'm hungry. I want some milk." He went with her into the tiny hall and she got out milk from the infinitesimal refrigerator behind the silvered panel. " Want some ? "

" Yes. Here . . . ." He put some glasses on a tray. " They're F.B.I. men."

" Oh." It wasn't news.

" I didn't want to go to them, Maida. I want you to understand. You see—well, you'll have to answer their questions, you know."

" Yes, of course."

" I . . . " He was having great difficulty getting it out. She touched his cheek with her hand. " Steve, it's all right. About the burned planes, you mean. And my being an— an accessory after the fact. That's why you didn't want to go to them. You knew I had got myself too involved ; incriminated—that's the word. Oh, yes, and the letter Smith had made so it looked as if I had written it ; you were right about that, you know. The dreadful thing is the planes. . . ."

" Maida, I was afraid of Smith. I didn't know what he'd do to you ; what they'd do. I hated to go to the F.B.I., yes. But I saw all at once that you were in more danger from Smith than from—anything else."

" Did you tell them everything ? "

" Yes. But they'll want to question you."

" You told them about the "—the word stuck in her throat this time but she said it—" about the planes burning ? "

"Yes," said Steve miserably. "There wasn't anything else to do."

"I know. I wanted you to, last night. I couldn't understand why you didn't. I ought to have known. Have I incriminated myself too much, Steve? I mean, will they—will they do anything? Arrest me . . . .?"

He put down the tray with the glasses, which was just as well, for they were clattering against each other. He put both arms around her and said: "Darling, don't. Don't even think. . . ." He stopped and held her so tight she could scarcely breathe. So he was afraid that they might do something; they would blame her, naturally. She had given—what was the phrase?—aid and comfort to the enemy; so she should be blamed. It didn't matter what had been her intention, six burned planes were the result. She put her arm up around his neck and said: "Why, Steve —Steve . . ."

It meant, it's all right; we've got to go through with this; there's no other course. Steve said something; she couldn't understand it, except the tone of his voice, which went right straight to her heart, just as if it were a bird singing its way direct to its home. It was a silly thing to think but that's the way it was. She moved her head so as to put her lips against his cheek. "It'll be all right, Steve."

Someone was coming to the door. Steve let her go and picked up the tray of glasses and took up the milk bottle. The F.B.I. man paused a moment and went back to the little living room and she and Steve went, too. The other F.B.I. man was talking quietly into the telephone and hung up without haste as they entered.

She didn't want to look beyond the sofa; she did, however, and a rug made a bunchy, long hump on the floor. The lights were on. The two F.B.I. men didn't look at all alike and the same description would have fitted them both; they were both young; both were slender, both inordinately quiet-looking, somehow, both very alert. Mainly both of them gave the same sense of power in reserve.

One said: "Good," looking at the milk. One of them unobtrusively manoeuvred a chair so when she sat down she couldn't see Smith.

Probably she heard their names, then. She never knew, though, what those names were. All her life, however, she

remembered their faces, their quiet kindness—their thorough-
ness and their untiring, inexorable, patient yet swift search,
search, search among the details they drew from her.   They
didn't start to question her at once.   They all sat and drank
milk just as if there was all the time in the world.

They didn't hurry her either about her story.   In fact,
they seemed to want her to take her time ; to tell it all ; not
to miss anything.

She stumbled a little now and then, merely because she
was trying to get everything in ; even her dinner with Bill
Skeffington and what he'd said.   When she came to his
question about the cause of the fight Steve and Walsh Rantoul
had had she stopped dead and looked at Steve, but he nodded.
" It's all right.   They know. . . . "

The thing she hated most though was when she told of the
burned planes.

She finished with the message on her table about the
transport planes.   All three men, so different in appearance,
looked exactly the same, somehow, when she told of that.

There was a long silence.   Then they began to question.
Rather to her surprise it was details they questioned about ;
small details ; descriptions ; they urged her to tell everything
she could remember.   " Try to think of it in pictures, Miss
Lovell," said one of them.   " Describe it as if you were
describing a picture.   Say, the library when you came down
and found Rantoul.   Describe it."

So she did.   Walsh had been behind the sofa ; there were
about ten feet between it and the bookshelves along the wall,
and he lay there, so he was visible from the door into the hall
where she stood ; not visible from the french doors.   There
was a question here ; she hadn't been actually in the room
when Smith entered it, presumably from the terrace, as he'd
claimed ?   No, she'd been putting the dog in the closet off
the kitchen.   Where had Smith stood when she returned ?
He was in the room, not near the french doors.   Go on,
please.   Well, nothing was disturbed in the room, really.
Except, there was the red carnation.   Oh, yes, and there'd
been a glass broken and on the floor.   Glass ?   Yes, a highball glass.   He'd poured himself a drink as she talked to him
before going up to Steve's study.   They nodded again.
What had happened to the glass ?   Malcolm, that was the
butler (there was a look of knowledge in their eyes as she

explained Malcolm's identity), Malcolm had picked it up. Had the room changed at all when she came back from taking Rosy to the kitchen ? (She noticed the swift precision with which they were both familiar with all the names, even the name of the little spaniel.) She thought not ; except Smith was there. And the revolver ? Yes, the revolver. This one ? They said. And Steve's revolver lay on a table, carefully shrouded to preserve fingerprints which probably, thought Maida, wouldn't be on it. She said heavily, everything lost now, all defence gone, " Yes."

They said nothing for a moment. Then they went on : Describe Smith in life, his words, his accent if any ; everything she could remember. Like a picture, they said again, listening and registering with those highly trained intelligences. Describe Mrs. Blake's house and why she thought someone looked out of the upstairs window. Describe the office when she went back to it that night. What did she do with the message on the typewriter ? Oh, burned it in the ash tray . . . Describe ; describe. Describe her visit to Walsh's cottage ; what had it looked like ? (She didn't tell them, and she hadn't told Steve of the thing Angela had said ; that was between her and Angela. Somehow she couldn't tell them either of the thing Angela had said, as if it burst from her, in her own car the night she'd brought Maida home. " I've been a fool," said Angela, swearing.) But at last they got to the murderer of Smith ; the person who had been there and whispered and whispered out of the thick darkness and then dropped Steve's revolver and fled silently into the night, at the little hum of the elevator, and escaped. She knew that by now a search was going on for that person, for someone hurrying from the apartment house at a given time ; someone hurrying from the vicinity of the apartment at a given time. Anybody at all wearing— perhaps—a derby hat. That was all they knew.

It was the most detailed bout of questioning. Was it a man or a woman ? Why did she feel it was a woman ? Could it have been a man ? What was said ; what did she see in that shadowy, flickering glimpse ; was she sure it was a derby hat ; did the person wear a skirt or trousers ? She couldn't be sure of that ; she wasn't really sure of the derby hat. Again because it was Angela—her rival ?—and some obscure and probably silly impulse restrained her (and because, too, she really did not think that Angela had murdered Walsh or Smith or by any flight of the imagination could be conceived in league with enemy agents of any country), she did not tell of Angela's visit to her apartment, clad in riding clothes : breeches and coat, and a hat with a round, hard crown.

CHAPTER TWENTY

TIME PASSED ; the telephone rang twice and each time was answered by one of the F.B.I. men who gave non-committal replies. In the end she had told everything except Angela's conversation with her in the cottage (when Angela had said flatly that she was to marry Steve), Angela's unexplained words to the effect that she'd been a fool, and Angela's visit to her in riding clothes that afternoon and what she'd said. She had told of Angela's arrival at Christine's house shortly after Walsh was killed ; she'd had to, and she'd have to tell Angela that she had done so.

She had told everything but those small facts—or at least she thought she had told everything.

Eventually, out of all the questioning, she began to perceive that one inquiry kept repeating itself, in different words, by way of implications in direct, and in all sorts of subtle and indirect phrases. It remained the same question and it was : "*Why* was Walsh Rantoul murdered ? What was the motive ? *Why ?* "

Steve had said it was important, too. Why was Walsh Rantoul murdered ? And who murdered him ?

She could answer many of their questions but not that one. She couldn't tell them, either, whom Walsh had planned to meet in Christine's house.

They wanted to know why Smith had been murdered, too. Obviously by someone working with him ; obviously by someone as determined as Smith to make her give items of information. Possibly by a higher-up, so to speak, someone from whom Smith took orders. Certainly by someone who had obtained possession of the revolver, and with whom there must have been some kind of quarrel.

" He was different," said Maida, suddenly remembering

her last conversation with Smith. They pounced on that. Different ? How ?

"Everything. His—his voice. What he said. I mean he seemed to know then, or at least to believe (when he hadn't been sure before) that I had talked to Steve and told him the whole story."

"As if someone had told him that you had ? " said one of them explicitly.

"Yes. Perhaps."

"Tell us exactly again what he said. Everything you can remember."

There was a short pause when she finished.

She was learning that the F.B.I. men never made comments. They only asked and listened. It was Steve who said : "Could he have learned, during the time to-day between his telephone calls, that she had talked to me ? Although nobody knew but Maida and me, so I can't see how . . ."

"Go on," said one of the other men, looking interested.

"Well, and also that the date she gave him was the wrong one ? That would argue that whoever he's working with had been involved in the burning of the planes, not Smith, and that would . . ."

Steve was looking very excited, and one of the men interrupted and said : "Possibly. Anything else, Miss Lovell ? "

"No."

"I'm afraid we'll have to use your apartment for awhile to-night. Perhaps to-morrow," said one of the men finally. Inspector, Steve called him. "Do you think you can take her to Mrs. Blake's for the night ? " he asked Steve.

So they weren't going to arrest her just yet. They knew, of course, that they could stretch out their hands at any time and find her. They weren't going to arrest Steve just yet, either. And Steve, she suddenly discovered, had an alibi for Smith's murder. It came out as the three men talked just then. Steve had realised that, as he'd said, she was in less danger from the F.B.I. than from Smith and had gone to them when she went to the movie. So he had been with the F.B.I. men while whoever killed Smith had been in Maida's apartment.

And then she was putting a few things in her dressing-case, and one of the F.B.I. men was standing in the room, being very polite and unobtrusive and watching every single thing she put in her case down to her toothbrush and powder puff.

One of them went to Christine's in Steve's car with Steve and Maida. He was quiet and had stopped asking questions ; only his eyes were alert.

She suddenly saw that that was in case she was followed. He left them at Christine's after coming inside barely long enough to telephone for a taxi. It was late, but Christine was at home and still up, and all curiosity. " A friend of yours, Steve ? But what's his name ? I never saw him before ! He's a very strange young man, isn't he ? I mean so—so much like a radio."

" Radio ? " said Steve, looking a little startled. They had gone back to the library again, after the inspector had taken his quiet departure. Christine was knitting again, and there was a tiny fire on the hearth. Yellow jonquils were on the table. Maida and Steve had not had a moment for talk. Christine had accepted Maida's presence with her customary unruffled kindliness. Maida saw that Christine had been crying ; her pretty eyes were puffed and swollen and pink. Two damp handkerchiefs were crumpled on the footstool.

" Of course," said Christine. " Ring for Malcolm to take Maida's dressing case up to her room, will you ? I mean he's so—so *listening*. Like when you tune the radio, and you can sort of feel it groping out into space for whatever it is that turns into sounds and words." She gulped. " Oh, Steve, Steve, I don't know what to do. You see I—I'm perfectly positive Angela's been taking money from . . . " She stopped and glanced at the door. " From somebody," she whispered. " And I think it was from Walsh Rantoul."

Steve went to the door and closed it. " What do you mean, Christine ? "

It proved to be a very simple exercise in deduction. " It's the money she spends, Steve. You see, we have exactly the same income. We inherited the same amount, divided between us, and invested exactly the same way. Neither of us has made any change in investments. Her income and mine are practically the same. I have something from "— tears welled up into Christine's round blue eyes again— " from Harcourt, enough to help run this house. The house was given to me because I was the elder. Also I liked it and wanted to live the rest of my life in it, and Angela never liked it. She thinks it's old-fashioned and stuffy, and she says the neighbourhood, now, is crowded and suburbanish. It isn't really ; it's just like any residential part of a city. . . . "

Steve brought her swiftly back to the point.

" Why do you think she's got money from Walsh Rantoul ? "

" Why, because she spends so much ! Things I can't afford and never think of, though I'm what you'd call moderately—well," Christine flushed a little. " Well, I suppose I'm what you'd call fairly—fairly . . . "

" Rich," supplied Steve dryly. " But so's Angela."

" Not that rich," said Christine with simple conclusiveness. " Furs, that penthouse, clothes that cost like everything, original models, and jewels; Steve. Jewels ! That big car of hers ! She gives money to charity, too—she's always being photographed doing it. She . . . Steve, somewhere she's been getting substantial amounts of money. Maybe not only from Walsh either, because "—she frowned and rubbed her forehead—" because from the way Walsh lived I shouldn't think he *could* give her enough to make up for all she spends over her income. Now there's no use in telling me I don't know, Steve, because I do. *You* wouldn't be so likely to notice but . . . And then there's the way she's been since Walsh died. Even since he—well, disappeared, she's been as nervous as a cat. Kept inquiring about him by telephone ; came to his cottage and went into it at least twice—I think to search for something, some clue to what had happened to him maybe, or maybe just to be sure there was nothing that would involve her, if something *had* gone wrong, of course. I'm talking about last week when he was gone, but we didn't know he was dead, unless Angela thought he might be dead . . . Oh," said Christine, caught in her own confusion, " *do* you understand ? "

" Why should she take money from Walsh ? "

Christine's eyes widened. " Why, for introductions, of course. I know it's terrible ! But I have heard of its being done, only *not* in Washington ! "

Of course. Unless . . . But Angela couldn't have been in league with enemy agents, thought Maida, with a kind of vehemence ; it simply wasn't possible. Angela was an American ; probably a fourth- or fifth-generation American at the least. She was Christine's sister, the sister of the

widow of a naval officer. She was a Favor ; one of a family
fairly well known, fairly well placed ; certainly it was a name
that carried with it a certain authority, a promise of integrity.
It was not a particularly distinguished name ; it was just
solid and substantial. But it was that.

Of course Angela herself, so beautiful and so energetic,
had by the force and charm of her personality made herself
well known. Angela did like money ; at least, she liked the
things that money bought.

"It's not a bit pretty," said Christine. "It's not a bit . . .
But I feel sure that's it. And she—oh, Steve, Steve, what
shall I do ? " she turned bright scarlet and began to cry.
"It's too horrible ! If it ever gets out . . . "

"You'd better ask her," said Steve, and went to put his
arm around Christine's heaving shoulders. "You'd better ask
her point-blank."

"She won't tell me," sobbed Christine. "She'd be afraid
to ! "

"Ask her anyway, Christine. Don't cry like that. Maybe
it won't come out. Angela's pretty smart."

"I *can't* ask her," wailed Christine, as if that settled it.
"She's gone to a party to-night."

Steve smiled a little. "There's always to-morrow."

There's always to-morrow.

In the night it rained, a light, gentle spring rain. Maida,
awakening at the sound of the rain, thought of that : There's
always to-morrow. What would it bring ?

There had been little chance to talk to Steve. It was late.
Christine stopped crying, and said they'd all better go to bed
and then went with Maida to fuss around the room, asking
about her breakfast tray and what time she wanted to get
up. Steve had come to the door in his pyjamas and dressing-
gown, at the prolonged sound of Christine's voice. "It's
two o'clock," he said. "Go to bed, Christine. Oh, and
Maida . . . "

"It's all right," she said. "You can open the door."
He did so. "I only wanted to say you're not to go to the
office to-morrow."

He couldn't say any more on account of Christine, and
Christine heartily concurred with that. "You're quite
right, Steve ! She never gets a day off and she looks dead
tired, keeping her up like this." It was exactly like Christine

not to inquire as to why Steve had brought her there for the night but simply to accept it. Days later she might come out with a theory as to the reason, and in this case it wouldn't be merely her own opinion; she'd know from the papers. It was better, though, to tell her nothing then. Steve glanced once at Christine, and then came into the room and put his arms around Maida and kissed her. "Well!" said Christine, perking up with interest. Steve led Christine firmly out of the room, turned to give Maida a reassuring look, and closed the door. She could hear him talking a little to Christine who, apparently, let herself be led away.

She would go to the office the next day, however. Naturally. Anyway, it would be better than to stay at Christine's, waiting for the telephone, waiting for the F.B.I. men to come, waiting for the police. Would the F.B.I. men and the police work together? She supposed they would; there would have to be some kind of collaboration. Two murders. Would an account of Smith's murder be in the papers the next day? And the place—her apartment—where he was found? Would they say it might have some connection with Walsh Rantoul's murder? What exactly would they say?

It was no use trying to answer those questions. In fact, it was no use trying to answer any of the questions that kept pulling at her as if they had fingers.

But when it began to rain and she awakened, she lay for a long time, listening to the light soft drone of the rain upon the roof and upon the brick sidewalk—and upon the garden and the hedge and the sloping roof of Walsh's cottage.

She began to think more and more of the question the F.B.I. men had reiterated so adroitly, in so many ways, with such careful indirection that if she had had any glimmer of its answer it must have come out. That was: why was Walsh Rantoul murdered?

Was it something out of his blank (covered and hidden) past? Was it some pressing, immediate quarrel? Was it because of something that had to do with Smith and Smith's activities? Much hinged upon whether or not Walsh had been an enemy agent or not. Much hinged on what—in that case—he had attempted to do as an enemy agent. It could have been Walsh on the second floor, prowling through

Steve's desk, hearing the door bell and looking at her out of
that window and then hurrying down to the library.

And why was Smith killed? Had he failed in some
project? But that would scarcely bring about his murder.
Then why?

She wondered whether or not the murderer of Walsh
Rantoul and the murderer of Smith (that thing that had
talked, whispering, out of the darkness) were the same. It
seemed to her likely, mainly because murder is what it is—
dangerous as a two-edged knife, too dangerous to be under-
taken except as a last and horrible resort.

Rain dropped lightly and steadily from the leaves. In
another week or so the lilacs would be out, scenting the air.
Already, in a week's time the little leaves made green haloes
everywhere. Had it been only a week since she had entered
that house and talked to Walsh Rantoul, and later found
him dead? And then met Smith?

The sheets smelled faintly of lavender. The curtains
were up and showed ovals of sky, and the outlines of dimity
curtains drawn back in loops. Watching one of those oblongs
she went to sleep, and when Malcolm brought up her breakfast tray and Christine came fluttering in ahead of him to
put a lacy bedjacket around her shoulders, she brought also
a note from Steve. He had already gone.

"You are not to come to the office to-day; Jane can
manage; she'll have to learn anyway, and may as well begin
now. You'll be all right. Men from the F.B.I. are guarding
you and the house. Their idea is that somebody will try
to get in touch with you. Telephones are tapped. They
insist on this; they say you are absolutely safe; I have
to follow their orders. They said to warn you not to
give anything away in your voice or what you say; they
were emphatic about this. They said to destroy this
letter. Would have talked to you but didn't want to wake
you. S."

She read it and read it again; and then read the first
sentence a third time. That sentence did a very strange
thing, as a matter of fact. All at once the actually dark
and rainy day seemed to be flooded with sunlight. It was
as if the birds burst into song and the buds into bloom and
everything was glorious and life was beginning and aware of
its own beginning for the very first time.

" What *is* the matter with you, Maida ? " said Christine.
" Your eyes look like stars.   What did Steve say ? "

Well, of course, he hadn't said. anything.   Except that
Jane would have to learn to manage at the office.

And some other things ; she thought of those things more
soberly, and, as soon as Christine had gone, burned the letter
in the ash tray.   As if Christine would have read it !   Or
Malcolm, or one of the maids !   Still that was what Steve
had said to do.   She read the newspaper and there was a
column about Walsh but nothing new, and there was no
mention of Smith anywhere.

At noon Christine fluttered in again, wondering if Maida
would mind if she, Christine went out.   " I've promised
lunch and bridge.   Of course, I'd just as soon not go ; rather,
in fact, only . . . "

Christine was induced not to change her plans.   Maida
explained that she couldn't possibly eat lunch after so late
and large a breakfast.   An odd look of something like relief
flitted over Christine's face.   " Really, Maida ?   Yes, I
quite see.   Very well.   Malcolm is so set in his ways that
it's just as well—that is . . .   Well, you see he's cross
anyway because a man from the police, I suppose, though,
Malcolm insisted he was an F.B.I. man !   Do you suppose
the F.B.I. is investigating Walsh ?   Well, anyway, this man
came and made Malcolm hunt in the rubbish barrel for a
highball glass that was broken the day they think Walsh
was killed.   Did you ever hear of such a thing ?   They found
it, too.   Since tyres are so precious they only collect trash
like that every two weeks.   And the man wrapped it all up
and took it away with him, of all things."

The broken glass.   Did they hope to find fingerprints ?
Walsh's would be there.   Christine went on : " I—well, I'll
be going on then, dear, if you're sure you don't mind being
alone.   There are some new books downstairs."

Eventually she went away.   It was only when an unusually complete silence settled over the house that Maida
understood Christine's first and enigmatic remark about
Malcolm.   He was set in his ways, and this was servants' day
out in Christine's house, for it was Monday again, and Malcolm
didn't like to wait to serve lunch.   For an instant Maida felt
a twinge of uneasiness.   It wasn't going to be pleasant to
stay there alone in that house, waiting for the telephone and a

voice at the other end of the wire.   Whose voice ?   It could
not whisper intelligibly over the telephone.   Would she
recognise that voice when it spoke naturally ?   But men
from the F.B.I. were there, somewhere.   She wondered
where, and thought of Walsh's cottage and of the empty
house at the corner beyond it.   What was the name of the
people who had lived there ?   She could only remember that
they were of German extraction and had little wax angels
on their Christmas trees.

She dressed.   She had worn the blue and grey plaid suit
to Christine's the night before, but she'd put in her dressing-
case, under the eyes of the F.B.I. man, another dress, a thin
yellow woollen, tailored and simple.   She tied a blue ribbon
around her hair, and wished she had torn off the first sentence
of Steve's letter, in order to keep it.   Well, she wouldn't
think of that.   She tried to put it out of her mind as she had
tried to put out of her mind and memory the moment in
Steve's office, days ago now, when he'd taken her in his arms,
and she'd been sure that he meant what he seemed to mean.
Then, what with work, what with people around all the time,
what with things that had to be done and done quickly,
what with her own terrible preoccupation, she hadn't ever,
really, been sure because there'd been nothing said.

She went downstairs, through the silent house and into
the library.   There were new books, none of which looked
interesting beyond their bright jackets.   She drifted presently
to the terrace.   The rain had stopped ; there was only a
soft kind of mist which felt cool against her cheeks.   A robin
was worrying a long worm, down on the bright green lawn.
Beyond the low fence Nollie Lister was working in his garden,
in raincoat and a sodden felt hat, with Rosy sitting on her
own side of the fence surveying him sluggishly but somewhat
purposefully.   He saw Maida and called across : " Nice rain."

" Yes."

" We needed it."

" I suppose so."

It was not a scintillating conversation.   Even Rosy
seemed aware of it, for she gave Maida a bored look over
her fat shoulder.   Nollie went back to setting out seedlings
and Maida looked at Walsh's cottage through the hedge,
now misty green with its small, delicate leaves.   The cottage
looked empty.   Again she wondered exactly where the men

from the F.B.I. were waiting. She saw no evidence of their presence anywhere.

After awhile she went back into the library. She discovered that she had a tendency to circle around the telephone, watching it, waiting for it to ring. She must be careful when it did ring.

She had thought the servants were all out and the house was altogether empty, so it was rather a surprise, sometime later, to hear someone walk quietly along the hall and out the front door which closed firmly. The footsteps were light, with clicking high heels. It must have been a maid ; odd she went out through that door ; something to do with latch-keys, Maida supposed. No concern of hers, certainly. She put down one book and took up another and read a chapter, and still the telephone did not ring.

What Maida didn't know was that the person who walked down the hall and out the front door was wearing a blue and grey plaid suit and carrying a large, red handbag. The suit didn't fit her very well and a black hat which did not belong to Maida was pulled well forward over her face. She walked rapidly toward the corner and got into a taxi which had already been called and was waiting for her.

The taxi had got well away from the vicinity of the house—and was being followed by another car—when Maida heard footsteps on the terrace. She looked up with a jerk.

It was, however, only Nollie Lister, still in his sodden felt hat and long raincoat. He was carrying Rosy in his arms and Rosy was struggling furiously. It was like a scene run twice by a motion-picture projector. He knocked at the french door and, as it stood open, came into the room.

" She was in my tulips again. Really," he said, " if this goes on . . . "

He stopped. He bent over and put Rosy down. As he did so three things slid out of Maida's memory and strung themselves together like beads on a chain. Then she saw that the long raincoat had fallen apart and Nollie was wearing a neat, unobtrusive grey suit and newly polished shoes—not muddy, gardening shoes, not a sweater and old flannels. He straightened up then, looked at her, and said : " So ; I see I was right. I thought I'd better cover my tracks. Before I go away. Always cover your tracks. It's one of the first rules. *I wouldn't touch the telephone if I were you.*"

CHAPTER TWENTY-ONE

HE wasn't any different.

He was thin and nervous and awkward with an ill-fitting collar, so his scraggly neck stuck out of it like an ungainly branch of a wizened and unhealthy tree. His sodden felt hat was still on his head and shaded his face as Smith's hat had shaded Smith's deep-set eyes and strongly marked face and the lines coming down from his nose to his cruel mouth. Smith had looked like a spy. Smith had looked powerful. Smith *was* powerful. And Smith was dead and she had seen him.

She shrunk back away from the telephone. He said : " That's better. A woman—a maid in my house—has just walked out the front door wearing your clothes. I've an eye for these details. You showed yourself on the terrace in a yellow dress ; you were wearing a jacket and skirt when you came last night. I believe you have told Blake everything. There was no mention of Smith's death in the paper this morning. Blake may not have reported it. On the other hand, a strange man came here with you and Blake last night and went away. So I took the precaution of sending the maid in case the house was under guard. I might say that I saw a man leave Walsh's cottage, join another man in a car parked across the street and drive in the direction of the taxi I had telephoned for. They looked like F.B.I. men. Were they ? And why didn't you tell them what you know ? Obviously, you didn't know until now—or didn't know that you knew. Have I made a mistake ? No—you would have remembered. You would have eventually come to the realisation that I saw just now in your eyes. How did I give myself away ? Not that it matters ; not that it matters at all. *Move further from the telephone.*"

She must have done so. She was looking at his hand— his white, thin, nervous-looking hand which held a revolver. A hand that had pushed itself down, as if nervously, as if in embarrassment, between the cushions of the sofa—that was to look for his gloves. The yellow gloves—a gardener's gloves !—that Malcolm had found in the cushions of the sofa

and given to her and that she'd thought belonged to Christine
and because they seemed so unimportant (so commonplace,
so completely removed from anything concerned with Walsh's
murder), she'd forgotten them.   Nollie had forgotten them,
too, and then remembered and tried to find them.   Of course
he'd worn gloves ; he hadn't wanted to leave his fingerprints
on anything.   Could fingerprints be taken from gloves ?   She
didn't know.   And anyway they were in her red handbag !
And even if the F.B.I. men found them they wouldn't know
their meaning.   They wouldn't know how they had come
into her possession until she told them.
     Until she told them !
     Probably only then she really understood what the thing
in Nollie's hand meant.   Cover your tracks.   Walsh—why ?
Smith—why ?   But there was no question about Maida
Lovell.   She knew too much ; it had flashed in her eyes and
he had seen it.   He had come to discover whether she knew
or not ; and now he knew.
     Before I go away, he'd said.   So he was leaving.   A quiet,
unobtrusive, nervous-looking little man ; nothing about him
to attract attention ; nothing to keep him from pursuing
his work against her country somewhere else.   His protective
colouration was perfect.   He was the man one cannot describe ; the man like hundreds of other men ; the man—why,
literally, the man next door.   Always somewhere near ;
always part of the landscape—literally, again, in this case,
for Nollie was constantly in his garden, coming and going,
unquestioned and all but unseen.
     He held the revolver as delicately and surely as a surgeon
holds a knife.   Behind him he was reaching for the french
door and closing it ; that was to muffle the sound of the shot.
The shot ?   Was she going to stand there and make a target
of herself, doing nothing to stop it, nothing to—didn't they
say that all spies were egoists ?   That all spies had to have
a flare for self-dramatisation ?
     But there was nothing she could do.   He wouldn't talk ;
he was too smart for that.   Besides, he didn't have very
much time.   Pretty soon the men following the woman they
thought was herself would discover the truth and return.
How had the maid entered ?   By the back door, of course.
The corner of the house would cover her few steps from
Nollie's house to Christine's ; sometime or other he must

have provided himself with keys to the house. That was because—why, because Steve had come there to live, of course. Suddenly she saw that there had been a whole programme, a plan, built upon the fact that Steve had come to live in Christine's house. Next door to Nollie Lister.

He said : " What is the right date for the transports to leave ? "

" It was you last night in my apartment."

" Of course. Tell me quickly."

" Why did you kill Smith ? Would you really . . . ? " She looked at the hand that held the revolver.

" Oh, certainly ; but tell me and I'll let you go." He said it readily, lying.

She said slowly, trying to think : " I don't know exactly. I can find out."

" How ? "

" By telephoning."

" He wouldn't tell you."

" Not to Steve. To somebody in the office. Steve wouldn't know I had asked."

" You lied once about the transfer of the Interstate planes. If I'd believed the message Smith sent me, they'd have been transferred and under government protection before my man got them. . . . "

" *Your* man," she cried sharply.

" My man, of course. It took me months to get him a job on the night force (he's a mechanic) at the Interstate plant. It was he who found out the right date. He used his ears and overheard some talk. If I had depended upon Smith— upon you—we'd have lost that chance."

Wings put themselves on her shoulders ; it was almost literally an impression of soaring. " *Your* man ! " she cried again. She hadn't been responsible for the burning of those six planes. The terrible thing she had done, she hadn't really done, then. She'd waited ; she'd concealed Walsh's murder ; she'd bargained with the enemy—*but she hadn't burned six planes.* Suddenly it seemed to her that nothing else really mattered.

" Unluckily—or perhaps luckily since I'm about to dis- appear—the F.B.I. rounded him up this morning. I just got news of it. I don't think he'll talk. He doesn't know much to tell, in any case. Still, I'm taking no chances.

Cover your tracks," he said again, and looked at her and added rather softly: "Hurry up, do. When do the transports leave?"

Again, as at some other time (some very distant time), she thought how incredibly simple and quiet were the crises of life. Even perhaps the last crisis of all. Well, she wouldn't die. She couldn't. This was real life, familiar, loved; she was herself, Maida, living and breathing. And she hadn't betrayed her country and the men defending it.

Nollie Lister said: "Look here. You'd better believe me and tell me that date. I can easily convince you that I'm in earnest. I killed Walsh; I'll tell you about that. When Blake came here to live I saw it was an excellent chance to add to our source of information; living right next door and knowing Christine from childhood . . ."

"You really are Nollie Lister?"

"Why, of course. Understand me, I'm not doing this for money. I'm doing it because I must do it. You see—I was taken abroad as a child. I was a frail, sickly child, never able to be like other children. I was put in school in Germany for years. I kept going back there; I am younger than Christine; I know more of the new Germany; I had always admired Germanic ideas—but the new regime—force . . ." Another tone came into his voice; his eyes glowed strangely. In a flash of understanding she caught the admiration in his face; it was the admiration of the weakling for the brute, for violence and slaughter, for burning and destruction. He said: "I have always been a kind of underling; never quite enough money; never achieving the place I deserve in life. But in the new order—when it comes . . ." He stopped, his eyes still glowing, and said in a whisper: "*Then I shall be great!*"

Like the traitors in Norway. Like the men in Hungary who listened to the siren song of the German propaganda machine. Like the men in too many places who were discontented, who were easy dupes, who believed that they would be rewarded, that they would be given the place in life that they thought they deserved when the Germans came. All of them weaklings, all of them malcontents and cowards—yet gnawing away like rats at the very supports of the country's war efforts.

"You believe that?" she said.

He didn't seem to hear her. He said rather quickly : " Walsh was sent for ; he was a new man, but he had certain talents."

Another weakling, she thought. Walsh. Another dupe.

" I knew of Christine's cottage. I told him to lease it and he did. He was to acquaint himself with Washington ; to try to pick up news items here and there. But when I discovered that Blake's job was really important inasmuch as, if we could arrange it, there would be a steady stream of information which could be of considerable use, I gave orders to Walsh to concentrate upon Blake. Blake likes Angela. I remembered her as a child and that she rather liked money, so I played on that weakness of hers. Walsh made her take money (as a present, I told him to say) for her kindness in introducing him to people she knew. I daresay it isn't the first time her kindness in that direction has been rewarded in just that way. However, the point is that Walsh failed. He tried to get news from Angela about Blake's affairs and Angela either didn't know or wouldn't tell him. Walsh stayed here for several months ; he was supplied with considerable money ; he accomplished exactly nothing. And he was dangerous. Fools—especially pretty fools like Walsh —are always dangerous. He knew me, you see. I mean he—and Smith—were my men ; reported directly to me. I began to see that Walsh had no brains ; in the end I saw that there was only one way in which he could be of any possible service to me. That was in the unlikely event that, somehow, I could—I believe the word is frame—Blake. So I instructed him to quarrel publicly with Blake, and planned his murder, in such a way as to involve Blake. I intended then to step in and tell Blake I'd keep quiet, in exchange for information."

" Steve wouldn't have . . . "

" Yes, that was the flaw. I was afraid Blake wouldn't fall in with my plan. It was an extremely dangerous plan and not very likely to succeed. Still I had to get rid of Walsh ; he was becoming more dangerous every day—very vain, very sure of himself, very prone to boast. I," said Nollie, " am not boasting. I am proving to you that the best course for you to take is to do as I've told you. Tell me the date and be permitted to escape uninjured. Three loads of ferry pilots . . . " said Nollie, his eyes glistening.

Maida said stiffly : " Go on."

" No, I've said enough. Except that night, Monday night,
I was on the terrace. I'd sent Walsh to search Blake's desk ;
again he'd failed. Although I'd searched it many times (keys
and locks are part of my business), so I didn't really expect
anything. However, he came down to tell me that you were
at the front door. I told him to talk to you. I am an
opportunist, one must be when one serves as I serve. I am
weak physically, but I have . . . However, you talked to
Walsh ; I listened from the terrace ; what I couldn't hear,
Walsh told me. I had rather thought that you were in love
with Blake ; then I knew it. Instantly I saw the way to
work it. Murder Walsh with Blake's revolver. Naturally,
I knew where it was kept. I've had constant opportunities
to know everything I wanted to know about this house. If
Blake hadn't come here to live with Christine—but he did
and that was what suggested the whole plan. However, as I
was saying, I knew I could make it look as if Blake had done
it. I thought I could count on your feeling for him. You
were in a position to get information and give it to me. Then
Blake himself came. I was still on the terrace. Smith was
there, too ; Smith was, in that respect, in my confidence.
Also he knew as well as I knew that hiring Walsh had been
a mistake that was likely to cost us our lives. He was very
pleased when I told him what I planned. It was the only
way either of us could make any real use of Walsh. Kill
him ; and trap Blake, by means of you. I was watching,
you know, when Walsh told you that you were in love with
Blake. Well, that's all. Blake played into our hands by
coming to the house. Walsh saw him arrive. While Blake
was talking to you in his study, I told Walsh to quarrel with
Blake again. He did. Blake knocked him out and left.
I came in and took the revolver and shot Walsh. Smith
knew what to do ; I didn't intend to appear in it. I had the
revolver all the time, not Smith. What is the date for the
transports to leave ? " He slid the question in without a
change of expression or voice.

" I don't know. . . . "

For the first time he looked faintly annoyed ; there was
nothing else in his expression at all ; he might merely have
missed a train, or stepped inadvertently in a mud puddle.
" But you must understand," he said. " I mean what I say.

You saw Smith dead last night. How can you doubt it when I say I'm going to kill you? That is, however, I won't, if you tell me all you know about the transports."

His voice had a kind of querulous tone. He said: " Smith and I met in your apartment last night. He'd been getting out of hand, too big for his boots. He wanted more money; he was moved entirely by venal motives. I began to see that I was in danger from him, even more than I had been from Walsh. When I came here Saturday night and you and Blake were here, I felt that you'd been telling him the whole story. You did, didn't you? I told Smith that you had. I felt sure of it, not only because of your faces and something in the air, but by the way Blake replied to the police; the way he tried to keep you out of the thing. I was sure you'd told him everything. Therefore I reasoned that Blake would go to the F.B.I. You knew Smith and could identify him and probably Smith would telephone to you or come to see you and they'd get him; and I couldn't trust Smith. As I say, he was swayed entirely by venal motives; and he knew me and could identify me. The man they picked up at the Interstate work yards this morning can't. He's never seen me, face to face. Smith could, and Smith, with all his readily identifiable physical characteristics, would be picked up almost at once. Saturday night, while I sat in this room, I began to plan. I told Smith the next day to send you to the movies; told him to search your apartment. I met him there and got rid of him. I'm much more use to my Germany than Smith was." His eyes slid to the watch on his wrist. " I've got to hurry. Have I convinced you? What is the date? When do they leave? Tell me quickly. I'll let you go. I promise you. Tell me. . . ."

His eyes flashed—he whirled. There was a quick little rush of feet. The french door swung open and Angela came into the room. Angela in her green dress again, and red sandals and a raincape over her shoulders. Her cheeks had two pink spots in them and her eyes were bright and she'd been running. She said, breathlessly: " Nollie, you'd better hurry! Quick."

His hand with the revolver, his right hand, was hidden from Angela by his raincoat.

Angela came quickly into the room and closed the french door and cried, but softly, urgently: "I tell you to hurry!

We've got to get away! I'm frightened. I'm—I'm going with you."

" *You !* "

" Of course. Oh, won't you understand ! I've got to go, too. I couldn't even get any clothes. I've got no money. You'll have to take me." She was close to him ; she was pleading ; her hand went out toward his arm. She cried : " Don't kill her—they'll get me for murder, too ! I'm terri- fied, Nollie. I didn't know it would be like this when Walsh told me. I wasn't warned. I—you must come now. You must come . . . "

Nollie Lister's small face was white with fury. " *Walsh told you !* " he cried.

" Of course, he told me ! I worked with him. Walsh wasn't very smart but I am. I've got all sorts of things to tell you. Only I won't if you kill her. I'll be afraid. . . . "

The gloves, thought Maida swiftly, and Nollie's hands trying to find them, trying to recover something he'd for- gotten—failing. Those two memories were two of the beads on that chain of conviction. And it seemed to Maida that a wave of perfume (of gardenias, Angela's favourite) came to her and reminded her of the third small bead. There had been no scent of gardenias the night before, when someone had whispered out of the thick blackness in her apartment. So it was not Angela.

Then, fascinated, Maida saw Angela's white hand close on his arm—close hard, close strongly, close too strongly. Angela flashed her a look. All at once she reached behind Nollie ; she dragged his other arm downward ; a deafening noise seemed to spring from the floor. It rocked the room and Maida had reached Angela's side ; she had closed her hands above Angela's hands. A man in a slippery raincoat was twisting and pulling and writhing and was getting away ; the revolver was making great waves of sound, firing into the floor, and then all at once the thing in the raincoat grew limp and fell heavily forward. Fell so heavily, so strangely that it was like a sack. She felt her hands moving away from him.

Angela had gone somewhere—it wasn't Angela beside her at all. It was Steve.

The terrace doors were open. Steve had the revolver. She saw it in his hand. No, it was a different revolver.

because Nollie's white hand, flung out in strange slackness on the rug, still had a finger caught in a revolver.

Bill Skeffington was there, too. And amid the noise, the confusion, the turmoil, two other men came running in from the hall. All of them were stooping over the huddle on the floor. She could only see part of a shiny raincoat.

Angela came from somewhere again and put her arm around Maida.

"You'd better sit down," she said, looking blue around her mouth. "I guess I'd better, too. I heard it all, you see, from the terrace. Or enough of it. Come with me . . ."

Rain had begun again and was beating against the windows and upon the terrace like so many marching feet. The marching distant feet of soldiers, thought Maida strangely, marching to victory.

She and Angela sat in the dining-room. Sat there looking at each other. Angela got out a handkerchief and said: "I was afraid it would take longer for them to come. I heard him tell about Walsh; I listened for a little and ran to Walsh's cottage and telephoned to Steve, but he wasn't there and Bill wasn't there. They must have been on their way here. The wire was tapped, I guess, because a voice cut in and asked what I wanted. I told them. Oh, Maida, I've been such a fool. But I'll never be that kind of fool again ! I've "—tears rolled out of her blue eyes and down her soft cheeks—" I've learned my lesson. Nobody was ever as ashamed as I am. I mean, I'll never, never . . ."

"Angela," said Maida with extraordinary calm really, considering the truth of it, "you saved my life."

Men were in the library ; men were in the hall ; they could hear their voices. The front door opened and suddenly a woman was there with another man. She was wearing Maida's blue and grey suit and crying. "I didn't know— I didn't mean—he told me to. He told me to. . . ." she sobbed.

"Will you come in, please ? Will you come this way, please ? We'd like to question you. . . ." The perfectly polite, perfectly cold and impersonal voice cut into the maid's protests.

"I wonder," said Angela as the maid and the man with her passed out of the range of their vision, "how much she knows. And how much she'll admit. There must be others

—still she may not be one of them. Well, I suppose I did save your life." She looked straight at Maida. " I didn't exactly mean to ; that is, yes, I did mean to when I heard him talking. I had come to Walsh's cottage. I was nearly beside myself, you see, thinking it "—a deep scarlet wave came up into her face, but her eyes didn't waver—" it would all come out. Not a pretty story, you know. One of the things that—well . . ." She shrugged. There was complete finality in the shrug. " Besides, no one is likely to believe that I knew nothing of Walsh's real intention. I— well, as I was about to say, I had come to the cottage again. I couldn't stay away from it. I was looking for any clues to—to me. And I came quietly across the grass and my shoes were so wet I suppose I didn't make any sound on the terrace. Then I saw someone close the door. It was done so—so oddly, somehow, that I tiptoed up to where I could hear. And when I'd heard enough I—well, I told you. I ran back and telephoned for help. Then I thought if I could upset Nollie—worry him, make him think I knew about Walsh and him, make him think anything that would—oh, stop him for a minute, or two or three minutes, it would give them time. Then I was so close, and he was sort of surprised, not really watching, so I—well," said Angela simply, " I just grabbed. I wasn't close enough for him to aim at me very quickly and besides he wasn't between me and the gun. And he really believed me for a minute. And then you came to help. It was Steve, though, that got him. Speaking of Steve . . ." she stopped. She looked at Maida and said, " I suppose you'll marry Steve, now."

" He hasn't asked me to."

" I "—she hesitated and then went on—" in the cottage you know, that day . . ."

Maida nodded.

" Well, I—look here : I like Steve. And it's time I married. But I—oh, the hell," said Angela, " I'm not engaged to him. He hasn't asked me either."

" Oh," said Maida.

Angela's blue eyes sharpened. " And you knew it," she said. She bit her lip. Then she sighed. " Listen," she said, leaning across the table. Her green dress and lovely white chin reflected dimly in the polished mahogany. " Listen. All I care about is getting out of the perfectly stinking

entanglement I've got myself into. When all this ghastly
story comes out . . . " She stopped again. She blinked
back tears. " Frankly, I'm not interested in a man at this
point. All I'm interested in is how much I can rescue of—
of myself," said Angela. She looked up as Steve and Bill
Skeffington came in.

Bill was jubilant, quite himself again, no longer white and
wild-eyed as he looked when he ran in from the terrace after
Steve. Steve came to Maida directly and just stood there
beside her. Steve looked the same, too ; brown-faced, quiet,
rather sober and thoughtful, however. Bill cried : " By
golly, it looks as if he's going to live. , Nollie, I mean. Steve's
shot got him through the shoulder. And if he lives they
think they'll get on to the trail of a whole gang of enemy
agents. . . ."

" Several," said Steve.

" You never know," cried Bill excitedly. " Maybe hundreds. Anyway," he said, " if it's only two or three, it's an
important two or three."

" Is that right, Steve ? " asked Angela.

" They think so." Steve looked down at Maida and put
his hand over hers. " Make you feel better ? And you can
remove the planes from your conscience."

" Planes ? " asked Bill sharply.

" Never mind," said Steve. His eyes went to Angela.
" I've been talking to the Inspector," he said. " He can't
make any promises. But he says that some of these things . . .
Well, don't worry too much about the newspapers. . . . "

" Steve, do you really mean . . . ? " Angela sprang up
and went to Steve, and put her hands on his shoulders,
searching his face. " Really, Steve ? Is there a chance ? "

" Chance of what, for gosh sake ? " muttered Bill.
" You're so damned secretive. If you hadn't been like that
in the first place about Walsh I wouldn't have—have tipped
off the police."

Angela, a strange look on her face, was still looking into
Steve's eyes. Bill said, half-apologetically, " I wouldn't have
got around Nollie and asked questions either. And, my gosh,
how he did lead me up the garden path. Managed to make
me suspicious of you, Steve, and still didn't tell me anything.
Why do you suppose he told me he'd seen you and Walsh
fight on Monday night, and then didn't tell the police ? Oh,

I see, naturally. It was to turn the screw a little tighter: Frighten Maida ; make her scared to death of more and more evidence coming out against Steve. So she'd be more willing to follow orders. We barely got here just now, you know, Maida. One of the F.B.I. men telephoned to Steve, saying you had left the house—at least a woman in your clothes had left. Steve said it couldn't have been you, that you wouldn't have gone. He collected me and my revolver and drove hell for leather. It's a queer thing," said Bill, " how Nollie's own actions worked against him."

Bill's brow was deeply furrowed. He smote the table with his hand and cried : " I've got it ! It's like the tragedies, you know. Elizabethan. Back in college days when you study and they tell you that man makes his own destiny. I mean—well, don't you see, if he hadn't made me think there was something suspicious about Walsh's disappearance, things wouldn't have come out just as they did. Don't you see ? I mean that's what he meant to do, just to put more successful pressure on Maida. And I fell for it. Sure, I fell for it. I didn't know it was anything like this till Steve told me about it yesterday and sent me to the movie to watch you, Maida, and watch for Smith, while he went to the F.B.I. Soon as Steve told me the truth, I knew I'd been barking up the wrong tree. . . . "

Maida said suddenly : " But you didn't suspect Steve ? "

" Of course I did. Why not ? A man has to make his own way. I mean I've always had to make my way the hard way." Bill stopped suddenly. He cleared his throat. He looked out the window at the rain. He looked back at Maida. At Steve. At Angela, who was still standing there, quiet, her hands on Steve's shoulders. Bill said : " Yes, I see your point, Maida. I—er—see your point. I—well, Angela, let's get along. They don't want us. . . . "

The front door opened again and in a flurry Christine swept in. She was pink and ruffled and questioning ; cars in front of her house, people on the sidewalk saying there'd been shots ; and what did they mean F.B.I., and why didn't somebody tell her ? Bill had one arm around Angela. He drew her into the hall and collected Christine, and they could hear his voice booming out cheerily. Quite recovered.

Steve said : " Come with me, Maida."

They went into the kitchen. Rosy was there, cowering under a table.

"She's gun shy," said Steve. He looked at Maida and took her tight into his arms.

"Listen," he said after a moment—five minutes; ten; time had quite happily just stopped marking the moments. "Listen," said Steve against her ear. "I've fixed things so we can leave day after to-morrow. We can be gone three days."

"Three . . ."

"And then I go into the navy. If they'll have me."

"But, Steve, you can't! Your job . . ."

"Ceases to exist." His eyes were shining and he laughed at her incredulous look. "Really it does. And soon. It was a temporary organisation to meet an emergency need. Everything now is being taken over by the army and the—oh, the point is, my darling, I've got three whole days of my own. I don't know about the licence. I never thought of that till this minute. I think there's some place over in Maryland, though, and then we'll drive down into Virginia where there's lilacs and dogwood and . . ."

"Steve, do you mean you want to marry me?"

"What do you think I'm talking about? We've been engaged for a long time," said Steve simply. "I think it's time we got married. Besides, I'll like it."

"But we haven't been engaged. You didn't . . . We haven't . . . I don't . . ."

"There's no point in being engaged anyway," said Steve. "Get your coat. I'll fix it with them. . . ." He nodded toward the library. "No, I'll get your coat; I'll be right back. But first . . ." He put back her head and kissed her again.

The rain drummed softly on the windows behind them. It was raining like that down in Virginia, she thought, softly and gently on the lilacs.

THE END